## "It's sweet and salty and creamy,"

Jay whispered, sliding her finger back and forth across his lower lip.

Maxi gave an awkward little smile. It was all the sophistication and pizazz she could manage, and she prayed it didn't give away the fact that he had her senses reeling out of control. *Sweet and salty and creamy*? Was he talking about the meringue? About her finger?

"Exactly," he went on, kissing her fingertip, "the way I know you're going to taste."

Maxi drew a shuddering breath. He definitely was not talking about the meringue. *The way she was going to taste*. He said it with quiet assertion, as if the taste of her on his lips was already a fait accompli. Excitement swirled inside her, along with confusion.

There were so many questions she wanted to ask him. What about his reason for being here? What about the rules, and playing it safe, and forever and ever amen, and the big risk he was taking just by kissing her?

She never got a chance.

Dear Reader,

The name Silhouette **Special Edition** represents a commitment—a commitment to bring you six sensitive, substantial novels every month, each offering a stimulating blend of deep emotions and high romance.

This month, be sure to savor Curtiss Ann Matlock's long-awaited *Love Finds Yancey Cordell* (#601). And don't miss Patricia Coughlin's unforgettable *The Spirit Is Willing* (#602), a deliciously different novel destined to become a classic. Four more stellar authors—Tracy Sinclair, Debbie Macomber, Ada Steward and Jessica St. James—complete the month's offerings with all the excitement, depth, vividness and warmth you've come to expect from Silhouette **Special Edition**.

Deeply emotional, richly romantic, infinitely rewarding—that's the Silhouette **Special Edition** experience. Come share it with us—six times a month!

From all the authors and editors of Silhouette **Special Edition**,

Best wishes,

Leslie Kazanjian
Senior Editor

# PATRICIA COUGHLIN
# The Spirit Is Willing

*Silhouette Special Edition*

Published by Silhouette Books New York

**America's Publisher of Contemporary Romance**

To Bill, again and always.


For fools rush in where angels fear to tread.
—Alexander Pope
*An Essay on Criticism* (Part III, 1.65)

**SILHOUETTE BOOKS**
300 East 42nd St., New York, N.Y. 10017

**Books by Patricia Coughlin**

Silhouette Special Edition

*Shady Lady* #438
*The Bargain* #485
*Some Like It Hot* #523
*The Spirit Is Willing* #602

## PATRICIA COUGHLIN,

also known to romance fans as Liz Grady, lives in Rhode Island with her husband and two sons. A former schoolteacher, she says she started writing after her second son was born to fill her hours at home. Having always read romances, she decided to try penning her own. Though she was duly astounded by the difficulty of her new hobby, her hard work paid off, and she accomplished the rare feat of having her very first manuscript published. For now, writing has replaced quilting, embroidery and other pastimes, and with a dozen published novels under her belt, the author hopes to be happily writing romances for a long time to come.

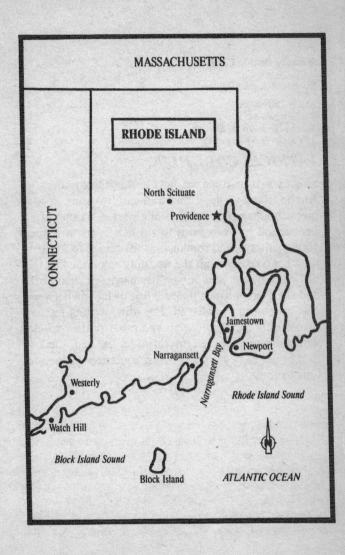

## Prologue

The whine of the siren sliced through the gray predawn stillness. Inside Miriam Hospital's emergency room the medical team awaiting the arrival of the ambulance fell silent. Until now their vigil had been punctuated by spurts of conversation about what lay ahead, marked by the offhand callousness necessary for survival when working so intimately with suffering and death. Now there was silence and a familiar tension that wound tighter and tighter as the shrill whine grew closer and louder.

The siren finally choked off in midwail directly outside. Almost instantly the swinging doors were thrust open, slamming against the wall with a bang that snapped the hairtrigger mood and fired everyone into action. With choreographed precision the group of residents, nurses and technicians, armed with state-of-the-art equipment, surged into position around the stretcher.

They had been fully briefed about what to expect by the ambulance attendants' radio report. Auto-accident victim.

Male, mid-thirties. Broken ribs, profuse bleeding from numerous lacerations, possible head and internal injuries, shallow breathing, rapidly falling blood pressure. Status: code red; the hospital term for the most critical emergencies. Still, there was a stunned, though almost imperceptible, intake of breath as they caught their first glimpse of the man lying on the stretcher.

The reaction wasn't prompted by the profusion of blood. The group of hardened professionals was long-since immune to the sight of a shocking spill of scarlet. It took a very different color to make their skin prickle. It took the unique grayish pallor that shaded the man's bruised handsome face. Even the film of moisture coating his skin was ominous, having nothing to do with the sweat of exertion and everything to do with death.

Working the frenetic eleven-to-seven shift in a city hospital emergency room quickly qualified a trained individual to sense the outcome of a crisis even before laying a hand on the patient. Each of them sensed it now, and as always the youth and obviously top-notch physical condition of the victim that fate had delivered into their care made his current broken state that much more tragic.

The seeming futility of their efforts did not lessen their speed or diligence, however. In a matter of minutes the man was connected to a battery of machines via a tangle of tubes and wires and was en route to an operating room, where a hastily summoned team of surgeons headed by Dr. Richard Mellor, chief of surgery, was already scrubbing.

A series of painstaking procedures was required just to repair the internal damage inflicted by the accident.

"What the hell did this guy do?" an exasperated Dr. Mellor muttered at one point. "Drive a truck off the Washington Bridge?"

"Not quite," replied the OR nurse, who had gotten a full rundown of the accident from the ER nurse, who had gotten it straight from the young police officer who'd been first on the scene. "He merely drove it straight into a tree . . . a nice big, solid oak, I'm told. And, just for the record, it was a Jaguar, not a truck.'' She slapped the proper clamp into the surgeon's open palm before he had to ask for it. ''Seems he was trying to drive, drink a cup of coffee and read some sort of business report all at the same time.''

''Obviously a type-A personality,'' remarked an assisting surgeon.

Someone snorted. ''Make that type I, for idiot.''

''It's still a damn shame,'' said the first nurse, her sigh expressing the regret they were all feeling.

It was four hours later, after 10:00 a.m., when Dr. Mellor peeled off his seventh and final pair of bloodstained rubber gloves and left the OR.

The supervising nurse handed him the patient's chart as he passed her desk, knowing that despite his fatigue the surgeon would dictate his notes while the session was still fresh in his mind. He glanced at the top sheet and for the first time learned the name of the man whose life he had been fighting to save. Jason Allaire.

''There's someone waiting to talk with you in the lounge,'' the nurse informed him almost apologetically.

''His wife?'' Dr. Mellor inquired, feeling the already-tense muscles at the back of his neck tighten. The last thing he felt like doing was delivering to a tearful wife the kind of prognosis he must deliver. Relief rippled through him when the nurse shook her head.

''No. He's not married. The man waiting to see you is a friend of the patient's. Actually he's the patient's business partner,'' she explained, ''but he's the closest thing to next of kin we could locate. Mr. Allaire has a brother in California, whom his partner—'' she glanced at the notepad in front of her ''—Ben Griffin, has promised to try to contact. Seems you've had the pleasure of working on one of the partners in Allaire, Cross and Griffin, a very big-deal advertising agency in Boston.''

Mellor grunted. ''Pleasure? Hardly. And he sure doesn't look like such a big deal right now.''

"How did it go in there?"

He shrugged. "It went."

She nodded, understanding. "I think Mr. Griffin would like to see his friend, if that's okay with you."

"Fine," Mellor replied, his shrug weary. If one picture was worth a thousand words, letting the man's partner see Allaire would spare the doctor from having to spell out the grim reality of his condition. He plucked at his soiled surgical scrubs. "But first I'm going to get rid of these and wash up. Have Mr. Griffin meet me in the recovery room in fifteen minutes."

The private recovery room where Jason Allaire had been brought was dimly lit. The click of the door opening jarred him from the frightening, confused jumble his thoughts had been ever since he floated to the top of a black well a few minutes ago. He wished his eyes would obey his command to open. He had a haunting impression of what was going on, and he didn't like it.

He remembered seeing that damn pothole and thinking how he'd just had the Jag's wheels aligned, and then the feel of the hot coffee spilling over his thighs—a tiny harbinger of the pain that followed, more pain in more places in his body than he ever could have imagined.

After that there were only lights and loud wailing noises and snatches of sentences that half made sense as they traveled through his brain, but then couldn't be recaptured. He decided that there had been an accident and he was in a hospital, and he burned with the need to know more. If only he could dislodge this two-hundred-pound weight from his chest and spit out whatever was holding his jaw wedged apart and somehow get his eyes to open, maybe he would be able to find the energy to ask.

"Jason?" The tremulous voice seemed to come from a long way away. "Jason, old buddy."

Ben? thought Jason. Of course, it was Ben. Who else would they call? They would hardly drag his brother, Steve, all the way back here from L.A. Unless . . . It was suddenly even more difficult to draw a breath. God, he prayed, please don't let me hear Steve's voice.

He strained to identify the second male voice wafting above him. He was introducing himself to Ben—Dr. something-or-other—and saying something about a spleen, about having to remove it. Was he talking about *his* spleen, for Pete's sake? Wasn't a spleen something vital, like your heart or your liver? The doctor had moved on to talking about something else. No! Jason wanted to shout. What about my spleen? God, this was frustrating.

He struggled to follow what they were saying, but it was like listening to a car radio with poor reception that kept fading into indecipherable static. He did make out the words *'always in a hurry.'* Oh, right, Ben, in a hurry to arrive early at that emergency meeting on the Hot Dog King account in order to keep *your* tail out of the fire. There's gratitude for you. *"Personal effects."* Personal effects? His? That sounded a little bleak. Like something an undertaker would say.

Now Ben was confirming that he recognized the key chain found near the car. He should. A solid eighteen-carat-gold brick isn't easy to forget.

*" . . . gift from his brother right after he bought the Jaguar. . . . Got a big kick out of the inscription. . . ."*

The words engraved on the back of the key chain wound a path through Jason's mind even before Ben started to read them out loud. *He Who Dies with the Most Toys Wins.* Yeah, he'd gotten a kick out of it all right. It was a joking acknowledgment of the friendly though fierce competition between him and his only brother.

It also summed up their shared philosophy of life, one forged during the childhood they'd spent being bounced from one foster home to another, dragging with them their few personal effects and the naive belief that sooner or later their mother was going to make good on her promise to get her life straightened out and reclaim them.

The old lady never did come through for him and Steve, but at least she had taught them a valuable lesson about where to put your trust. Not in people, and certainly not in women. Women were immensely pleasurable but not to be taken too seriously. And love? Jason would have chuckled if he had the strength. Love was an all around bad investment. He hadn't become a millionaire at the age of thirty-four by making bad investments. The only things that counted in this life were those for which you could hold the bill of sale in your hand.

The voices of Ben and the doctor seemed to be moving farther away from him now, becoming wavery. Yet with this new, peculiar consciousness he seemed to have somehow acquired, Jason sensed that it wasn't they who were moving. The darkness around him was brightening, shifting in strange murky patterns. He felt as if he were drifting through a long tunnel of some hazy stuff, like clouds, for heaven's sake.

*For heaven's sake....* What an apt choice of words. But then, words were his business. Leave it to him to capture the essence of the moment, an expressive genius to the end. The end.... Is that really what this was all about?

The voices were even farther away now. Jason was glad. They were too far away to frighten him with their solemn forecast. *"Coma induced by severe cranial trauma...bruised brain stem...surprisingly normal brain waves considering...amazing really...medical miracle...next few days critical."*

## Chapter One

He blinked and looked around, startled to find himself standing at a busy intersection.

On his right was a skyscraper that looked as if it had been carved from a solid sheet of glass. On his left stood a not-so-dazzling but still-impressive granite building with square lines and solid Doric columns. Directly across the four-lane street in front of him was a neat green rectangle of city park bordered by wooden benches and slender young maples.

Nowhere in sight were the legendary gold scales that he expected would be on hand to weigh the good and bad deeds in his past life and deliver a verdict. Not that he was in any big hurry to find out what that would be.

The traffic light turned red, followed by the squeal of rubber on pavement as the flow of cars halted, parting like the Red Sea to permit those who stepped quickly enough to cross the street. He let himself be swept along with the tide of pedestrians and, once on the other side, impulsively turned in the direction of the clock on the next corner and started walking.

Scales or no scales, there was something vaguely familiar about his surroundings, which ruled out his being in the ethereal place he'd always hoped he would end up. He guessed he wasn't dead after all. On the other hand, he wasn't sure he was exactly alive, either.

What he was sure of, with an inexplicable resoluteness that might account for his fatalistic calm, was that he was where he was supposed to be and that he was here for an important reason.

There were several names for what he suspected was happening to him. Near-death experience. Out-of-body experience. Occasionally when stranded in the dentist's waiting room he would pick up a copy of some popular magazine and read accounts of such things. And laugh. He'd been so sure they were nothing but the products of weak minds and strong imaginations. This must be what was meant by learning the hard way.

He glanced at the street sign above his head. Kennedy Plaza. The name fit comfortably in his mind, like one he'd heard before.

Feeling curious enough to risk appearing foolish, he reached out to touch the sleeve of an older man walking slightly ahead of him. "Excuse me, sir, could you tell me what city I'm in?"

The old man frowned. Reaching up to fiddle with his hearing aid, he glanced warily over his shoulder, looking right through him as if he were . . .

Invisible, he thought, seizing the most obvious explanation under the circumstances. All things considered, he supposed he should have expected as much.

The clock up ahead read 11:15, and the digital display beneath it alternately flashed the temperature and the date. September 14. At least that seemed right. It occurred to him that, for that matter, so did he.

He drew encouragement from a quick glance down at his lean six-foot frame dressed in a pair of dark slacks and a black-and-white woven silk sports jacket. Hand-tailored. Great taste. And not a mark on it, he observed with surprise, suddenly recalling the accident in a series of fleeting impressions: the sound of glass shattering, the acrid smell of smoke, the pain.

He tried reaching back past the accident for something more—his name, his date of birth—but met a frustratingly blank wall. The accident was all the history he had. Like one of those toys where you lift the cellophane to make everything disappear from the gray sheet below, his past had been wiped clean. As he continued walking, he gradually became aware that in its place he'd been given a bizarre new consciousness. He knew all sorts of things he didn't understand how he knew.

For example, he knew that somehow, for some reason, he was being given a second chance—make that a *last* chance— to tip those missing scales in his favor. He could help himself by helping someone else, and as the crowd on the sidewalk ahead thinned slightly he felt his gaze mysteriously drawn to the someone else in question. With his new gift of insight he had no doubt that the dark-haired, slightly offbeat-looking woman walking directly ahead of him was the one he was meant to watch over.

He couldn't stop the smirk that claimed his lips. She wasn't at all what he would have chosen if left to his own devices. But then, he wouldn't have chosen to be a . . . a guardian angel—there was no better name for it—in the first place. His smirk edged wider as he took a closer look.

She was short, although that wouldn't be so bad if she didn't overcompensate by wearing those ridiculously high narrow heels. And that getup she had on. He wondered if she knew how much she resembled a pumpkin from the back. Not that she was heavy—quite the opposite. But in his opinion no woman's backside looked its best squeezed into a tight, burnt-orange denim miniskirt.

The orange-and-white striped top she wore with it was draped off one shoulder to reveal the strap of an orange tank top beneath in a fashion he supposed was intended to be alluring but looked only sloppy to him. The pièce de résistance, however, was her handbag. Satchel would be a better name for it. Nearly as big as she was, it was clearly a flea-market relic from the sixties.

His appraisal was interrupted by the doubletake that occurred in him naturally as a lean, leggy blonde strolled by in the opposite direction. He instantly and guiltily short-circuited the response. Another lesson learned. Angels—if, indeed, that's what he was—were evidently fully capable of inconvenient physical throbs if presented with the right stimuli. Succumbing to them didn't seem like the most impressive way to get started, and he caught himself foolishly glancing skyward, wondering how closely he was being monitored.

Maybe he should be thankful he'd gotten Ms. Pumpkin after all. At least he wouldn't have any trouble thinking of her not as a woman, but as a . . . What?

Shrugging off the problem of semantics, he decided that for now he'd settle for mastering step one by not regarding her in the way he had a hunch he usually regarded members of the opposite sex: as prey. True, he couldn't recall specific details of his past life, but he knew in his heart that this role as protector of women was a new one for him. And one he couldn't afford to screw up.

He trailed along for several blocks, vaguely uncomfortable in such a passive role but unsure just how actively involved he was supposed to get in protecting her. He found himself watching for his chance, straining to pick up on any new feelings or impressions that would tell him irrevocably what to do.

Then it happened. He saw her lift her foot to step over the sewer grate in the sidewalk, told himself that if her skirt weren't so damn tight even her short legs could have made the stretch, and then winced as her heel came down, the narrow point of it plunging into a slot in the iron grate and catching.

At once it occurred to him that this was going to be easier than he thought. He didn't even pause to think. His duty clear, he hustled the few steps to her side and hunkered down to do it.

Maxi Love stumbled as the sewer grate snagged her heel, and she swore under her breath as she flailed for balance. She'd learned long ago to walk around these metal booby traps. Of course there were those, her dear family among them, who would say she had it coming for walking around with her head in the clouds. But at least this time she had a good reason for being preoccupied: her upcoming lunch with Peter Duvall.

With more colorful muttering she switched her shoulder bag to the other hand and reached out to brace herself on the brick wall beside her. Fortunately she'd made this same mistake often enough to have mastered the perfect twisting-pulling motion required to free herself. She was attempting it when she felt fingers close around her ankle. Instinctively she let loose with a scream registering somewhere in the shrill soprano range.

Maxi wasn't paranoid, but she wasn't stupid, either. While Providence might not be afflicted with a skyrocketing crime rate, it harbored its share of perverts and deviants, and who else but one of them would crouch beside you in broad daylight and latch on to your ankle?

Without stopping to think, she quickly followed up the scream with a wild swing of her shoulder bag, connecting solidly with the head of the man crouching at her feet. With a loud grunt, he toppled to his knees. Only then did Maxi remember that she had tossed her wrist weights into the bag before leaving home, in case she had time to stop at the gym later.

Rubbing his head with the hand not clutching her ankle, he mumbled, "For crying out loud..."

"You better let go of me, mister," she ordered.

The man jerked his head up, his irritated frown giving way to an odd look of disbelief, as if she were the crazy one here.

"You can see me." His words were more of a surprised observation than a question.

"Of course, I—" Maxi broke off, hesitating a second before continuing in the calmer tone she'd heard one was supposed to use with such people to avoid alarming them further. "Yes. Yes I can see you . . . but I don't have my glasses on . . . and I have a very poor memory, honestly. So if you'll just let me go, we can both forget this ever happened. See? I'll even close my eyes now so I won't get a real good look at you."

"That's not what I meant." He grimaced. "Dozens of people on the street, and I pick an old deaf guy," he muttered.

She flicked her eyes open to look around. "What old deaf guy?"

"Forget it."

"Fine. If you'll just let me go. . . ."

"You think I'm holding you?" he interrupted, his tone hotly indignant.

"I know you are."

"I'm not."

"Well, it sure feels that way."

"I'm not *holding*. I'm *helping*. You got stuck here all on your own."

"I know that." A deviant for sure. Even if he had been simply trying to help at the start, any normal man would have backed off when she hit him in the head to signal that his assistance was not wanted. Maxi forced a smile. "It's very gallant of you to offer your help. Thank you. But I don't need it."

"Yes, you do."

He now had his other hand clamped across her instep and was squeezing her foot as he rocked it back and forth.

"Ouch! I don't. As you pointed out, I got it stuck in here all by myself," she said between gritted teeth, "and I can get it out the same way."

"Never happen. Did you ever think of having new soles put on these shoes, lady? You've got a little piece of rubber hanging off, and it's hooked in there good. Will you hold still?"

"No. I want to do it myself."

"Watch it," he admonished as she attempted to shake him off. "You're pinching my finger."

Without a trace of guilt Maxi noticed that his finger was, indeed, trapped between her shoe and a strip of metal. She leaned purposefully to that side. "Then we're even, because you're pinching my foot."

His grip on her instep tightened, forcibly stilling her. "Move it just once more, honey, and I'll shove the other heel in, too."

"Gallant," she muttered again, but decided that holding still might be the wisest approach until she was free. If he was right about her heel being caught on something, it might not be so easy to loose it all on her own after all. Bracing one hand on the wall, she endured the quizzical, amused smiles of passersby.

All she needed now was for Pete Duvall to stroll past on his way to meet her at Simon's Landing. One look would confirm his opinion that she was a total scatterbrain, incapable of handling the new project she still couldn't quite believe was hers. Peter had made no secret of the fact that he opposed her getting it, and she was sure he wouldn't hesitate to lobby to have it yanked away from her for the slightest provocation.

"Why?" she entreated softly and of no one in particular. "Why today of all days?"

"Stop griping," her stubborn rescuer ordered without glancing up. "I'm the one doing all the work."

"And whose fault is that?"

"Believe me, you don't want to know."

Maxi shook her head. Just her luck to be accosted by a glib deviant. "I don't need this."

"Well, unfortunately, I do." He grunted, and before Maxi could decipher that last cryptic remark, she was free. "There."

He stood. Maxi, regaining her composure, took her first concentrated look at him. Even without her glasses she could see that the man's packaging was nice. Very, very nice, actually. She tried not to let her reaction show as she tipped her head back to take it all in. He was also very tall. Of course, from her five-foot-three viewpoint, most men looked tall.

However, most men did not have thick, wavy black hair that made your fingers itch to thread through it or eyes so deeply blue that you felt as if you were lost at sea when he riveted them on you as he was doing to her now.

Fewer still were blessed with features as finely drawn and expressive as this man's, so that even his aloofness was conveyed as a palpable emotion. The artist in Maxi heralded the perfect alignment of those features. So perfect, in fact, that only the self-assurance and strength he projected so effortlessly rendered a face that might otherwise have been called too pretty, unmistakably sensuously masculine instead.

The fact that she had never been to Paris did not deter Maxi from whimsically concluding that he looked like a Parisian. His nose was straight, his cheeks slightly, dramatically, alluringly hollow and his mouth . . . His mouth, fully capable of a devastating sulk and now resting in an ever-so-slightly challenging smile, gave rise to all sorts of fantasies.

Maxi quickly jerked her thoughts onto a safer path.

Well-dressed and *GQ* handsome he may be—clearly the man still had problems. Besides, any smart woman knew that too-handsome men were seldom worth the tummy flutters they incited. And this man looked not only too-handsome, but slick. Her education about slick men had started at home, with her father and brothers.

She'd learned to distrust their motives and to chafe at the awkwardness they could reduce her to with simply the condescending arch of an eyebrow, the way this stranger was now doing. His was a look laced with smugness, as if she'd forgotten something when she was getting dressed this morning and he knew what it was.

She positioned the strap of her shoulder bag with defiant crispness. "I suppose I should say thank-you."

"It would be nice."

"Thank you." Startled to hear the note of uncharacteristic waspishness in her voice, she softened—he had helped her, after all—and added, "I mean it, really."

His distracting mouth twitched.

Maxi's mind wandered. She caught it. She had to stop thinking such things.

"You're welcome," he told her. "Really."

"Well..." She grasped the shoulder bag firmly. "So long."

"So long?" he echoed as she turned to walk away. "That's it?"

"That's it." Her back was to him now, and she resisted the urge to see if his expression was as satisfyingly incredulous as his tone. Apparently being shot down by a woman was not an experience life dealt him very often.

"After I saved your life?" he called after her. "Do you have any idea what would have happened if I hadn't come along when I did?"

"Sure," she called back. "I'd have pulled my foot out, just like I always do."

"Guess again. You probably would have fallen through that grate. What then?"

Maxi smiled without meaning to. "Then the trolls would have gotten me."

Trolls? His face was tightly drawn in an irritated frown as he watched her stride away. She'd been joking, of course. No normal person believed in such things as trolls. He tried to turn off the part of his brain saying "And this situation is normal?'' As well as the part reminding him that *normal* was not the first word that popped to mind when describing the woman he'd just encountered.

Trolls. He shook his head and started walking. Of course it was a joke. He hoped.

## *Chapter Two*

Maxi's smile faded along with all thoughts of her recent rescue as she glanced at her watch and realized that even if she ran the rest of the way she would be late. Simon's Landing, the trendy, upscale café Duvall had chosen, was located on South Water Street, a showpiece strip of urban renewal overlooking the Providence River's reclaimed waterfront, about eight blocks from where she was.

Peter was already seated at a corner table when Maxi walked in breathing heavily. He'd probably made a point of arriving early, she thought, the better to put her at a psychological disadvantage. Peter had not become the manager of Robert Chandler's gubernatorial campaign by being ignorant of power moves and how to execute them to his advantage. His huggable teddy-bear appearance was deceiving. Beneath Peter's sandy-haired, square-jawed, all-American pleasantness hammered a heart of solid avarice.

Supposedly he wanted to meet with her today to discuss the time frame for the project. Maxi felt certain, however, that what he really wanted was to make the point that even though Robert Chandler had gone against his campaign manager's recommendation in selecting Maxi to produce these three do-or-die commercials for his campaign, in the day-to-day scheme of things he was still the man in charge.

Stealing a few seconds behind the ficus tree in the cramped entry to catch her breath, Maxi glanced at Peter's rigid posture and remembered the first time they had met, six months ago, when she'd walked into Chandler campaign headquarters and volunteered her help. Apolitical by nature, she had been motivated by her childhood friendship with Robert Chandler's daughter, Lynn, and the conviction that the man really cared about the future of Rhode Island.

Unfortunately, all his strongest qualities and most innovative ideas were not being made clear to voters. To be too direct about the issues was "too risky," in Peter Duvall's words. Privately Maxi had once asked Robert why he had chosen someone as ruthless and calculating as Duvall to head his campaign. "Because I'm not," had been his answer.

Maxi had understood the rationale, but then, as now, she hadn't agreed with it. In her opinion, one oft expressed to Robert and shared by several others among his hard-core volunteers, the heavy-on-rhetoric-light-on-substance campaign style orchestrated by Duvall spelled disaster.

When last week's polls had shown Chandler trailing his opponent by twenty percentage points with barely eight weeks to go until election day, he had finally been forced to listen. Hence the decision to launch a television blitz in the final weeks, spearheaded by his participation in a televised debate he had previously avoided, and reinforced two dozen times a day by the eye-catching, evocative, foolproof commercials it was now Maxi's job to produce. She was still amazed at how her impulsive decision to volunteer to help with the campaign had led to this, the biggest project of her career—one every bit as crucial for her as for Robert Chandler.

Gathering her determination about her like a suit of armor, she stepped from behind the ficus and started across the crowded room. The daunting feeling that this lunch was a make-it-or-break-it opportunity to prove herself to Duvall was stronger than ever. Peter said nothing about her being late, letting his quick glance at his watch as he rose smoothly to his feet say it all. Tardy. Unprofessional. Strike one.

"Peter, hello," she said, struggling to maneuver herself and her shoulder bag through the narrow space between their table and the next.

"Oh, excuse me," she apologized as her bulky bag bumped the woman seated at the table beside them. She repeated the apology when she swept the napkin from the lap of the man behind her, sending it floating to the floor. "I'm so sorry."

She bent to retrieve it, and as she finally slipped into the chair Peter had been holding for her, she observed him quickly mask his disgusted look with one of generic civility. It confirmed what until then had been only a vague suspicion. It wasn't simply that he considered her inexperienced. He didn't like her and he wasn't looking forward to working with her any more than she was with him.

"I'm sorry I'm late," she told him, surreptitiously kicking her bag into an out-of-the-way spot beneath her chair. "I got . . . caught up with something."

"No problem. Of course, I do have another appointment at one."

And, of course, there was no question of *his* ever being late. Maxi smiled at him across the small table. "Then perhaps we should get right down to business."

"I think perhaps we should order first to ensure we're not held up later. You'll find that pacing means survival in this business."

Was that a warning? Maintaining her smile in spite of his subtle little zing, she opened her menu, already knowing she was too anxious to swallow more than a glass of water. She quickly decided on the arugula-and-tomato salad with basil vinaigrette, then, in an effort to appear relaxed, pretended to peruse the rest of the menu for a minute or so. When she looked up, he was staring at her expectantly, his own menu already closed. Ah, pacing.

"So," he said after their order had been taken and they had exchanged a few superficial words about the unseasonable heat wave gripping the city, "let's talk deadlines."

"Actually I thought we already had," Maxi pointed out. "The day we held the strategy session at headquarters. It's my understanding that I'm to have the commercials ready to air by October 1, the night of the debate."

He nodded. "Yes, that is the date agreed on as a *final* deadline. But I feel we need to set up some intermittent meetings, for progress reports, you might say, to help you with pacing."

Not even attempting a subtle counter-lunge, Maxi fell back on her usual forthrightness. "Let's drop the facade, shall we, Peter? We're not here to talk about pacing, but control. Yours."

"I've already cleared this plan with Chandler," he informed her, effectively defusing the all-out attack building inside her. "Of course, you can go over my head about it if you like, but in these final crucial days, it seems his interest would be better served if we all tried to work together harmoniously."

Maxi gazed at him through narrowed eyes. "Why don't you spell out for me exactly what that entails?"

"For starters, you provide me with a schedule of when you're shooting and where," he replied so quickly and succinctly that Maxi knew he'd given all this a great deal of thought. "That way I can stop by and lend moral support if I'm in the vicinity. And I'd like to review all the unedited tapes. And I'd like to be kept fully informed of your ideas as they develop."

"I've already shown rough storyboards for all three commercials to Robert, and he likes them. I don't foresee any major changes, and, frankly, I don't see the need for any further collaboration."

"I do." He smiled. "Admit it, Maxi, you've bitten off a great deal here. Sure, you've worked on commercials before—"

"Among many other projects."

"But always as the art director. Frankly, it concerns me that with our tight, last-minute budget constraints we have to depend on you to be something of a jack-of-all-trades."

"I can handle it."

"No doubt," he countered in a tone that made it clear he had many. "But on the remote chance that you don't pull it off, I'd like to know it before I turn on my TV on October first."

"Why? So you can say I told you so?"

"Let's just say I like being prepared." His smile, artificial as it was, disappeared. "Get it straight, sweetheart. I haven't worked endless days and even longer nights for months so that you can waltz backstage at the last minute and come out looking like the star."

Understanding brought with it amazement and then a rush of the buoyant, go-for-it confidence Maxi had been trying to talk herself into for days.

"Of course," she exclaimed. "You're not worried that I'll cause Robert to lose, but that I'll be responsible for him winning."

"That's absurd." He laughed, but behind the wary brown eyes she could see him reevaluating her worth as an opponent. "I want him to win more than anyone."

"Right. You just don't want to share any of the credit for it."

His chuckle was softly admonishing. "It's a bit early for a discussion of credit, Maxi. But then, considering how new you are to the game, I suppose it's to be expected that you would forget there are eight long, hard weeks remaining before credit—or blame—is assessed.''

She knew that. Wasn't much of that hard work to be her own? But she had revealed her inexperience by letting him twist her into a corner with her own words. Strike two.

''Now,'' he continued, evidently mistaking her thoughtful silence for surrender, ''why don't you give me a clearer grasp on these revolutionary ideas of yours.''

*So you can better articulate them as your own, if the occasion arises?* Mindful of the truth of what he said about the need for harmony, she kept the thought to herself.

''My basic idea is to let the voter watching the commercial get to know the real Robert Chandler.''

Peter nodded. ''Noble aspiration, risky reality. Give me details.''

''I'm going to emphasize the reason he decided to take a leave from his very profitable business to run for governor in the first place, because he has old-fashioned values that this state needs to rediscover in order to move ahead.''

Duvall made a scoffing sound. ''Old-fashioned values? That's your revolutionary idea? That's been done to death, sweetheart.''

''So what? In Robert's case it happens to be the truth. And he has the vision to make those values from the past work in the future. For instance, he cares about families and in the 1980s that translates into childcare and health care and job training for young mothers.''

''Those are women's issues, Maxi.'' The dismissive emphasis he put on the word *women* made her burn to think that someone so close-minded could wield such power. ''If Robert emphasizes them, he'll be targeted as pandering to a special-interest group.''

''What about the environment?'' she demanded. ''Robert was concerned about ocean pollution long before it became trendy. He cared about it as long ago as when he used to take Lynn and me to Eastern's Beach and teach us to dig for clams, and he cares about it now that some beaches have had to be closed because of the debris washing up. That's the kind of man he is, and that's what I plan to let the voters know. Or is that pandering to special interests, too?''

''Could be. I won't know for sure until you start spilling the exact details of what you plan to show in these commercials. You can do that, can't you? I mean, that is what you art directors do...organize the props and the people and exactly what we see on the screen?''

''That's a big part of what I do, yes.''

''Then let's hear it.''

Maxi drew a deep breath as she struggled to organize her thoughts, nervous that no matter how she presented them, her ideas would earn only derision from Duvall.

''I intend to start shooting this afternoon at Roger Williams Park....'' she began.

Maxi took pleasure in the look of surprise that flickered briefly across his face. Clearly he hadn't expected her to move so quickly.

''Why the park?''

''Because Robert has been instrumental in its revitalization, in turning what had been a dangerous place no one would visit after dark to a place where families can go to picnic, ride the paddleboats, stroll through the zoo or the Japanese Gardens.'' Her voice quickened with anticipation. ''And visually it's a perfect spot to shoot. Full of color and texture and—''

''That should thrill the people of Providence,'' Duvall interrupted with a wave of his hand. ''But what about the other seventy-five percent of the voters? Politics is a game of demographics, sweetheart. Winning is the bottom line. You need significant identification factors to propel an unaffiliated voter to vote, and in terms of—''

Maxi turned the tables by interrupting him this time. ''That's politicalese, Peter, and you know it. You're trying to intimidate me. But guess what? I'm not intimidated. Although you are laying it on so thick I could choke on it.''

Her flair for the dramatic led her to emphasize the point by making a little coughing sound, accompanied by a hand delicately clasped to her throat. Instantly she felt herself grabbed from behind and yanked from her chair. Even before she turned her head, some sixth sense told Maxi whose strong arms were locked so tightly across her ribs.

"Oh, no," she groaned, recognizing the man who less than an hour ago had held her just as immobile by her ankle.

"Relax," he commanded. "You're going to be all right."

"I'm already all right," she insisted, the last word blasted from her as he gave her rib cage a violent squeeze, forcing all the air from her lungs.

Peter was on his feet now, too, glancing around uneasily at the attention they were attracting. Some small corner of Maxi's mind registered the thought that this sort of bizarre scene might reflect badly on the candidate, constituting a resounding strike three.

"What do you think you're doing?" Peter demanded.

"Heimlich maneuver," came the terse reply as Maxi felt the man behind her brace to repeat it.

Before she could gather breath to yell stop, Peter spoke again.

"Why? She isn't choking."

"She's not?" Maxi's Galahad muttered.

"No," snapped Maxi, finally able to speak. She glared over her shoulder at his doubtful expression. "She's not. Although she wishes she were. That would be the least embarrassing way out of this."

"You're sure you're really all right?" he persisted.

"Positive. At least I will be as soon as you let go of me so I can slink back into my chair. Or maybe," she added in a stinging whisper, "I'll just crawl all the way under the table. How could you do this to me?"

"I didn't do it *to* you," he whispered back. "I did it *for* you."

"Well, do something else for me—stop doing things for me. And let me go."

"Of course." Instantly the man dropped his arms to his side, apparently as eager as she was to end this, but when Maxi tried to sit, she couldn't.

"Let go," she repeated.

"I did."

"Then what . . . ?"

"I think we're stuck."

"To what?"

"Each other. Or rather, my belt is caught on your... What do you call this thing anyway?"

"A belt," she snapped.

"Could've fooled me." His fingers moved along it exploratorily. "Feels like hunks of granite."

"Those are crystals...expensive crystals. Don't chip them, for heaven's sake."

"Don't worry, I'll buy you a new one." He paused, then muttered what sounded like "Someday."

"You can't buy me a new one. These crystals were specially chosen to augment my own natural energy."

"Your what?"

"Natural energy. I draw strength from them."

"Sort of like Popeye and spinach?"

"No." She glanced around with growing impatience, praying his fumbling around back there would produce quick results.

"Then how does it work?"

"They provide energy," she snapped, conscious that every ear—as well as every eye—in the place was on them. "Healing strength. Confidence. Good things. Would you mind not rubbing them that way? They can pick up negative energy."

"You're making all this up."

"I certainly am not."

"You really believe it?"

"Of course."

"Oh, no." He sighed, as if what she did or didn't believe had something to do with him personally. "This is going to be a lot tougher than I thought."

"What is?"

He hesitated, then said, "Getting our belts unhooked. In fact, I think we're going to have to go someplace more private. Turn slowly and head for the door. Trust me . . . I'll be right behind you."

Maxi wasn't in the mood to laugh. "How reassuring," she snapped, obeying his instructions because she had no other choice.

"Should I . . ." Peter began, making a reluctant move to accompany them.

"No," Maxi hurriedly replied. "Please just wait here, and I'll be right back.

The short walk to the door was the most excruciating of her life.

"I can't believe it," she muttered several times. "I can't believe this is happening to me. Did you follow me here?"

"Not intentionally. Maybe we're meant to be thrown together."

"What a gruesome thought."

If he was telling the truth about not following her, then this was no more than a horrible coincidence. Or fate. Maxi flinched. She believed strongly in the latter. But if this were her fate, she'd rather not think about it.

Once outside the restaurant, she glanced around, then led him to the relatively private alley between that building and the next.

"How are you going to do this?" she asked.

"Very carefully. It may not be made of magic crystals, but this is the only belt I've got."

"Right, Slick," she drawled, turning her head to run a pointed gaze over the sleeve of his obviously expensive jacket. "That's the only belt you own. Tell me another one."

"All right." His fingers, which had been working to undo their belts, stilled. In that smooth, deep voice that sounded the way expensive Scotch tasted, he said, "I'm your guardian angel."

## Chapter Three

Maxi shook her head, her faint scoff mocking. "Right. Sure. You're my guardian angel. And I'm Miss America."

It was his turn to scoff. "Not likely. But I really am your guardian angel."

"For your information, guardian angels are supposed to help people, not attack them." She glanced over her shoulder in time to see the edges of his mouth tip downward.

"I know that," he said.

"Then try helping by getting my belt unhooked."

"Try wearing a normal belt and maybe I could. I think walking out here jammed them together worse."

She threw her hands into the air. "Oh, no. I should have known better than to listen to you."

"Will you keep your voice down?"

"No. I always shout when I'm frantic."

"Well, try and curb it, will you? The last thing we need is to draw attention to this."

"Whose attention? In case you haven't noticed, we're standing in a deserted alley."

"Forget it. You wouldn't understand."

"Gladly." She was quiet for as long as her self-control would allow before asking, "How are you doing back there?"

"Swell. Don't rush me."

"Sorry. But did I happen to mention that I was in the middle of a very important lunch when you intruded?"

"Really? He doesn't look your type."

Maxi guessed the conclusion he had jumped to and laughed. "Thank you, I'll take that as a compliment. Actually, it's a business lunch."

His knuckles kept rubbing against her back as he fiddled with the belts. It wasn't an unpleasant sensation.

"What sort of business are you in?" he asked after a moment.

"Art."

"Figures."

Sensitive to disapproval on the subject of her chosen vocation, Maxi stiffened and shot him a lethal look over her shoulder.

"I only meant that you look like the creative type," he explained quickly.

The creative type. She decided she liked the sound of that, liked the idea that the talent she valued so highly was somehow discernible in her appearance. "Really?"

She kept her eyes on him, pleased by his solemn nod.

"Really." He returned his attention to his fingers. "Sell much? Of what you paint, I mean."

"Oh, I don't paint," she replied. "I'm actually an art director... free-lance. I have my own company, Artful Purpose." Accustomed to having to explain her work, Maxi continued. "When you see an advertisement or a TV commercial or even a movie, the art director is responsible for just about everything you actually see... the choice of locations, the design and construction of the sets, the props, the wardrobe, even the special effects.''

He listened patiently as she delivered her obviously pat spiel, already knowing exactly what an art director did, wondering how he knew, wondering what other knowledge and insights were inside him waiting to unfold.

He also found himself listening to the music of her low-pitched voice. It was smooth but husky, bringing to mind the sensation of stroking velvet against the nap. Such a sexy sound was a surprise coming from such a tiny woman, and it made him curious about what other surprises she might harbor. He tried not to think about it.

''Sounds like a lot of hard work,'' he said when she had finished.

''It is, but it's also a lot of fun to create a whole new fantasy with each job. I love it.''

''I guess you have a lot of help with the drudge work, too, being the head of the company, I mean.''

''Well, actually I'm the head and the tail ... and all the parts in between. Artful Purpose is a one-woman show...for now, at least. Someday I plan to have my own crew, maybe several. I want to do videos and work on special programming for public television and, eventually, movies. More and more producers are shooting their films around Rhode Island and—''

She broke off with a wide, self-deprecating smile that did nothing to dim the glow of excitement that had lit her eyes as she talked about her work. ''Of course, all of that is dependent on the project I'm working on now, which is dependent on the lunch I'm missing right this minute.''

''Keep your shirt on. I've almost got you unhooked.''

It was a lie and he winced a little as he delivered it. The truth was that he had already untangled their belts and now had one finger looped through hers, tugging on it periodically so she wouldn't suspect she was free until he'd come up with a way to forge a different sort of connection between them. It was clear he couldn't keep traipsing around after her, upsetting her, causing scenes. And telling her the truth obviously had not been the answer. Finding out more about her life might provide him with some sort of idea as to how he could fit himself into it.

"I take it that guy in there is a big client?" he ventured.

"Sort of," she replied. From the time she was small, Maxi had had trouble heeding the warning not to talk to strangers, and it took only the rumble of sympathetic interest in this man's deep voice to start her talking about her challenging campaign assignment and about Duvall's lack of confidence in her and about how the future of Artful Purpose hung in the balance.

"So you can see how it would make my life easier if I could win Peter over to my side," she concluded. "And why I just have to make these commercials the best ever."

"Success is very important to you," he observed, wishing he could share with her his newfound comprehension of how pointless such single-minded ambition was. Unfortunately, as he well knew, it was a lesson not so easily learned.

"Yes, in a way I suppose it is," she concurred quite deliberately.

"There's no denying its advantages, the BMW and the condo and the trips to... what's in this year? Sydney? Excursions into the outback?"

"Sounds like success is a place you've been, Slick."

"Could be."

"Well, just for the record, the BMW and the condo and the trendy vacations aren't the reason I'm working twenty-hour days. To me success means being offered quality projects and having the freedom to choose the ones that will really be a kick to work on."

He leaned forward, tilting his head so he could look deeply into her eyes. His slight smile reflected his mood, a blend of wistful and skeptical. "You really mean that?"

Her hair was cut like a china doll's, straight across her forehead and curving to frame her delicate chin. As she nodded vigorously in response to his question, it swung back and forth, gleaming in the sunlight, then once again settled into a flawless silky black bell when she stopped moving. He thought how a woman with hair cut like that would never mind a man running his fingers through it.

"Yes, I really mean it. Although I have to confess, I do have one ulterior motive for wanting my company to be a huge financial success."

Her sheepish smile distracted him from thoughts of how it would feel to let her hair sift like cornsilk through his fingers. He already knew how it smelled, like the fragrance of patchouli oil, although again he wasn't sure how he was able to identify such a thing.

"An ulterior motive? Are you going to tell me you're plagued by a secret fetish for designer silk dresses?"

"No," she replied with a throaty little chuckle. "I'm going to tell you that I'm plagued by a family of super-achievers who are all of the opinion that I'm wasting my life in a nowhere business and are more than willing to tell me what I ought to be doing instead."

"It doesn't sound to me as if your business is nowhere," he told her, startled by how defensive he felt on her behalf. "I'd say landing the opportunity to do this sort of political commercial at . . . what are you? Twenty-four? Five?"

"Nine," she corrected, squaring her shoulders in a way that signaled annoyance at being thought younger.

"Landing a job like this at twenty-nine is still a pretty big deal."

"Thanks. Unfortunately, my family does not concur. They are steadfast, practical types. The bank book is their only yardstick for success."

"Don't listen to them, because they're way off base. Believe me, I know. As you said, I've been there. And back. Or something."

She twisted around, arching her neck so she could meet his gaze. The top of her head rested lightly on his chest. He knew he wasn't especially tall—five-eleven was stretching it—but she made him feel tall, and powerful, and protective. Or maybe that was just how he was supposed to be feeling. He had to try to keep all this in perspective, and somehow that was hard to do when he was touching her.

"Do you know that so far you've saved me from trolls, given me a break from an awful lunch, and now you're waxing philosophical on me and I still don't even know your name?" she said.

"It's Jay." The name rolled off his tongue quite automatically. Jay.

"Jay...?"

The rest didn't come so easily, and rather than lie to her, he smiled and said, "Just Jay. What's yours?"

"Maxi. Maxine, actually, but I hate that. Maxi Love."

"Well, Maxi Love," he said, unable to keep from smiling as he said her name, "your break is over. You're free."

His announcement brought Maxi a rush of relief, quickly followed by disappointment. She gave her belt a cursory examination, straightened her shirt and finally turned to face him, strangely reluctant to walk away. She tried telling herself it was only because being free meant being free to rejoin Peter inside.

"Well, thanks again," she said.

Jay smiled and moved one shoulder in a small shrug. "It was the least I could do."

"You're right," Maxi countered with a laugh, "it was. The next time you get the urge to rescue me, do me a favor and restrain yourself."

"I'll try."

"Well..." She smiled, suddenly awkward.

His smile, she decided, was unique. Sort of sweet and sort of sexy. Make that very sexy. Like the man himself. Jay. Even his name sounded sexy to her. She'd never known a Jay before.

He was standing with his head tilted slightly to one side, eyeing her thoughtfully, as if debating with himself whether he should say something more. Maxi found herself wishing he would. Ask, she urged silently, surmising what was on his mind. She touched her lucky piece of rose quartz, part of the pendant she wore on a gold chain around her neck, and focused all her positive mental energy on him. *Just ask me.*

Allowing strange men to pick her up on the street was not something she did, ever, but Jay no longer seemed so strange to her. Trust in fate—wasn't that what she was always advising others to do? Undeniably fate was hard at work here. The reason this didn't feel like your ordinary, run-of-the-mill pickup must be because...

Because the man doing the picking up was so darn slick, she thought suddenly, the trusty piece of good-luck quartz feeling stone cold against her fingertips as she came abruptly to her senses. What in the world was she thinking of, letting herself be taken in so easily? Just because the man had high cheekbones and heavy-lidded eyes and the most gorgeous mouth, soft and full...

"See you," she said without preamble, spinning around to head for the sidewalk a few feet away.

She half expected—no, more than half—that he would call out to her as he had the last time, ask her to wait, ask her something. His only response to her abrupt "See you," however, was a softly uttered, "Right, you will," as she rounded the corner of the building.

Maxi told herself she didn't have time to ponder the mysterious note of promise in his tone. It was going to take every ounce of her concentration to salvage what remained of her lunch with Peter.

The unexpected and embarrassing interruption did nothing to alter the course of their luncheon...unfortunately. It continued to slide downhill in a strained semblance of cordiality, ending with Maxi smiling determinedly, resolved not to let Peter goad her into losing her cool and with Peter cheerfully promising to see her at the park later that afternoon. He was, he announced, scheduled to be in the area, anyway.

Maxi gritted her teeth until she swore she could taste ground enamel. Obviously, Peter was not going to delay enacting his role as her self-appointed watchdog. Let him. She had nothing to hide. And although she refused to go running to Robert with complaints about his campaign manager's attitude, she did plan to document her ideas and to let enough people know about them, so that Peter couldn't possibly steal her thunder later.

She had scheduled the shoot at Roger Williams Park for two that afternoon, which gave her a little more than an hour to pick up the props she would need before meeting the cameraman at the park. Ned Parker was a genius with a camera, which meant his services didn't come cheap. He also was experienced in shooting political spots and was open to trying new approaches. Maxi had decided he was worth the major crimp his fee put in her operating budget. She would cut corners elsewhere.

Several quick stops were all it took to collect the props she had scouted around for earlier in the week. As she steered her ancient gray Volvo, a hand-me-down from her brother, onto Interstate 95 south, she finally shook the oppressive feeling, left over from lunch with Peter, no doubt, that something was going to go wrong.

She had the Miami Sound Machine tape in the cassette player turned all the way up and the windows rolled all the way down so that the hot breeze, which felt more like July than September, could lift the hair from her neck. Piled on the seat behind her were a traditional wicker picnic basket to be used in the "family picnic" sequence of the first commercial, along with a red-checked tablecloth and assorted picnic paraphernalia. Beside the picnic basket were several loaves of bread for the "feeding the ducks" sequence and a straw hat with a wide black band that—after being used to enhance the "young couple" sequence she had planned—would fit nicely into Maxi's personal wardrobe. One of the perks of the trade.

The only thing she didn't have were the photogenic families and young couple who would be seen enjoying themselves on camera. Actors' salaries were one of the corners she was cutting. She'd decided to opt for authentic by plucking her "stars" from among the park's visitors. After enhancing reality by painting in a few eye-catching details with the props, she would step back with fingers crossed and let them tell in their own words their feelings about having a clean, well-maintained park and one of the best small zoos in the country in their home state.

Later, using voice-overs and shots of Robert, which she was counting on Ned Parker to edit into the finished commercial, she would link the showpiece park with the candidate's work on the development committee responsible for its revitalization. She knew the finished look she was aiming for would be effective, and she knew that, with Ned's help, she would get it.

She entered the park through the towering ironwork gates off Elmwood Avenue and followed the curving road as it wound past the restored casino, which was sometimes used for city galas, and skirted a small pond inhabited by wild ducks. She came to a stop on a hilltop overlooking the Temple of Music, where she had arranged to meet Ned. The bandstand, with its white stone columns, was nestled in a shell of grassy slopes. Each Fourth of July it was the stage for a pops concert and fireworks display that drew thousands of spectators.

Today, as on any nice day, people had spread blankets on the lawn to enjoy a lunch break from tramping around the zoo, or simply to lie in the sun. Maxi ran a subtly discerning eye over those she passed as she lugged the props down the hill, taking note of several families and at least one couple who personified the images she had in mind.

Ned hadn't arrived yet, but his assistant Mickey Crowley, a skinny nineteen-year-old with frizzy red hair, was already setting up equipment. Maxi found an out-of-the-way spot to dump the props and introduced herself. Wearing a wide grin, Mickey wiped his palm on the leg of his faded jeans before shaking her hand.

"I can see why Ned's rates are so high," she remarked with a smile. "He has to pay an assistant to do the back-breaking work."

"Don't kid yourself," Mickey returned, matching her light tone. "I'm virtually a volunteer. Ned refers to it as my 'internship.' But, boy, someday…" He let the comment trail off, but his eager expression as he adjusted the dial on a light meter said much about his ambitions.

Maxi chuckled. "Yeah, I know the feeling. Mickey, would you mind keeping an eye on those props over there while I go forth to practice my powers of persuasion on the crowd?"

He squinted at her. "How's that again?"

Briefly Maxi explained her plan to use real people in the commercial.

"Oh, no, not amateurs. We'll be here all night trying to get it right," groaned Mickey, but he was laughing as she walked away.

Just as she had hoped, the prospect of being on television was more than enough compensation for people to volunteer for what she was careful to warn them might be several hours of repetitious work. Within half an hour Maxi had recruited what she thought of as her starring cast, as well as backups for all of them, not bothering to tell them which was which. She would have them all sign release forms, tape everyone and make her final decisions later. Experience had taught her that sometimes what seemed perfect live was a zero on film.

When she returned to the wide marble steps of the bandstand, where she planned to begin shooting, Ned still hadn't shown up. She made a joke about saving a bundle by docking him fifteen minutes' pay and then delivered a pep talk to the eager group she had rounded up, making it clear they weren't expected to sing Robert Chandler's praises on camera, simply to tell in their own words why they enjoyed coming to the park.

The watch on Maxi's wrist was lime green, with a tiny plane at the tip of the second hand. Gradually, as the plane circled, chronicling the passing minutes, the pep drained from her pep talk. She was certain Ned knew what time he was supposed to be here. The children started to fidget. Bored with running up and down the steps, they began whining about how long it was taking. One of the fathers was pacing restlessly, and at least one of her young couples was murmuring between themselves about changing their minds.

At two minutes past three Maxi scanned the area for at least the hundredth time and could have cried at what she saw coming over the hill. Ned was still nowhere in sight, but Pete Duvall was. The premonition of disaster, which had returned and grown more insistent, suddenly exploded, incinerating her hopes of knocking Duvall's socks off with her brilliant command of the situation. It was hard to appear in command when half your troops were AWOL.

Forcing a smile she hoped radiated confidence, she rose from the step where she'd been sitting and walked down to the terrace below to greet him.

"Peter, I didn't expect you this early."

"We finished up with that senior-citizens group sooner than anticipated." He had been glancing at the tableau on the wide steps behind her as he spoke, but now his gaze swung to meet hers, razor sharp. "Seniors are a major voting block, you know."

"So I've heard."

"Then why don't I see any included in that mass of humanity you've gathered over there?"

"Because senior citizens don't happen to be central to the thrust of this particular spot. They are included in the next one," she added, then could have kicked herself. She owed him no explanations. "I'm sure I don't have to tell you that young families, college students and single parents are also important voters."

His murmured response was noncommittal. "So," he continued more forcefully, with another frankly curious glance around. "What's happening?"

"Nothing terribly riveting at this point," Maxi replied, her tone bright, her heart in a vise of panic. "We're still in the preliminary stage of production."

Mickey, who had ambled down to join them, gave her a vacant stare at her glib reference to a stage that was clearly new to him. It was new to Maxi, too. Luckily he didn't comment, however. She suspected he had picked up on the undercurrents of animosity between her and Peter.

"Who's he...the cameraman?" Peter inquired with a nod toward Mickey.

"Ah, no. He'll be arriving a little later," Maxi countered quickly. Too quickly, she fretted. "Mickey is his assistant."

She introduced the two men, and there followed a stilted moment. Finally Mickey broke the silence and won a permanent place in Maxi's heart.

"Maxi, I know you said you want to double check those props again," he said, eyeing her meaningfully, "so I thought that while you're doing that, I would call and check on that other matter for you. You know, the one that wasn't ready on time." His look grew more pointed. "Okay?"

He meant he would call to check on Ned, she realized.

She nodded vigorously. "Yes, yes, fine. Perfect."

Excusing herself, she went to tend to the trumped up task, blessing Mickey for providing her with an excuse for a moment alone to gather her thoughts. A sideways glance as she pretended to examine the contents of the picnic basket told her Peter was engrossed in conversation with the pacing father. Swell. No doubt he was getting an earful about how disorganized this whole operation was. She hoped Ned would turn up soon or at least, that Mickey could pin down exactly how late he was going to be so that she could appear to be on top of the situation here.

If it got much later, she would be forced to reschedule, in spite of the fact that the camera equipment was all set up and the cast ready and waiting. That would also put her at the mercy of the weather—a picnic in the rain simply didn't have the same charm—and delay the shooting of the other spots, thereby cutting into the time she had to edit them before the deadline. Not to mention the fact that, after her performance at lunch, she couldn't afford to let Peter witness another fiasco. Oh, Ned, where the hell are you?

All too soon a sober-faced Mickey was back with the answer to her question. He hurried over to where she was standing at the far corner of the bandstand, positioning himself so his back was to Peter.

His tone was hushed. "You're not going to believe this, but—"

"Just tell me," Maxi interjected, her stomach tightly knotted.

"Ned's at the emergency room. He left a message with his service, knowing that when he didn't show up one of us would call and check on him. Something about twisting his back playing racquetball this morning. They think it might be a slipped disk or something. Anyway, he can't make it today. He said he's sorry and he'll call you later."

"Sorry?" Maxi hissed, then felt her irritation drain as quickly as it had erupted. Ned hadn't injured himself on purpose. She glanced across the bandstand and saw Peter watching them intently. Ned's excuse was certainly legitimate and not anything she could be held responsible for, yet she dreaded the smug, condescending smile with which Peter would greet the news that she was forced to cancel.

Her mind grappled for some way to avoid it. She even briefly considered pressing Mickey into service as a replacement for Ned, then recalled that she had already identified him as the cameraman's *assistant*. That would be all the reason Peter needed to dismiss whatever film he shot as second-rate.

She stared at the waiting equipment and restless group of people, the optimist in her determined to delay the inevitable. "Oh, Mickey, I hate to give Duvall the satisfaction of cancelling the shoot."

Mickey offered a weak smile of commiseration. "I don't really see what else you can do."

"I do."

Maxi spun around at the sound of the deep, familiar voice coming from the other side of the massive post directly behind her. Taking only a half step to the right brought Jay into her line of view.

He was grinning, standing with one shoulder resting on the stone pillar. Even with his jacket draped over his arm, tie loosened and the top button of his white shirt undone, he looked like an advertisement for expensive menswear. The latest in rumpled chic.

"Oh, no."

"Don't groan," he admonished, straightening and coming toward her. Maxi controlled the urge to back away. "It looks to me as if you need rescuing . . . as usual."

"Well, if it's 'as usual,' it means my situation will go from bad to worse now that you've shown up. What on earth are you doing here?"

"You mentioned you'd be here this afternoon and that Duvall might drop by. I just figured you could use someone in your corner. I can see I was right."

"No. You were wrong," Maxi insisted. "The last thing I need right now is to have to deal with you. I have a major catastrophe on my hands."

He was still smiling. "Why do I get the feeling that's an hourly occurrence with you?"

"Please, Jay, just go away. This isn't anything you can fix."

"Of course it is, Maxi Love." His voice was low, crooning, a velvet rebuff. "You just have to learn to trust me."

"Fat chance," she snapped. "I don't even know you . . . and don't call me love."

"Why not? That's your name, isn't it?"

"You know that's not what you meant."

"It certainly is."

"You know what I mean."

"Maxi, I don't even think *you* know what you mean."

Mickey, observing the exchange in fascination, cleared his throat loudly. Speaking from the corner of his mouth like a character in a low-budget detective film, he muttered, "Look sharp."

Maxi glanced over her shoulder and saw Duvall approaching at a rapid clip.

"Maxi, I hate to interrupt your... whatever's going on over here," he said, his expression subtly disapproving, "but you do have people waiting. Now, do you or do you not have a cameraman scheduled to arrive here sometime this century?"

Maxi faced him squarely. "Peter, the fact is that I—"

"Do," interjected Jay. "And not just scheduled. I'm here." Maxi watched in horror as he extended his hand to a wary-looking Peter. "How are you doing? We didn't get a chance to meet at lunch."

Peter nodded, shaking Jay's hand automatically. "Of course, you're the joker from the restaurant. But, how... what..."

"Small world, hmm?" Jay's smile was unflagging.

"You mean you're the cameraman?"

"You got it, pal."

Peter turned to Maxi, his look accusatory. "You didn't say a word at lunch about knowing him."

"That's because we'd never met before," Jay answered for her. "Quite a coincidence, wouldn't you say?"

"Yes, yes that's the least of what I'd say," Peter retorted. "Is this true, Maxi?"

Maxi drew a deep breath and hesitated, seeing her choices very clearly etched in the annoyed expression on Peter Duvall's face and the audacious grin on Jay's. Even Mickey's overbright eyes seemed to be urging her on. At that moment she would rather have shoveled cow manure into the wind than hand Peter Duvall even a small victory.

"Of course it's true. Allow me to introduce you to the cameraman I'll be working with today." She put an ever so slight emphasis on the word *today* as she glanced in Jay's direction. "Peter Duvall, this is Jay..."

"Angel," he said as she let the introduction hang expectantly. "Jay Angel."

Maxi met his smile with a frosty glare, shifting rapidly to a smile of her own as Peter glanced her way, his brow furrowed by a quizzical frown.

"Angel, Jay Angel," he repeated. "Funny, I know most of the photographers and cameramen in the area at least by name, and I don't recall the name Angel at all."

Jay met his challenging gaze. "Really? Perhaps you're more familiar with my partner, Strumpet. Angel and Strumpet. We did a lot of work for your opponent last time around."

"That's hardly going to impress me."

"I wasn't trying to," Jay told him, his quiet tone an effective counterpoint to Peter's terse one. "I work for the lady."

Maxi winced, and not for the first time since the two men had squared off. Peter stiffened but withheld comment.

"Whereabouts are you located?" he asked Jay.

"Actually I'm on the road a lot. I guess you could say I work out of my truck."

"Truck?" Peter ran his gaze over the nearby road in both directions.

"It's in the shop," Jay offered. "That's why I'm late."

"I see."

There was a wealth of undercurrent in the two words, and in Jay's smile as he said, "Good, then we can finally get to work around here." He slapped Mickey on the shoulder. "We all set to go, Ricky?"

"Everything is set up just the way you like it, boss," replied the younger man, his delighted grin totally out of control.

"I knew I could count on you," Jay told him, crossing to where the camera was set up, surrounded by an orderly array of cables and cases containing lenses and videotape.

"Always," Mickey said, adding more quietly, "and just for the record, the name's not Ricky, it's Mickey."

Maxi, following along behind, sighed. It was going to be a long afternoon.

They could not possibly pull this off. Peter was too sharp. It would take only minutes for him to deduce that Jay was not a professional cameraman. If that long. Her heart clenched as Jay lifted the camera and proceeded to peer into the lens end.

Immediately he lowered it to flash her that disarming smile. "Relax. I was only teasing. I know what I'm doing."

"You're sure?"

Her expression was vulnerable, almost beseeching, as if everything hinged on his reply. Abruptly Jay realized that, in essence, it did. This project was a turning point in Maxi's life, and it was why he was here to help. He knew that now. Knowing gave him a sense of purpose and an understanding of how much time he had to work with. Maxi's deadline was his own, as well, looming less than three weeks away. In a way, this project was a turning point for both of them.

Maxi's suspicions about Duvall were right on target. Just those few moments of conversation had been long enough to convince him of that. Duvall would prefer to see Maxi fall flat on her face with these commercials, but, barring that, he wanted to carve out a piece of her glory for himself.

He would hang around, exerting pressure, maneuvering her into compromises that would ultimately make the project less her own. Jay knew all about those kinds of compromises. Somewhere along the line he'd made them himself. But Maxi shouldn't have to. Not if he had anything to do with it. Which, it appeared, he did.

"Yes, I'm sure," he answered finally, hoping she would believe him. The tight set of her jaw eased only slightly.

He was sure about what he was doing. Although that hadn't been the case when he brashly presented himself to Duvall as her cameraman. Not until he actually touched the camera and felt the way his fingers molded to it as if from long habit had he known for sure that he could handle what had to be done.

So it seemed cameras were part of his life, or at least had been at one time. He did find it necessary to draw Mickey aside for a few specific questions about the equipment before they got started, but he could tell from the kid's expression that they weren't the questions of an amateur.

When he was ready to begin, he looked up to find Maxi busy positioning one of the families around the red-and-white table cloth spread at the base of the steps, valiantly trying to keep two rambunctious toddlers from sticking their sneakers into the bowl of strawberries she had placed in the middle of the cloth. Assorted other goodies peeked picturesquely from the open wicker basket.

"What's this?" he asked, calling her over to where he was standing, "instant picnic?"

"Uh-huh. Add one wholesome family and stir."

"Well, you're going to have to add and stir somewhere else."

"What are you talking about?"

"You've set it up too close to the steps."

She frowned. "That's where I want it."

"Well, it's all wrong."

"Says who?" She laughed derisively. "You?"

"That's right. Me. Your cameraman."

She glanced to where Peter was speaking to another man a short distance away. "When Peter's around you're a cameraman," she allowed in a hushed voice, "but when we're alone, you're just you, a pest."

"A pest who's pulled your ass out of the fire," he reminded her. "Three times."

"Bull. Once. And even that remains to be seen. I'll still be surprised if we manage to make it through the afternoon without him suspecting the truth."

"Which is?"

"That you have no idea what you're doing."

Bristling under her dismissive glare, Jay retorted, "I told you, I know what I'm doing. Now if you'll move the damn picnic and let me do it, I'll prove it to you."

"I'm not moving it. I want the bandstand in the background. Without it the commercial could have been filmed anywhere."

"I agree. But it ought to be farther in the background so it doesn't diminish the importance of the people who are speaking. I can zoom in, get a little footage of the kids chasing each other up and down the steps, then pull back and use the bandstand to frame the shot of the picnic. It will work. Trust me."

Her look expressed the unlikelihood of that happening anytime in this millennium. If not for Peter's shouted inquiry about what was holding things up, Jay suspected she would have stood her ground against his suggestion indefinitely. As it was she gave him a long, cold warning look before stalking off to move the tablecloth.

It took about an hour to shoot the first scene. Maxi never actually got around to admitting he was right, but Jay could tell from her smile as she stood beside him looking on that she was pleased by the way it was shaping up.

It wasn't difficult to read what Maxi was feeling from moment to moment. Her pale green eyes, her mobile smile, even the way she tossed her head gave it all away. Anger or joy, it was right there up front for the world to see. Didn't she realize that was an invitation to be hurt?

No. Jay could see that she didn't. There was nothing guarded about Maxi, nothing held in reserve. She was alive, sparkling, like a glass of ginger ale poured too quickly and threatening to overflow the glass. Around her he felt as if he were perpetually holding his breath in anticipation of her overflowing the restrictions of ordinary, safe, sedate behavior. To his chagrin, it excited him.

The kids were especially attuned to her élan, he observed with a certain amount of awe. Probably because, in their estimation, she had her priorities in order, displaying more concern when one of the little boys lost his good-luck marble in the grass—even holding up shooting until it was located—than when they spilled fruit punch on her tablecloth. He was quite certain he'd never known another woman who would react that way while under such tremendous pressure.

As the day wore on she progressed from her initial irritable acquiescence to his suggestions to considering them willingly, and finally to asking his advice about such things as light angles and placement. Jay did his best not to look smug. He was in too good a mood to risk spoiling it with another argument, and it wasn't just because of the easy rapport developing between them.

The work itself filled him with satisfaction. It was an indescribable feeling, as if he had recaptured something so special that he feared probing too deeply might mean losing it all over again. He knew it had something to do with his hunch that the tape he'd shot was good, damn good. Mickey's boss's equipment was the latest in technology, right down to the capacity to let the tape be viewed on site... a fact he and Mickey kept to themselves until Maxi had thanked the last of the participants and tactfully gotten rid of Duvall.

The three of them crowded around the back of Mickey's van to view it. Even in black-and-white and on a small screen it was obvious Jay had captured precisely the upbeat, evocative images Maxi wanted.

"So, boss," Jay said as the final frames of the couple on the veranda of the Victorian-era casino wound to an end, "what do you think?"

She grinned at him, satisfaction shining in her eyes, and said, "Not bad, Slick, not bad at all."

He waited until they had thanked Mickey and helped him pack up the rest of the equipment—Maxi promising to be in touch with his boss later—to ask again.

Following her to her car, he caught her arm so she was forced to face him. "All right, now I want to hear it. What do you really think?"

"That you're good," she admitted. "No, better than good. Wonderful. I mean it, Jay, you saved my life this afternoon."

"Now, that's what I wanted to hear. And..."

Her eyebrows lifted as his voice trailed off expectantly. "And? Oh, and thank you."

"And..."

"And...I give up."

"And that you trust me, finally."

She smiled. "I trust you."

"Enough to give me a lift home?"

She looked around in surprise. "Don't you have a car? And don't give me that bit about your truck being in the shop." She shook her head, remembering. "Angel and Strumpet."

"As a matter of fact, I don't have a car right now."

"How did you get here from downtown?"

"Hitched."

"No. Really?" His narrow-eyed glare silenced her burst of laughter. "I'm sorry, you just don't look like the type to hitchhike."

"I'm not sure I am," he admitted. Resting his hip against the car, he asked, "What type do I look like?"

Her teeth clamped down gently on her bottom lip as she pondered the question, tilting her head to one side to appraise him carefully.

He sighed. "Forget it, Maxi. The fact is, I'm not like any man you've ever known."

"Oh, please." She chuckled. "Where do you get these lines? Next you'll be offering to prove to me just how different you are."

Jay found his gaze riveted on her mouth. "Would you like that?"

Instantly she stopped laughing. Her tongue skittered across her soft-looking lips, severely testing his self-control. "I . . ."

Her inarticulateness hardly mattered. He could read her now as easily as he had earlier. Her wide eyes and trembling lower lip kept no secrets. She would like it, all right. As much as he would.

"Cat got your tongue?" His voice was a low-pitched, intentionally suggestive drawl, which he found came very easily to him. "I can fix that for you."

He caught himself as his head bent toward her. Hell, what was he thinking of?

Her eyes had fluttered shut, but they opened as she sensed him jerk away. She blinked in confusion. "Jay. . ."

"Sorry," he said in a tone far rougher than she deserved. He forced a smile. "I forgot I'm supposed to be proving to you that I'm trustworthy enough to merit a ride home."

"Don't lose any sleep over it," she snapped. "You're doing a terrific job."

The unmistakable trace of disappointment in her retort transformed Jay's labored smile into a genuine one. She unlocked her door and allowed him to open it for her, then reached over to lift the lock on the passenger side as he walked around to get in.

As they pulled away from the curb in the direction of the main gates, she glanced over at him. "You'll have to tell me where we're headed."

"I already did. We're going home." When she smiled as if she once again believed him to be teasing, Jay added in a sober and very deliberate tone, "Yours."

## Chapter Four

Seated in the wicker swing chair suspended from a ceiling hook in one corner of her living room, Maxi sipped a glass of zinfandel and watched Jay amble about perusing her belongings. With the gentle push of one toe against the darkly patterned Persian carpet, she kept the swing swaying in time with the vintage Beatles music that softly filled the room.

Every now and then she smiled as Jay stopped dead in his tracks for a closer look at some object that caught his eye or to check out the record albums in her admittedly eclectic collection or to study the titles of the books overflowing the antique barrister cases lining one wall. The bookcases definitely represented a coup for Maxi. She had rescued them from the iron jaws of the garbage truck bright and early one morning and then begged, wheedled and finally bribed the sanitation crew to haul them up the three narrow flights of stairs to her apartment.

With six rooms, her apartment was a rarity in this neighborhood of subdivided old homes, a blessing she never failed to exploit whenever she found herself on the receiving end of a condescending glance from some terribly upscale type at a party. During the past several years the terminally trendy, as her friend and downstairs neighbor, Rudy, called them, had descended on the area in swarmlike fashion. This once comfortable counterculture district was known as College Hill because of its proximity to both Brown University and Rhode Island School of Design.

Maxi had neither the resources nor the inclination to compete with their designer life-styles, but she did have a long-term lease on six rooms in a location to die for. When provoked, she would oh-so-nonchalantly let the fact drop: *Six rooms. Yes, that's right, directly on Prospect Street, but of course the north end, and yes, the view from the living room is appallingly breathtaking.*

Naturally she always neglected to mention that the rooms were only slightly bigger than a bread box, drafty as a dungeon in the winter and steamy as a sauna from June to August. Make that September, she thought, straining to catch the meager breeze wafting through the window behind her. One thing she never exaggerated about was the view of the city below. It *was* spectacular, outweighing any petty inconveniences as well as the outrageous rent, and Maxi found the neighborhood, with its stalwart core of students and artists, energizing and inspiring, not to mention convenient for her work.

Besides, in the three years she'd lived here she'd managed to fill every square inch of space with mementoes from trips, relics from past projects and an odd assortment of treasures she'd happened across and simply couldn't pass up because the price was right and because someday, on some job, she just might need a pink leather bucket seat salvaged from a custom '63 Thunderbird. Relocating was not something Maxi considered lightly.

Over the rim of her wineglass she watched Jay examining one of the small ceramic cottages gathered on a shelf. Miniature houses, of all designs, held a particular allure for her, and she'd collected enough to create a sprawling, if somewhat eclectic, village. Maxiville, Rudy had christened it, insisting it symbolized her subconscious search for the happy home she'd missed out on as a child. Maxi considered his opinion proof positive that anyone who graduates from college with a psychology minor ought to have a warning to that effect stamped on his forehead.

She had no idea why the small houses called to her and preferred not to waste time pondering things she had no control over, like her childhood. She had her hands full trying to figure out the present. For instance, what lapse of judgment had prompted her to agree to bring Jay home with her, and for dinner, no less?

It was simply good manners, she tried telling herself, unsuccessfully. Good manners didn't suggest, much less require, a woman to extend a dinner invitation to a man she hardly knew simply because he had helped her out of a tight spot. All right, two tight spots. But that's as much as she would concede. No matter what Jay said, she refused to consider his behavior at lunch anything other than a major intrusion.

If she were honest, there was only one explanation for why she had brought him here: She wanted to. All things considered, she wasn't sure what that said about her character. She supposed on a certain level she'd wanted to spend the evening with him from the moment he suggested it but had bristled at the way he seemed to be taking so much for granted. Her resentment quickly disappeared when, as they were driving out of the park, he very debonairly invited her to discuss matters over dinner and then was forced to awkwardly rescind the invitation. Right away Maxi guessed that, along with lacking a means of transportation, Jay had a cash-flow problem.

Considering his style and the way he was dressed, the discovery added to her growing curiosity about him. Unfortunately, it also spoke to the softheartedness that had led her astray a time or two in the past. Before they had reached the highway she heard herself inviting him home to dinner.

He had now worked his way around the living room as far as the ancient pump organ, which took up more wall space than she could spare. Gingerly he lifted the cover and glanced around at Maxi.

"Do you play?"

"No. Which is just as well, because neither does it. Something about cracked bellows. I plan to learn someday, though, as soon as I have it restored, which will be whenever I can afford it. Even as is, it would make a great prop for the right job, don't you think?"

He responded with an indecipherable movement of his head and moved on.

The totem pole was next. Another of her finds. Positioned between two windows, it made a great rack for drying clothes, although at the moment Maxi wished she'd thought to remove the white lace teddy hanging from the top totem's nose before Jay caught sight of it. Too late. Her fingers tensed around the stem of the wineglass as she saw his hand lift.

With his fingertip he traced one narrow silk strap, slowly, attentively, as if caressing a flesh-and-blood lover. Watching from across the room, Maxi felt the contact as surely as if she were that lover. It's all in your imagination, said a little voice inside. It didn't help. Her eyes widened in shock as he slid his fingers unhurriedly along the path of lacy trim. Her skin tingled in response. She felt the rough, gentle scrape of his touch across the top of her breasts, in between, lower. My god!

Her head fell back and her stomach muscles clenched as his fingers continued to wander downward. She squeezed her eyes shut, hoping that out of sight really did mean out of mind. It didn't. Even with eyes closed she knew the exact instant when his fingers claimed that spot where the teddy came together in a row of tiny satin-covered snaps.

There was an explosion of heat between her legs, brought on by a tactile sensation so real it was scary.

She opened her eyes to see him rubbing the soft fabric between his thumb and forefinger. With a squirm she sat upright, spilling wine on her leg and sending the swing chair lurching back and forth. The commotion caught Jay's attention. He turned, still fingering the lacy undergarment, and when their eyes met, the undercurrents in the room surged, making it difficult for her to breathe.

The warm night air suddenly had a scorching edge. If a second ago she had felt as if his fingers were caressing her, she felt now as if his eyes, so dark blue they appeared black in the waning light, were looking through her, reading the excitement beating within her and liking it. Their gazes clung, neither of them saying a word, and the silence would have been enormous if not for the music that seemed to escalate, overflowing its background role with words about places remembered for a lifetime.

Yes, thought Maxi, places and moments. Like this one. It was true that she had a very active imagination, but she certainly wasn't imagining this. This was happening. It was as if the two of them had picked up the script from some old black-and-white movie from the forties and decided to act it out. There was the sweetly compelling musical score and the smoky gaze that refused to quit, and Jay was unquestionably the perfect leading man. He stood there so confidently, so expectantly, so silent. Of course he was silent. The next line must be hers. But what was it?

"Why did you want to come home with me tonight?" she asked.

Wrong line. She knew it the instant Jay removed his hand from the silk-and-lace teddy, breaking the spell. His smile appeared to be an act of labor.

"Dinner," he replied. "That was the invitation, wasn't it?"

Impatiently Maxi put her wineglass aside, annoyed that he could manage so light a tone when she was haunted by this sense that there was something happening beneath the surface here. She was a great believer in inner senses, and all hers were clamoring that more lay behind today's events than either her romantic imagination or the heavy hand of coincidence. She was certain that a few seconds ago Jay had been equally attuned to the vibrations between them, and she had no intention of letting him off with so glib a reply.

"All right, then, why did you stop and help me in the first place?"

"Because your foot was stuck."

"Right. And you just happened to be there. And then again at lunch. I suppose you charged in that time because I was choking?"

He shrugged. "I thought you were. You looked like you were. How was I to know you would sit in a restaurant and pretend to choke?"

"How was I to know I was being stalked by a nut with a Sir Galahad complex?"

"Tell me, do you get your kicks at the beach by pretending to drown?"

"I'll bet you get yours by forcing mouth-to-mouth resuscitation on unsuspecting swimmers."

"All the time." He took a step toward her, which in a room that small was enough to bring him close indeed. Beneath that phony lazy smile he was clearly provoked. "Care for a demonstration?"

Allowing impulse to outweigh common sense was a bad habit Maxi had all but despaired of breaking. Instantly she was on her feet, standing with her hands propped on her hips, her head tilted back to meet his gaze. "Why not?"

Despite the forcefulness of his hands closing on her shoulders, hauling her against him, Maxi wasn't the least bit anxious. She was excited and honest enough to admit to herself that she wanted Jay to kiss her now, just as she had a while ago in the park.

Instinctively she went up on her toes, arching closer to him. Maxi was a chest woman, and as she pressed her palms to his she felt the wonderful, uniquely male firmness of muscle over bone, along with the telltale throb of his heartbeat. She wasn't the only excited one. Pressing her tightly against him, Jay bent his head, and for one glorious instant Maxi basked in the dark glow of desire lighting his eyes. It vanished as quickly as she had incited it. She could actually see him reining himself in, fighting the feeling even as his fingers continued a hungry caress of her shoulders. She could have shaken him in frustration.

"I think not," he said finally, removing his hands and, with them, any polite excuse for her to remain so close to him. "At the moment I'm too hungry to spar with you."

"Oh? Is that what we were doing?"

"More or less. At the risk of sounding like a pushy guest, what time do you usually eat dinner?"

"Whenever the spirit moves me."

His mouth twitched. "Do you have any idea when that might happen tonight?"

"No better idea than I have about what's really going on with you."

"I already told you, but you wouldn't listen."

"Tell me again."

He started to speak, then stopped and eyed her speculatively. "I think it's the sort of thing that's better discussed on a full stomach."

"Are you bartering with me?"

"It takes two to barter. I think I'm begging."

She sighed loudly. "Oh, all right. What do you want to eat?"

"What do you have?"

"Whatever you like. Italian, Mexican, Japanese."

"You have the stuff on hand to make all that?"

"More or less," Maxi replied, pulling a stack of well-thumbed takeout menus from the bookcase and fanning them before him.

Jay grinned. "I take it you don't like to cook?"

"Actually I don't mind. It's just that it would probably be more fun if the results were occasionally edible."

"I'm not fussy and I really don't want to put you to the trouble of going out again."

"Don't worry, all these places deliver. That's my personal criteria for a four-star restaurant."

"I can find my way around a kitchen. Why don't I just fix us something from what you have on hand?"

"If you like. Do you know any recipes that call for wilted lettuce and half a frozen chocolate torte?"

Smiling weakly, he plucked one of the menus from her hand and looked at it. "Mexican food sounds perfect."

Jay assured her he shared her asbestos palate, so they easily agreed on what to order and Maxi phoned Tortilla Flats.

"I should offer to pay," Jay said after she'd hung up, "but—"

Maxi interrupted to spare him the embarrassment of making excuses. "Absolutely not. This is the least I can do to repay you for helping me out today. I'll pay you for your time, as well, of course—the going hourly rate for free-lancers, if that's all right with you?"

"That's fine." His expression revealed that in spite of his obvious cash shortage, he hadn't considered that she might pay him or how much. New questions chased after old ones inside Maxi's head. She knew her curiosity must be palpable because as if to avoid it, Jay moved away from her, settling into one corner of the sofa and giving the room another lengthy look. "This is some place you have here."

"I'll take that as a compliment. Most people seeing it for the first time just smile and look confused."

"It is a little overwhelming—sort of a visual assault. But I think I like it. How many people would think to place a headless mannequin wearing an old military uniform beside a Wyeth print of an old military uniform?"

"Don't you love that painting?" she asked, shifting her gaze to the framed print hanging above the bookcases. It was a limited edition that represented the entire profit from her first free-lance project. "The deserted house, the old uniform, the tattered lace curtain blowing in the breeze from the open window. I look at that picture, and a thousand different stories come to mind. I can feel the wind and smell the mustiness of the jacket...it gives me goose bumps," she confessed, rubbing her hands over her arms. "That's my criteria for four-star art, incidentally, whether or not it gives me goose bumps. Movies, too."

Jay was listening intently, looking not at the print but at her, his expression beguiled. "I don't think I've ever met anyone like you before."

Maxi shrugged, her smile rueful. "That's not surprising, considering."

"No, I suppose not, considering." He looked away, his mouth twisting into a perplexed frown as if he were trying to figure out something very important. It didn't appear to Maxi that he had much success, but he finally turned his attention back to her and smiled. "Anyway, this place is definitely you."

"I'm not sure that's a compliment. My brother refers to it as 'the little home of horrors.' But then I have much the same feeling about his condo full of glass and chrome and white leather. His walls are all white, too, and he's hung lots of very startling modern art, the sort of paintings that I'd swear were hanging upside down if they belonged to anyone but Dave."

While she was talking about her brother's home, Jay was struck by another of those fleeting, crystal-clear images, this one of himself looking very much at home in a place exactly like the one Maxi described. If that's where he belonged, then how was it he felt so comfortable here in Maxi's cluttered fun house of an apartment? His tone was distracted as he said, "I take it your brother has a knack for hanging paintings."

"Dave has a knack for everything he attempts. Everyone in my family does ... with the exception of me, that is. The last time any of them made a mistake was when my mother didn't order enough champagne for Dave's college graduation party, and that was back in 1971."

Jay gave a soft whistle. "Sounds like they deserve to be in the *Guinness Book of World Records*."

"I'm sure they would be if they went in for anything so trite. As it is, either my parents, my sister or one of my brothers is included in every 'who's who' book ever printed...you know, *Who's Who in Medicine*, *Who's Who in American Law*." She made a toasting motion with her wineglass as she added, "In the universe."

"How about you?"

"Me?" She grinned. "I'm the baby. By the time I showed up, the Love family had used up its share of genius genes."

"Don't be so rough on yourself."

"I'm not, really. Not anymore, anyway. I used to be intimidated by all their successes. I was constantly trying to measure up and constantly falling short. Finally I learned to be honest and just accepted it. They can all do things that I can't."

"Maybe you just choose to do different things."

Maxi stared at him in amazement. "That's it exactly." She was so pleased she could have hugged him, except, given their track record with that sort of thing, it was bound to lead to another ego-bruising rejection, which she could live without. "My interests and dreams are so different from theirs. It's as if we come from different planets. Actually, I don't think they have dreams, only agendas and short- and long-range goals."

"Are you always this cheerfully biting where your family is concerned?"

"Cheerful, yes, but I certainly don't mean to sound biting. I love them. I'm just not like them. That's why it thrilled me that you understood that I just might actually want something different from what they have. Most people smirk and think it's sour grapes when I explain that I don't want to be the world's most successful surgeon or attorney or stockbroker.''

Her smile became self-deprecating. "Of course, I'm not exactly conquering the world of commercial art, which is no doubt what any one of them would have done by this time. I can just see old Dave sitting behind a big desk in some fancy downtown office—make that downtown Boston, it's a bigger market—overseeing his own very lucrative, very glitzy advertising agency.''

Immediately a new image erupted in Jay's mind: big office, big desk and him sitting behind it surrounded by a bevy of very bright-looking, very deferential associates. He tried to shake it. "I have a feeling that conquering the world isn't all it's cracked up to be.''

Maxi nodded, struck by his quiet tone. "Guess what? I have more than a feeling about it: I have firsthand eyewitness knowledge. I've spent my whole life watching these people I love most climbing and climbing and never realizing that they're there, that they've made it. Finally it occurred to me that they're addicted to the climb, nothing will ever be enough, and that's when I finally sat back and said, no thanks, that's not for me.''

"Not much of a climber?''

"I'm more of a floater, I guess. Don't get me wrong, I'm very ambitious in my own way, but I want to see things as I float along, and if I don't make it all the way to the top, well, that's the choice I've made." She sighed heavily. "Now, if I could only get my family to accept that and stop trying to push and pull me every step of the way to fame and fortune...'' She threw up her hands. "Enough. This subject is like the weather, you can discuss it forever and not change a thing. I'd rather talk about something else...you, for instance. Where do you come from, Jay?''

He gave her a look that said she wasn't as smooth as she was trying to be. "Nowhere, really.''

"Everyone comes from somewhere. The sky didn't just part and drop you into my life.''

"Wanna bet?"

"All right, fine. Keep your secrets. Can you at least tell me how you happen to know so much about photography?"

"I used to do quite a bit of it, I guess."

She made a face. "You guess?"

"It was a long time ago."

"How long?"

He seemed to shrug, then replied almost quizzically, "Fifteen years?"

"Are you asking me or telling me?"

"Fifteen years."

"Did you do it professionally?"

There was a thoughtful pause, and then, "Yes."

"Around here?"

"No."

"What do you do now?"

"Whoa...doesn't that question fall a little outside the parameters of name, rank and serial number?"

Maxi laughed in response to his teasing tone. "Yes, I suppose it does. I'm sorry if it sounded like I was—"

"Grilling me?"

In embarrassment she realized she'd been leaning forward in her chair, expression intent, doing precisely that. She forced herself to lean back. "You can't blame me for having a few questions."

"I don't. I'll do my best to answer all of them later so that you'll understand everything."

Why later? Maxi was about to ask when the doorbell sounded. She stood, pausing on her way to answer it. "You promise you'll explain everything?"

Jay flashed a smile, that smile that had the power to wilt her knees, and shrugged. "Everything I can explain. I promise you'll understand as much as I do, how's that?"

"What more could I ask?" she said, rolling her eyes.

It required a massive harnessing of willpower for her to avoid quizzing him between bites of quesadillos and Tortilla Flats's special burritos, which they ate at the kitchen table. As soon as they started cleaning up afterward, the telephone rang. It was Ned. Maxi picked up the phone and paced into the living room as she talked with him. By the time she returned to the kitchen a few minutes later, Jay had finished washing the dishes. He glanced at her as he tossed the towel over the rack, accurately reading her expression.

"Bad news?"

"The worst. Ned has definitely injured his back, and he's in traction. God, I hate racquetball." She kicked the leg of the table. "Can you believe such rotten luck?"

"Whose? Yours or Ned's?"

Maxi looked up in time to see Jay give her an arch glance. She lifted her chin. "Both. Of course I feel sorry for Ned, but, darn it, I need him."

"Not anymore you don't. You have me."

Lord, he was serious. Maxi tried not to laugh. "Forgive me, but it's hard to be reassured by that when I don't have the slightest idea who you are or where you came from or what your qualifications are...."

"You know what my qualifications are. You saw the tape I shot today."

"Yes, but—"

"And it was good."

"Very good," she admitted.

"And I'm available on short notice."

"So I've gathered."

"And willing to work within what you've said is a very tight budget."

Maxi tried not to reveal what a silver lining that would be. The money she would save on Ned's fee would cushion a lot of potential tight spots. "You would have to. No matter how good your work is, you don't have Ned's reputation."

"Maybe not, but at least I'll have his equipment... and his assistant, if you can talk him into letting us borrow or rent them for the duration."

Maxi groaned. Of course, Jay didn't have his own equipment. That was a problem she hadn't even considered.

"Smile, Maxi, love. It's a sure bet Ned isn't going to be needing cameras while he's flat on his back, and this will keep Mickey working. Ned will probably be willing to do it just to make up for letting you down at the last minute."

Maxi thought about the sympathetic nature that had caused Ned to squeeze her project into his busy schedule in the first place. "Maybe."

"Then why do I still hear a 'but' in your voice?"

"I'm sorry, *but* how do I know I can depend on you? That you'll be around when you're supposed to? That you'll—"

"Believe me," he said, punching the words out, "I'll be around."

"Maybe." She tossed her hair back and eyed him challengingly. "And then again, maybe the sky will open up and suck you back in again."

Jay didn't smile. "Yes, but that won't happen any time soon...at least, not as long as you need me here."

"Look, Jay, I'm sorry, but this project is too important for me to take chances."

"You won't be taking a chance on me. In fact, this is probably the least chancy thing you've ever done." He studied her frankly skeptical smirk and sighed. "All right, you want answers? Brace yourself. Do you remember earlier today, outside the restaurant, when I joked about being your guardian angel?"

"I remember."

"I wasn't joking."

Maxi regarded him in silence for a moment before walking purposefully to the door and yanking it open. "Good night, Jay. It's late. I'm tired. I have a genuine catastrophe on my hands and major decisions to make before tomorrow morning, and I don't think I care to waste time playing Name that Fantasy with you."

Jay's palm landed against the door and slammed it shut again. "Think again."

He glared down at Maxi without the slightest twinkle in his eye to suggest that this was in any way a joke. More alarming questions about him began to take shape.

"You think you have no time?" he demanded, chin thrust forward. "Baby, you don't know the meaning of the words. You think you've got problems? Honey, your life—as wacky as it is—is a cream puff. The toughest thing in your life is me, and you're going to hear me out."

Before she had a chance to say "Go to hell," he dropped his hand from the door and shook his head, looking more disgusted than anything else. "Great. Perfect. See what you did? You made me yell at you when all I was trying to do was get you to listen."

Maxi folded her arms across her chest and tried to look formidable. "All right, I'm listening."

He moved away from the door a few inches, stared at her, tugged at his collar.

Maxi stared back. "Well?"

"Okay, okay, this is complicated. It all started when I was in a car accident...this morning, I think it was. I woke up in the hospital, very badly hurt...." He watched Maxi's gaze skim over him. "I know I don't look hurt, but I was...I mean, I am. I must be." Impatiently he shoved his fingers through hair. "Anyway, I could hear people talking, a doctor and...I can't recall who else, and then all of a sudden everything got all weird."

Her eyebrows lifted. "All of a sudden it got weird?"

"Yes. It was—don't laugh—it was like I was moving through clouds."

"Clouds?"

"Right. Sort of white and fluffy."

"I know what clouds are, Slick."

"I'm not saying they were clouds. It might have been an illusion of some sort, all in my head."

"I think you're finally on the right track here."

"Cut it out, I'm serious. Look, have you ever heard of out-of-body experience?"

"Of course."

"Well, I know it sounds crazy, but that's what I think I'm having."

"You're right about the crazy part, but that's not what I think you're having. And I'm just as crazy for standing here listening to you."

"That's just it, you're not listening. You're acting as if I'm bothering you, asking to borrow your car or something." He gripped her tightly by the shoulders. "Maxi, I'm trying to tell you that I'm having a very mystical experience."

"Well, you'll have to have it somewhere else," she replied through gritted teeth, "because I don't have time for this right now."

"Wrong. What you don't have is a choice. Believe me, I know how frustrating this is. I think I was probably a very take-charge type before this happened. You know, successful, important, always in control, always knowing exactly where I was going and how to get there."

"I've got to admit, you sure dress the part." She shrugged off the annoyed look he flashed her. "Sorry, but I told you I have firsthand knowledge of that type."

"Then maybe you can understand that this has been a real bitch for me. I mean a real pain," he amended uneasily.

"Okay, assuming I understand that, and assuming this is all true, what does it have to do with me?"

He sighed, as if he weren't any happier about this than she was. "You're the one I've been sent to help. You know, guard."

Maxi propped her shoulder against the door and folded her arms across her chest, her smile smug. "I have to hand it to you, Slick, that's the most outrageous line I've ever heard. Although I'm not sure why you bother, when you obviously don't have the urge to take matters any further."

His expression darkened with indignation. "What is that supposed to mean?"

"You didn't kiss me."

"Of course I didn't," he countered with impatience that seemed to border on disbelief.

"Twice."

"And it wasn't easy. Hell . . . heck, I wanted to kiss you, maybe I still do, but I'm not sure that sort of thing is—" he shrugged "—allowed."

"Allowed?" Her quizzical expression quickly smoothed. "Ah, I see, now we're getting to the guardian-angel part."

"I'm not sure I'm your guardian angel exactly, only that I'm definitely here to help you. I figure it must be because of this new project you're starting. It's the only thing that makes sense."

Maxi straightened, her eyes brightening as she was struck by a new insight into what was going on. "You're right. That makes perfect sense, in a convoluted, busybody sort of way that I'm all too familiar with, and you can tell my father the same thing I told him a week ago, I don't want his help."

"Oh, no." Jay's eyelids lowered briefly as he gave a weary shake of his head. "You think your father sent me?"

"Didn't he?"

"No. It's nothing like that. I told you—"

"All right," she said, "then it must have been Dave. He's been driving me crazy for days now about hiring a full crew of professionals to handle everything for me so I don't blow my big chance, as if I can't handle it on my own. How much is he paying you?"

"Nothing. Think about it, Maxi, if anyone was paying me, I would have been able to buy you dinner!" he shouted. "I swear, I was not sent by anyone in your family. I never met any of them, never spoke to them. You have to believe me."

"Why? Do you have some proof what you say is true?"

Jay's mouth crooked into a sardonic smile. "Not on me. They didn't issue me an angel ID, if that's what you mean."

"Well, come back when they do." She swung the door open as she spoke and caught him off guard with a shove forceful enough to maneuver him out of her apartment and into the hallway. "Good night, Jay."

The toe of his designer loafer stopped the door from closing. "Please, Maxi, you have to trust me on this. It's very important."

"Sure, a matter of life and death."

"Way beyond that, actually."

The manner in which he shifted uncomfortably and groped for words did not add credence to his story. "I can't tell you how I know, because I don't understand it myself, but I know that it's very important that I look out for you for the next few weeks. I think..." He wet his lips, his expression endearingly abashed. "...I think I've been given some sort of last chance to atone for mistakes in my life, and I'm not going to let anybody get in the way of my doing it. I'm going to help you even if it kills you."

"What sort of mistakes?"

"I don't know," he shot back, swallowed hard and added, "but I have a feeling they were biggies."

"You have a feeling they were biggies? You don't know?"

He shrugged. "It's as if my past has been wiped clean. I can only remember as far back as this morning when I somehow materialized on the street behind you. Aside from that, there are occasional quick flashes—images, sort of—but nothing I can grab hold of."

"It's called amnesia, Jay. If what you're telling me is the truth, you should see a doctor."

"It's not amnesia. I'm sure of that because I have these—" he swallowed hard "—things that I just seem to know without knowing how I know. Insights, I guess you could call them."

"Or delusions. See a doctor, Jay. Here..." She grabbed her purse from the top of the pump organ where she'd tossed it after paying the delivery man, pulled out several bills and shoved them into his hand. "Here's what I owe you for the work you did today. There's a phone booth on the corner. Go call a taxi and go to the emergency room."

"No." The set of his jaw was suddenly stubborn, reminding Maxi of a spoiled child. "I—"

"Maxi? Is everything all right up there?"

It was Rudy calling to her from his apartment one floor below. She hadn't heard his door open, but he'd obviously overheard them arguing.

"Yes, fine, Rudy," she called out. "I was just talking with a . . . a friend, but he's leaving. Right now."

Jay responded to her pointed look with one of intense frustration. "Maxi . . ."

"Goodbye, Jay."

Maxi quickly closed the door and leaned against it with indrawn breath. Finally she heard his steps on the stairs, the front door clicking shut, and only then the sound of Rudy's door closing.

She let out a deep breath. So, now she knew why someone as great-looking as Jay had come traipsing after her. The man was certifiable. Letting him know where she lived had been a big mistake. Thank heavens Rudy had intervened. She hoped Jay had caught an eyeful of Rudy's intimidating muscular build on the way past. Good old Rudy, she thought with a rush of bittersweet affection. For all that had been and almost been between them, he had never stopped being a good friend.

Determined to put the episode from her mind, she crossed the room to turn off the lamp. It was only a little after ten, but she was exhausted. Hopefully she'd be able to keep her eyes open long enough to make a list of the antique shops she wanted to scout out in the morning. She'd had a good lead on the penny-candy display counter she wanted to use in the next commercial, and as long as she was going to be in Scituate, a rural town that was an antique lover's paradise, she planned to check for a few other props, as well.

With the list completed, she leaned over to turn off the bedside lamp, then lay awake, turning and tossing for what seemed like hours, more unsettled by Jay than she wanted to admit even to herself. Why did throwing him out the way she had leave her with this lingering guilt? His story was preposterous, even to someone with as open a mind about such things as she had. Actually she was fascinated by the possibility of near-death or out-of-body experiences and never passed over an article on the subject. In all her reading, however, she'd never once come across a case where a person having such an exerience tried to drag someone else—a stranger, no less—into it along with him.

The whole thing was so...Jay had hit upon the right word earlier: *bizarre*. And so had she, for that matter: *crazy*. The man was crazy. She snuggled into her pillow and closed her eyes, only to have her mind instantly conjure up a vivid image of Jay's face, his blue-black eyes and incredible, sulky mouth. She sighed. Absolutely crazy. Still, it would have been interesting to find out if he kissed as good as he looked.

It seemed to Maxi that she had just drifted off to sleep when a sound in the living room woke her. She raised herself to her elbows and listened. The noise wasn't repeated. The old house was full of strange creaks and groans, she reminded herself, and she was still edgy from the events of the evening. Those three-alarm burritos she'd eaten weren't helping, either. What she needed was a glass of cold water.

Ordinarily she would have trotted out to the kitchen in the dark, but tonight she flicked on every light she passed, so that as soon as she rounded the corner into the living room she was able to see him, sprawled on the sofa as comfortably as a tall man could sprawl on a small sofa. Only at the last second did she manage to stifle the scream that instinctively rose in her throat.

She wasn't afraid, exactly, but just to be on the safe side, she grabbed a brass bookend as she crossed the room.

"Jay?"

He made a snuffling noise and rolled over.

"Jay?" She jabbed his shoulder and he squinted up at her with one eye.

"Mmm?"

"What are you doing here?"

"Sleeping."

"I know that. I mean, how did you get in?"

Reluctantly he sat up, following her gaze to the front door, which she specifically remembered locking and bolting. Even the heavy-duty chain lock was still in place. "Not that way," he said, his voice rough with sleep. "Not through the window, either. I told you . . ."

Maxi cut him off, trying to keep the fear coiling within from her voice. "I don't care. It's obviously a trick of some sort. I don't care how you got in, just get out."

"Again?" he groaned, swinging to his feet and stifling a yawn. "Maxi, I'm not trying to be difficult, honest, but this materializing out of thin air takes a lot out of me. Frankly, I'm beat. Couldn't I just spend the night here on the sofa and we'll talk about it in the morning? I know that once you—"

"Now." She had the door open. "Out."

He came closer, clearly intent on getting her to change her mind.

"I mean it, Jay, I want you out. Or else I'll . . ."

"What? Call the resident bouncer?" The sleep had left his eyes and with his chin lifted in challenge and his broad shoulders squared, he suddenly looked more than a match for Rudy.

"Yes," she told him, trying not to sound as concerned about that prospect as she felt. "And the police, as well. Is that what you want?"

"No. That is definitely not what I want." With a sudden docility that startled her, he walked past her and out the door. "See you."

Maxi slammed the door behind him without replying and with clumsy fingers twisted the dead bolt and hurriedly slipped the chain back into place. Next she ran from room to room, shutting and locking the windows. She would just have to swelter for the rest of the night. She ended up in the kitchen, where she checked to make sure that the back door was also secure. Just for good measure she wedged a wooden chair beneath the doorknob.

There, she thought, let him try and get back in now. She stood for a moment with her forehead resting against the door, then turned to go back to bed. As she did, she rammed directly into Jay, who was standing close—very close—behind her.

His arm curled around her, corralling her against his chest; his hand covered her mouth firmly. "Oh, no, you don't," he whispered. "No screaming."

## Chapter Five

He was holding her too tightly, with one arm slanted much too intimately across her breasts. Maxi's heart was pumping as hard as if she'd just run a marathon, but mysteriously she wasn't afraid. Under the circumstances, that didn't seem like such a good sign. She was probably beyond panic and into hysterical paralysis. Forcing herself to stand still in his arms, she waited for her heartbeat to slow before finally trying to speak.

"You promise?" Jay asked, in spite of the fact that the sound she managed to mutter from behind his cupped hand was indecipherably garbled.

Maxi nodded vigorously.

"Okay." He released her but continued to eye her as warily as if she were a cornered rabbit that might bolt at any second. "I'm sorry about grabbing you that way, Maxi. I didn't want to scare you, but I also wasn't about to hang around outside on your doorstep all night."

"I locked all the windows, the doors, everything," she said in a slightly dazed tone.

He looked as if he felt very sorry for her. "I know you did."

"You're telling the truth, aren't you? About... everything."

Jay nodded.

"Oh, my God, it's incredible." She glanced at the locked door and then back at him, trying to come to grips with the situation. "Do it again."

"What?"

"Whatever you do... walk through the wall."

"No!" His expression was indignant.

"You don't have to shout."

"Maxi, this isn't some damn...I mean darn parlor game. This is serious."

She clasped her hands together contritely. "Of course. You're right. But can you at least tell me how you do it?"

"I'm not sure how it works. It's as if I blink and I'm here. The first time you threw me out, I didn't know it would happen. Now I know. Somehow I have the power to be wherever I'm supposed to be. I guess that's the key to it. Bad pun, sorry."

"Don't be. It's comforting to know that some things, like bad puns, endure even after death."

"I am not dead," Jay snapped.

"Well, excuse me," Maxi snapped back. "I mean, just because you walk through walls and claim to be my guardian angel is no reason I should assume that you're... you know."

"No, it isn't. Because I'm not. Not yet, anyway. All right?"

"All right." Silence. The scene was so mind-boggling Maxi was at a rare loss for words.

"So, what else can you do?" she asked finally, conversationally, ridiculously. What on earth were you supposed to talk about with an angel? "Have you tried leaping tall buildings in a single bound…okay, sorry. Seriously, though, if you suddenly wanted to, say beam yourself downstairs into Rudy's apartment, could you just focus on that and…?"

He was shaking his head. "It wouldn't work. Rudy is none of my concern."

"And I am?"

"That's what I've been trying to make you understand. I don't know why or how, but like it or not, we're in this together, kid."

"I'm not sure I like the sound of that."

"How do you think I feel? I can think of a million people who would be less of a pain in the as—neck to watch over than you."

"Then why don't you go find yourself one of them? Whoever you choose is sure to be more appreciative than I am. I have this thing about being watched over, you see, and—"

"Tough. Like I told you, you…"

"Don't have any choice," Maxi finished along with him, ending on a deep sigh. If he was telling the truth, if this wasn't all a bad dream that she might wake up from any second, then he was right; she didn't have any choice. "Just for the record, if I did have a choice, you're not what I would choose for my guardian angel."

"Oh, no? Who would you choose? Somebody more like the bearded hulk living downstairs? What's he suffering from, by the way? Severe lumberjack complex?"

She shook her head at the obvious reference to Rudy's affinity for wearing red suspenders and plaid shirts. "My, my, that was certainly a rather unangellike comment. And yes, I would choose somebody more like Rudy. He's sweet and compassionate and doesn't argue with everything I say. And he even looks more like an angel than you do and— Oh, my God, I can't believe I'm having this conversation."

"Me, either," admitted Jay, smiling abashedly. "Truce?"

"Truce."

He glanced around the kitchen. "I think we should drink to it. I know I could use a drink. Have you got anything stronger than wine?"

"I'm not sure."

Jay watched as she walked across the kitchen and stood gazing into the nearly empty freezer as if it were totally foreign terrain. Who kept liquor in a freezer? Probably someone who used a totem pole as a clothes dryer, he thought, and went along in silence until she pulled from the freezer the leftover chocolate torte she'd mentioned earlier.

"When I asked for something stronger, that's not what I had in mind," he told her dryly as she grabbed forks from a drawer.

Maxi plopped the torte on the table and sat down. "I can't help it. I always eat when I'm under a lot of stress, and you definitely qualify as a lot of stress."

"Well, don't." He slid the plate from beneath her rapidly descending fork. "Do you want to put back on all that weight you worked so hard to lose?"

Her eyes narrowed suspiciously. "What weight?"

"The twelve pounds you took off last summer."

"Fifteen." She shrugged in the face of his unwavering stare. "Oh, all right. Twelve."

"It's bad enough that you ate that Snickers bar in the bathtub the other night.

Maxi stared at him. "No one knows about that Snickers."

"I do."

"Oh, no. Now I need a drink, too." She banged cupboard doors open until she found a half-full bottle of Scotch, then stood considering the selection of drinking glasses on the shelf below.

"You're right," Jay said, "we might as well use the water glasses, they hold more. Don't worry so much about propriety."

She glared at him. "I don't."

"As a matter of fact, you do. You just pretend not to. The same way you pretend not to be bothered by your family's disapproval."

Instinctively she pulled the edges of her loose cotton robe closer together, wishing she'd taken time to look for the belt and realizing even as she did so what a furtive effort it was. "This is going to sound insane, but…are you by any chance reading my mind?"

"Not exactly. Not intentionally, anyway. I told you, I have these sudden insights. I don't know how or where they come from, just that they're the truth."

Setting the glasses and the bottle on the table, she slipped into the seat across from him and folded her hands in front of her. "All right, tell me what I'm thinking now."

"Maxi…" he said, his tone admonishing.

"I'm sorry, I forgot, it's not a parlor game." She frowned. "But how will I know when you know what I'm thinking?"

He looked up from pouring the Scotch and flashed her a grin that was not at all angelic. "You won't."

"That's an invasion of privacy."

"Sorry, but I doubt the Fifth Amendment applies in cases like this."

"Then what does?"

He gave it some thought and shrugged. "I don't know. I didn't get a rule book, either."

"It all seems pretty slipshod to me. I mean, here you are, supposedly sent to help me, and you're feeling your own way."

"Maybe that's the point. During the last few hours it's occurred to me that I might need your help as much as you need mine. It's to both our advantages to cooperate."

Leaning back in her chair, Maxi regarded him with a narrowed gaze. In spite of what she'd seen with her own eyes, she couldn't completely shake the thought that this might be a trick of some sort. "How do you figure that?"

"You need a cameraman, right? And quickly, or you'll lose all credibility with Duvall and, maybe if he has his way, your shot at this project. By stepping into Ned's shoes, I can save your as—hide, and it looks as if at the same time you'll be helping me save my—" He floundered.

"Soul?" she said, eyebrows arched as she suggested what was both most obvious and least believable.

"Well put," he said, saluting her with his glass.

"Jay, do you really think that's what this is all about?" She suddenly felt overwhelmed by the enormity of what was happening. "That you've been given some sort of last chance to make amends before..."

"Before I check out?"

She smiled weakly. "I didn't want to say it and upset you."

"I'm certain that's what it is. I just don't know all the dos and don'ts, so until I figure out the rules, I'm going to play it nice and safe. This is not the sort of opportunity to take chances with," he remarked dryly. "Whatever it is, it's only for a couple of weeks, Maxi. I'm going to give it my very best shot. Will you cooperate?"

Maxi reached for the glass in front of her and took a swallow, letting the liquor burn its way down as she thought it over. "All right," she agreed finally, "but on one condition: I'm still in charge."

Jay's eyes glittered. "Theoretically. Under the circumstances, I'd say neither of us can really claim that distinction."

"Then I'll settle for theoretically. Now, as long as we're going to be working together, maybe you'd better tell me everything again. From the beginning."

It was over an hour and a good portion of the Scotch later when he finished, stopping frequently to answer Maxi's questions or listen to her theories on the situation.

When she'd finally heard it all, she shook her head. "It's unbelievable."

"But you do believe me?"

"Yes."

"Then I think that's where we should leave it for tonight. We both need some sleep." He got to his feet. "Now that you believe I have nowhere else to go, may I sleep on your sofa?"

"Yes, of course. I'll get you a pillow and blanket." She found them in the closet and handed them to him with an apologetic smile. "I just wish I had someplace more comfortable to offer you. I keep meaning to buy a bed and turn the spare room into a guest room, but something else always comes up."

"A bed would be a lot more practical than that purple leather jacket you bought instead. Sorry," he said when she shot him a resentful look. "If you'd prefer, I'll try and keep your thoughts to myself."

Maxi considered that and shook her head. "No, I'd rather know what you know."

"In that case, yes, I can see through that nightgown you're wearing. And truthfully, Maxi Love, the sight is enough to tempt an angel."

"Which I'm not at all convinced you are," she snapped, crisscrossing the wayward robe in front of her and anchoring it there with folded arms. "Good night."

"Sleep tight."

"I will." She took a step toward her bedroom, paused and glanced back. "Jay?"

He gazed up at her from the sofa, knees bent, arms tucked behind his head. He looked a little like a *Gentleman's Quarterly* accordion, and Maxi felt a pang of sympathy. "Yeah?"

"Speaking of sleeping tight," she said, backing into what concerned her, "all this walking through walls and reading thoughts has got me wondering. I mean, I'm not going to wake up and find that you— You're not going to pull anything spooky on me while I'm sleeping, are you?"

Again there was nothing the least bit angelic about his grin or the look he raked over her. And, for that matter, nothing innocent about the tremor it set off inside her. This was conventional man-woman stuff, and very earthy. If Jay was worried that an occasional spontaneous curse was going to count against him, Maxi feared for his soul at that moment.

"I don't know," he told her, his low-pitched voice, soft and caressing, drifting to her through the shadows. "This is my first night on the job. We'll just have to wait and see."

Maxi couldn't decide if she was more alarmed or intrigued. For a long time she lay awake, waiting, but it seemed the night was going to be disappointingly uneventful, and eventually she fell asleep. Several hours later she came awake to find her room still dark and Jay by the side of her bed. She could swear he had been simply standing there watching her sleep, but as soon as she moved so did he, taking a purposeful step closer.

"Jay? What are you doing in here?"

"I was too hot to sleep," he said softly, opening his arms as he planted one knee next to her on the mattress.

Instantly Maxi was upright, grabbing for the sheet she had kicked to the foot of the bed and clasping it to her chest. "Stop," she ordered. "Don't do anything you'll regret."

Jay froze. His face only inches from hers, he peered at her with a startled expression that slowly gave way to a sardonic smile. "Maxi, love, you're jumping to conclusions again. I said I was hot, not hot for you."

"Oh." Her hands clenching the sheet were clammy. "I didn't say you were. As a matter of fact, that's not even what I was thinking. Exactly."

"Oh, no?" He tilted his head, making a great show of looking perplexed. "Then maybe it was me who got signals crossed." His voice dropped. "Maybe what you were really thinking is that you're hot for me."

"Don't be absurd...and don't forget why you're here."

"I haven't. Have you? I'm here to take care of you. For all we know that might include fulfilling your fantasies, satisfying all your most secret desires."

"What secrets?" she grumbled.

"Exactly."

Feeling suddenly breathless, she began fanning herself with the sheet, careful not to let it slip. "Gosh, you know you're right, it is hot in here."

There was a sly, knowing cast to the grin Jay flashed her. "I can take care of that for you."

"No, really, that's not necessary," she protested as he leaned closer.

"It's my pleasure."

"Don't bother. I'm not that hot."

"Liar. But don't worry, relief is at your fingertips."

Maxi was debating whether the situation was desperate enough for her to risk making an idiot of herself by running, when he continued.

"Or maybe I should say *my* fingertips." As he spoke he reached past her and opened the window over her bed, obviously the action he'd intended all along. "Better?"

"Much," she replied, though the fresh air did little to lower her temperature. The truth was she wasn't able to draw a real breath until he was safely off the bed.

"You shut and locked every window in the place," he reminded her. "I've already opened the others. I came in here to take care of this one for you."

"Thanks. I didn't realize how stuffy it had become. I feel a little light-headed."

"Mmm?" he responded, the glint in his eyes rendering the murmur a full-blown suggestion.

"I meant from the heat," Maxi shot back much too defensively.

"Of course. What else?"

"Us."

"Mmm?"

"Don't 'mmm' me. It's our auras. I think they're in opposition. There seems to be this tension in the air whenever we're together. I felt it right away."

"Yes, I've been feeling it all night myself. I just didn't think it was coming from my aura." His catlike smile implied where he did think it was coming from, and Maxi pulled the sheet a tad higher.

"You're just like my brother Dave," she told him, "scoffing at anything you can't see and touch and dissect. Not that *you* have any right to be so smug. After all, you're proof that things aren't always what they seem."

"True."

"And don't try to deny that there is a certain tension in the air whenever we're together."

"I wouldn't dream of denying it. You attribute this tension to the fact that our auras are in conflict?"

"Not conflict necessarily. Opposition. And yes, it's possible."

"So is Pee Wee Herman being elected president. It just isn't very likely. Where did you spend puberty, Maxi? Locked in a crystal ball? Has it occurred to you that there's a much more likely explanation for the tension between us?"

It had. "No."

"Want me to enlighten you?"

"Not especially."

"In that case, I'll say good-night." Still smiling, he turned to go. "Sweet dreams, Maxi, love."

"I've already told you not to call me that."

"And I've already pointed out that it's your name."

"No. My name is Love with a capital *L*. You were saying Maxi, love, with a small *l*."

"How can you tell if I'm saying it with a small *l* or a capital *L*?"

"I just can. And I don't like it."

"Fine." He gave in with a weary wave of his hand. "Have it your way. Good night, Maxi."

"Good night." She paused, not feeling particularly satisfied by the victory, punched her pillow into a comfortable shape and settled her head on it before adding, "Slick."

It took Jay a long while to fall asleep once more. It was still plenty hot in here, he thought, rolling to face the back of the sofa. Almost without pausing he rolled back the other way. The sofa was too short. And lumpy. The pillow was no prize, either. He wasn't sure he could take three more weeks of this. Lying flat on his back, knees in the air, gaze focused on the shadow spheres cast on the ceiling by the streetlights outside, it suddenly occurred to him how absurd it was to be getting all bent out of shape about the sleeping arrangements. He certainly had bigger things to worry about. Much bigger.

Maxi Love, for instance. No doubt about it, she was the wild card in this hand he'd been dealt. Sure she had agreed to cooperate, but would she? Even if she was willing to, would her idea of cooperating be the same as his? All he wanted was to play things nice and safe, get these campaign spots shot for her—which had to be his purpose for being here in the first place—and be on his way. Whatever that might mean. He closed his eyes, drawing a deep breath and savoring it. What worried him was that *nice* and *safe* didn't appear to play big parts in Maxi's life.

Her driving habits alone were enough to make him shiver. He could still hear the chorus of horns blaring behind them as she jackrabbited between lanes on the highway. "Signal," he had shouted. "You have to signal when you change lanes."

"I did," she'd retorted, sending him deeper into panic as she took her eyes off the road ahead to glare at him. "Can I help it if my left-turn signal is out of whack?"

Of course she insisted that she meant to have the signal light fixed, the same way she meant to shop for groceries, have the organ restored and buy a bed for the spare room. Her total lack of organization ruffled something deep inside Jay. He might not be able to recall the specifics of his own life, but he was certain that it had been scrupulously organized, planned down to the last detail. That was the only way to get things accomplished. It was obvious why

Maxi resisted so much as scheduling a time to eat dinner, however: she was rebelling against her family.

What she needed was for someone to take her in hand and prove to her that organization wasn't a dirty word, that careful planning brings results. Not someone, he thought suddenly. Him. It was so obvious he wondered why he hadn't seen it sooner. It wasn't simply the campaign ads he'd been sent to help her with, it was her approach to life. Folding his arms behind his head, he grudgingly revised his opinion of this whole operation. Things might have been a little slow getting off the ground, but obviously whoever was pulling the strings up there knew what they were doing after all.

Thinking of all the ways he was going to bring order to Maxi's life was as effective as counting sheep. He would have to devise some sort of chart, he decided, outlining her life in neat time blocks brief enough for her to handle. His mouth twisted. Like, say, an hour. Of course he would have to find room around here to hang the chart where she would be able to see it. Come to think of it, the apartment could stand a little organizing, as well. He drifted off to sleep pondering whether her books ought to be arranged alphabetically or by size and woke to the sound of someone hammering on the front door.

The hammering was eventually joined by the rapid patter of Maxi's footsteps. Jay lay on his stomach, resisting the urge to open his eyes except for the slits necessary to see his wrist. He could envision the slender, distinctive gold watch that ought to be there and wasn't. It didn't matter. Every bone in his body told him it was too early to wake up. Even if it had been time, this was no way to go about it.

There ought to be an alarm ringing, subdued but persistent, and conveniently located so he could reach out and hit the snooze button and take another fifteen minutes while the house slowly filled with the aroma of brewing coffee from the pot he'd set the timer on the night before. That was the civilized way to start the day. This was not.

Now Maxi and whoever was at the door were talking in that low-pitched sort of tone that made anyone within ear-shot intensely curious. Against his will Jay strained to make out what they were saying. He had a glum suspicion that the visitor was the lumberjack from downstairs. What had Maxi called him? Robby? Ronnie?

"There's nothing to tell," Jay heard Maxi say. From the sound of it they had moved closer. "I mean it, Rudy, he's just a friend."

Rudy. It was the lumberjack, all right.

"Yeah? I never knew you to let some guy friend spend the night before," Rudy said, sounding none too pleased that she had seen fit to do so this time. Jay wasn't sure why, but he took pleasure in both the other man's comment and his disgruntled tone.

"Well, he's from…out of town," Maxi explained, "and it was late…and he had some car trouble, so I let him spend the night."

"Well, it's not night now," the bearded Einstein pointed out. "Why isn't he up?"

"I guess he's tired."

"I'll say. I was really banging on that door."

"I'm sorry, I had the water running in the bathroom."

"That doesn't explain his not hearing it. Hell, this guy sleeps like the dead."

"Yes, he sure does." There was a distracted quality to Maxi's response. It almost sounded as if she were turning away. Then Jay heard her mutter, "Oh, no," and felt her hands land on his shoulders.

"Jay? Jay? Are you all right?" she exclaimed, shaking him with more force than he'd have thought someone her size could muster. "Can you hear me?"

"As clearly as if you were screaming in my ear," he muttered, reluctantly turning his head and opening his eyes to look directly into her wide-open pale green ones. "Oh, I see that you *were* screaming in my ear. Any particular reason?"

"You were lying so still I was afraid you were—" She glanced over her shoulder at the man standing there, eyeing them both curiously. "I just wanted to make sure you were all right." Raising her voice, she added, "I remembered you said you weren't feeling well last night."

"What was the matter with him?" asked Rudy.

Maxi and Jay looked up at him and spoke at the same time.

"He had indigestion."

"A headache."

They glanced at each other, then back at Rudy.

"I had indigestion, and it gave me a headache," Jay explained. "Now I only have the headache."

"Well, that's a good sign," remarked Maxi, wearing a starched, determined smile as she stepped between Rudy and Jay, who had now gotten to his feet. The two men were staring at each other with a look that was at once assessing and defensive and which Jay had no intention of breaking first. "Rudy, this is Jay...Angel," she said with the barest bubble of laughter. "Jay, this is my neighbor and friend, Rudy Bannon. Rudy came up to borrow a cup of coffee."

"Fine. There's an unopened can on the top shelf." Jay, having had the good fortune to notice it there last night when he was putting the dishes away, anticipated that such a proprietary remark would get under Rudy's skin. He wasn't disappointed.

With a warning look back at Jay, Maxi grasped one of Rudy's beefy arms and headed for the kitchen. "Come on, I think we could all use a cup of coffee."

Jay followed, noting that Rudy looked much the same as he had last evening when he'd stood glaring at Jay from his doorway: same threatening scowl, same faded jeans and red suspenders. Except this morning, instead of woodsy plaid he was wearing a T-shirt with something emblazoned on the front. Ah, yes, a beer slogan. Obviously a very classy guy. He was tall and muscular, with curly hair the same coppery hue as his beard, and he lowered himself into a kitchen chair as if he planned on being there a while.

Jay found a piece of wall to lean against and looked on. Maxi, her hair still damp from the shower, was dressed in an outfit unlike anything he'd ever seen. It was a dress, he thought, definitely a dress, in spite of the fact that it looked more like an overgrown lavender undershirt. It had a long row of tiny white buttons down the front and several layers of ruffles above her knees—well above her knees, he noted with interest. With it she was wearing a short black vest and a black leather belt slung low on her hips and—of course— the usual assortment of bangles and crystals.

Part of Jay thought she looked ridiculous. But another part, a part of himself he was still getting acquainted with, thought she looked absolutely beautiful, in the way a rainbow or butterfly did. He was so distracted by her that it took him several minutes to realize that she was measuring the coffee not into a cup Rudy could take with him, but into the plastic basket of the coffeemaker on the counter.

"I thought he wanted to *borrow* a cup of coffee," he said inquiringly.

Rudy looked at him. "I do."

"A cup already perked," Maxi added, without breaking stride—scoop and dump, scoop and dump. She finished, hit the On switch on the coffee maker and put the cover back on the can of coffee. "It's become sort of a joke. You see, Rudy doesn't own a coffeepot."

"Very cute," Jay responded. Then, thinking ahead, he added, "You mean he comes here for coffee every morning?"

Rudy smirked. Clearly he saw this as his revenge for Jay's knowing something as personal as where Maxi kept the coffee. "Like clockwork," he said. Tipping his chair back so it was balanced on two legs, he ran his gaze from Jay's rumpled dress shirt to his sock-clad feet. "So. Maxi tells me you're from out of town. Whereabouts?"

"Nowhere you've ever been," replied Jay, still chafing at the prospect of having coffee with this belligerent stranger every morning for what might well be the rest of his life.

Maxi shot him an admonishing glance. "Rudy's just trying to be friendly."

"Sorry," Jay felt compelled to say.

Rudy shrugged magnanimously. "No problem. So where are you from?"

"New York," Maxi replied at the same time Jay said, "Dubuque."

"Dubuque by way of New York," Jay clarified.

"Oh, yeah?" Rudy landed the chair on all four legs. "Why do I have the feeling something funny's going on here?"

"Because you're an acutely sensitive guy?" suggested Jay.

"Jay, don't you think you should go and get ready?" Maxi quickly asked.

He looked at her. "Ready for what?"

"Work." She pinned him with a very pointed glare before turning to Rudy. "Jay is going to help me out with the spots I told you about." Briefly she explained about Ned's mishap.

"That's a rough break," Rudy said, shaking his head. "Have you done this kind of thing before?" he asked Jay.

"Dozens of times." He rested his hips against the counter. "How about you, Bunyan? What line of work are you in?"

"That's Bannon," Maxi corrected, slanting Jay a look that said she knew the error was intentional and didn't think it was funny. "Rudy is a drummer."

"For Wild Horses," the other man added, looking expectantly at Jay.

Jay shrugged. "Should that mean something to me?"

"They're a very popular local band," Maxi told him.

"Not for long though," added Rudy. "Local, I mean. We just signed our first record deal, and Maxi's doing the cover design. Actually I wanted to talk to you about that, Maxi.

Grecco and I were talking it over, and we think the smoke thing is going to work after all. Can it be sort of shooting up from behind the amps and curling around the guitars?"

"Sure. How about the road signs?"

"We like that, too. We even thought that Yield might make a good title. But the guys don't like the feathers."

"But then the horse makes no sense," Maxi protested. "It was supposed to be horse feathers, get it?"

"Yeah, I get it, but . . ."

"Oh, never mind." She sighed. "I guess I can come up with something else."

"We tossed it around a little among ourselves and thought—"

"You know," Jay interrupted, "I think I will go and get ready or else we might not get any work at all done today."

Hearing the implication in his tone, Maxi pointed out, "This is work. But you're right. I want to check out that penny-candy counter as soon as possible in case it isn't right and I have to start looking all over again."

"Now that's being sensible."

"You sound surprised."

"A little." Jay thought he might as well let her know how he felt up front. "I have noticed that you have a tendency to be a little disorganized at times."

"Oh, you have, have you?"

"Yes. Nothing major," he said, telling himself an understatement wasn't the same as a lie. "Nothing a little coaching can't cure."

"Let me guess who you have in mind to play coach."

"It so happens I do have a knack for planning things."

"Well, so do I. As a matter of fact, I even made a list of all the shops I want to check out while I'm in that area today. Listed in order by location, I might add."

"You did?" he asked, amazed.

"Yes." From the pocket of her vest she pulled a crumpled piece of paper and looked at it. "First I want to stop by The Sugartree . . . if it's open on Wednesdays, that is. Then

Lillian's Attic. I know that one is open, I just hope I can find the turn for it. I remember it comes either right after a big red barn or right before that ice-cream stand with the big silver can out front. Anyway, I'm sure I'll know it when I see it.''

"Maxi, that's not a plan," Jay said. "It sounds more like directions for a scavenger hunt. Bad directions."

She tossed her hair back, and it was like someone waving a black silk flag in the morning sunlight. When she stopped moving, it settled above her shoulders in a line as straight as a military procession. "It will all work out," she told him. "You'll see."

Jay, utterly exasperated, found himself exchanging looks with Rudy. Any port in a storm.

"It probably will work out," Rudy offered. "You know what they say about God watching out for kids and kooks."

"That's right, Jay," Maxi chimed in, "*you* know what they say about that."

Jay squelched the urge to point out that she sure could look smug when she wanted to. "Yes, but I thought it was drunks and fools."

She shrugged. "And I thought you were off to take a shower."

"I changed my mind. I'd only have to climb back into these same dirty clothes afterward."

Maxi chewed her lip for all of five seconds before her expression turned as bright and full of promise as a new penny. "I know, you can borrow a few things from Grecco. It would only be for a week or so," she continued, turning to Rudy. "I'd say he and Grecco are about the same size, wouldn't you?"

"Close."

Jay frowned. "Who's Grecco?"

"Our bass player," replied Rudy.

Chuckling, Maxi added, "And, more pertinently, his roommate."

"Why not?" Rudy agreed, getting up. "The Grec won't care. In fact, his room is such a mess he probably won't even notice anything missing. I'll run down and see what looks clean."

"Nothing with too many studs or sequins," Maxi called after him.

Jay hoped she was joking.

When he finished his shower, he knotted a towel with pastel rainbows on it around his waist and walked into Maxi's room to find the borrowed clothes on her bed. There were a couple of pairs of pants and a few shirts and shorts. Apparently "the Grec" didn't wear socks. Jay held up two of the shirts, thinking it wasn't always easy to discern the lesser of two evils. True, neither was covered in studs or sequins; they were still about as close as a pink tutu to what he would choose to wear. Somehow he just knew he wasn't the black-jeans-and-Grateful-Dead-T-shirt type.

He refused to complain, though. Why give Maxi a chance to point out the truth, that beggars can't be choosers?

Resignedly he dressed, listening to the noise coming from the kitchen. It reminded him of a diner at rush hour. There was the clatter of dishes and flatware and the duel of raised voices competing for attention. Obviously the ranks of early-morning visitors had swelled.

He rounded the corner from the living room, still tucking his shirt into the jeans, and collided with a man wearing a charcoal pinstripe suit and a white shirt bright enough to read by. One look at the guy told Jay his suit was hand-tailored and his tie made of hand-printed silk. He suddenly felt more foolish than ever wearing a T-shirt with neon decals. It caused a physical ache in his chest to keep from blurting, "These are not my real clothes."

The newcomer adjusted his tortoiseshell glasses and peered at Jay with eyes as brightly inquisitive and as green—although not nearly as friendly—as Maxi's. Aside from Maxi's sweetness, he also didn't have lashes so dark and lush they made prime sable look shabby.

"Dave," Jay heard Maxi say, "this is Jay, the man I was just telling you about."

"The videophotographer?" he asked as skeptically as if she had just introduced Jay as the heavyweight champion of the world.

Jay, knowing how to seize control of a situation, stuck his hand out. "Cameraman, actually. My guess is that you're Maxi's brother Dave."

The other man accepted Jay's hand but said nothing. His lips were pressed together tightly, contemplatively, and the emotions emanating from his eyes—disapproval and suspicion—were totally foreign to Jay.

The extrafirm handshake Jay delivered did nothing to change the look he was getting, and suddenly he was struck by the realization that nothing he did or said would change it. Dressed as he was, without the outward badges of success that enabled men like Dave Love to distinguish one another from the mass of ordinary humanity, Jay would never win the approval or trust of Maxi's brother. Indignation welled up inside him. How dare he judge a man based on something as petty as the clothes he was wearing?

"Nice to meet you," Dave Love recited finally. "So. You're the videophotographer...cameraman that Maxi has chosen for the biggest project of her career."

"That's right."

"Hmm." It was a very eloquent *hmm*. "What studio do you work for?"

"None. I work for myself."

Dave's eyebrows appeared above his glasses, like twin black caterpillars arching their backs. "Oh?"

"That's right," Maxi confirmed. "And I was really lucky Jay could take the job on such short notice. He usually has more work than he can handle."

"I hope he also has good references," Dave said, still watching Jay.

"The very best," she countered with a drollness Jay knew no one else could appreciate. "My, look at the time. Aren't you going to be late for work, Dave?"

"A little. I told my secretary to forward my calls here. I thought it was important that I check in with you this morning."

"You mean check up on me, don't you?"

"Don't be so defensive, Maxi. This project for Chandler is the biggest thing you've ever handled, and I don't want to see you—"

"Screw up?" Maxi interjected.

"I don't want to see you make any impetuous or imprudent decisions as those faced with their first undertaking of any magnitude are sometimes apt to do."

"In other words," added Rudy, swigging the coffee remaining in his cup, "screw up. You know, Dave, old buddy, I once consulted a right-brain adviser who explained to me that there are no mistakes. That what sometimes appear to be mistakes at the moment are really just moves the spirit needed to make for whatever reason. So maybe you ought to just step back and let Maxi do her thing here."

Dave Love's expression remained immobile as he endured Rudy's lecture; he saved everything for his retort. "Thank you for sharing that insight. Aside from the pure pleasure of being blessed with such highly credible advice, it's enlightening. For all the years my sister has seen fit to endure your company, I've never once suspected you had any need for either a right- or left-brain adviser."

The put-down was so finely cutting that Jay caught himself beginning to smile in admiration and froze. Whose side was he on here? His gaze volleyed from Dave, still savoring his own brilliance, to Rudy, whose shrug said he couldn't care less what Maxi's big brother thought. The truth was, Jay wasn't sure which side he was on now. He knew only that at one time or another in his life, he'd been on both of them.

Giving his red suspenders a loud, no doubt intentionally irksome snap, Rudy stood. "Well, folks, I hate to enlighten and run, but I have to get some practice for our gig tonight."

"Don't let us keep you," Dave said. "After all, there just aren't enough hours in the day to accomplish some things."

Jay felt a new sympathy for Maxi for having grown up with a brother whose tongue had obviously been manufactured by Wilkinson Sword. Old Dave must have been a barrel of laughs as a surly adolescent. And if what Maxi had told Jay was true, the rest of her family was equally armed and dangerous. Dinner-table conversation at the Love house must have all the charm of bayonet practice.

"I hope you're not seriously considering doing any work for that motley band he's part of," Dave said to his sister as soon as Rudy was gone.

"No, I'm not considering it, Dave."

Inside the expensive suit his shoulders seemed to relax. "Thank goodness."

"I'm not considering it because I've already agreed to it."

"You mean you've signed a contract? Don't worry, Janet can handle it for you. She could find a loophole in Genesis."

"Janet is my sister," Maxi explained for Jay's benefit, confirming what he had already deduced on his own. "She's the women's movement's answer to F. Lee Bailey." To Dave, she said, "I don't need Janet to handle anything because I haven't signed a contract."

"Good. Don't."

"I have no intention of it. Rudy, Rick Grecco and the others are my friends. We don't need a piece of paper to guarantee that I'll do a favor for them."

"Favor? This, such as it is, is your life's blood, Maxi, your bread and butter, business, pure and simple. Do you think Donald Trump's friends ever ask him to build them a skyscraper as a favor?"

"I don't know, but the next time I see him I'll ask."

"Don't be a wise ass."

"Don't you. I can handle my own business affairs. When the time comes, the guys and I will work out suitable compensation for whatever work I put into their album cover."

"Like what? A quarter ounce of pink tourmaline and a gift certificate for a session with Rudy's right-brain adviser?"

Maxi shrugged. "I could do worse. Pink tourmaline is very powerful."

"Oh, please," groaned her brother. "Maxi, please, just let me handle your books for you, make sure your billings are—"

"No. I can take care of my own books."

"If you refuse to accept my help, at least talk to the friend I told you about. He's a Harvard MBA and a consultant to some of the top small businesses in New England. He'll be able to—"

"To what?" Maxi interrupted. "To break down what I do into bits and pieces? To label and compartmentalize and evaluate and prioritize everything?"

Jay, looking on, tried not to cringe as he mentally dismissed the chart idea that had seemed so brilliant last night.

"Well, the day that happens," Maxi continued, her angry gaze keeping Dave pinned in place, "your MBA buddy can just go ahead and do it all, because I won't want any part of it anymore. Try and understand, Dave, I do what I do because I like doing it this way. Because it's fun."

"It's not supposed to be fun." The words exploded from Dave, and as they settled in the quiet room, he had the grace to chuckle charmingly. He straightened his tie. "I meant to say that fun isn't the only consideration in running a successful business."

For the first time since Rudy left, Dave showed some sign of remembering Jay was alive, turning to him with a beseeching smile. Any port in a storm, Jay thought dryly.

"Jay, you're a businessman," he said. "Surely you agree with me that a business must be run in an orderly, unemotional fashion?"

Jay did agree with him, wholeheartedly, and the words to say so were already stringing themselves into a sentence in his mind when he noticed the look on Maxi's face. He didn't need any special powers to know what she was thinking this time. The question in her eyes was as real and easy to read as the clock on the wall above her head. *Whose side are you on?*

## Chapter Six

The turn for Lillian's Attic came just before the ice-cream stand with the big silver milk can out front. And just as she had known she would, Maxi recognized the narrow road that slanted off to the left as soon as she saw it and easily found her way to the small white-clapboard building that housed the antique shop.

The shop's owner, Lillian, remembering Maxi from previous visits, smiled and called hello when she and Jay walked in. Tall and slender, with intriguing flashes of silver buried in the short gold waves of her hair, Lillian was the sort of woman who cause manufacturers of skin-care products to drool. Stick Lillian in front of a camera with a bottle of moisturizer in her hand, and sales would skyrocket. In some ways she reminded Maxi of her mother, who also gave vital new meaning to the phrase "growing old gracefully."

The crucial difference, Maxi had realized the last time she was here, was that Lillian laughed. Maxi's mother only smiled. Oh, occasionally she made a small sound that passed for a laugh. It had a breathy, almost rusty quality, as if it hadn't been used in a long time. On the rare occasion when something slipped past her defenses and threatened to produce an out-and-out guffaw, you would see her take the trouble to press her fingers to her lips and smother it.

Lillian, on the other hand, truly laughed. Out loud. What's more, her eyes twinkled when she did it, letting you know that she was as comfortable with the sound and with the way it made the wrinkles near her eyes deepen as she was with everything else about herself; as comfortable as she was to spend her days in a small out-of-the-way shop surrounded by things she loved and that she quite honestly confessed she had mixed feelings about seeing go out the door. A sale wasn't everything, she'd once said with a shrug. To Victoria Love, who had turned a part-time job selling real estate into a highly profitable operation with offices statewide, a sale was everything.

When Maxi explained that she had just stopped in to browse, Lillian put aside the issue of *Colonial Homes* she had been reading to make them iced raspberry tea with honey and invited Maxi to explore a treasure trove so new she hadn't gotten around to unpacking it yet: two huge cardboard boxes full of old dolls.

"Look at this one." Maxi laughed as she uncovered one of the dolls. Each doll had been meticulously wrapped in tissue paper so long ago that the paper had grown as dry and crumbly as fallen leaves. She fluffed the doll's gathered skirt with her fingers. "This dress is great. It reminds me of one Ann-Margret wore in an old Elvis Presley movie. And these pearl earrings are a classic."

"That's a Ginny doll," Lillian told her. "I remember my daughter had one . . . still does, actually. I never was one to throw anything away."

Maxi stared at the doll in her hands, but her thoughts shifted to the parade of dolls in her own past, from cuddly soft babies to Barbie and Ken. Dolls with strings to pull and mouths to feed, dolls who walked and talked and gave rise to impossible-to-fulfill fantasies. All gone...where? Disposed of, given away, banished to make room for the next year's model, which in turn would be replaced by something newer and better, with hair that grew or changed colors. Of course as a child she had always been thrilled by the newest addition, and she couldn't remember ever being terribly conscious of or bothered by the quiet but relentless weeding out of the old. So why now, sitting around an oak pedestal table at the rear of Lillian's shop, should she suddenly feel this sadness, as if those old dolls had been a family wrenched apart?

Maxi tried to push aside the feeling. Why ruin what showed signs of being a perfect day in spite of the bad start Dave's surprise visit had given it? She reached into the box for a larger tissue-swathed bundle and rested it on her lap, wondering if she ought to call Dave later and soothe his hurt feelings. Yes, she would, even knowing full well that if things were different—if Jay had sided with him in criticizing the way she handled her affairs and she'd been the one who had stormed out in a huff—Dave would never make the same gesture.

Not that Jay had been as wildly gallant and enthusiastic in leaping to her defense as she would have liked. "I guess it's all a matter of style" fell more within the category of lukewarm and reluctant. But at least he hadn't come right out and said that she was the most disorganized, impulsive, befuddling excuse for a professional he'd ever met. He had waited and said it later, when they were alone in the pickup truck she had borrowed for the day.

Peeling away the final layer of tissue, Maxi caught a glimpse of white lace. "Oooh, a bride doll!" she exclaimed. "Look, she's perfect, right down to the white satin slippers and these tiny white roses in her bouquet."

"She is lovely," Lillian agreed. "Such detail. The man who sold them to me said he thought there was a bridesmaid and a flower girl packed away in there, too, but I hadn't dared to hope they would be in such mint condition."

Maxi quickly located and unwrapped those two dolls, as well, smoothing the ruffles on their matching pink-flowered dresses. Even before she had them lined up before her on the table, her vision of the next campaign spot highlighting old-fashioned values was expanding in her mind. What was more old-fashioned than the sort of love and commitment symbolized by a shining-eyed bride? She wasn't sure yet exactly how she would work them in, only that the fragile, old-fashioned look of the dolls would mesh perfectly with the nostalgic mood she was hoping to create.

"These are exactly what I was looking for," she said, savoring the rush of pleasure she felt whenever creativity and reality came together without too much trouble.

She glanced up to find Lillian smiling at the excitement rippling in her voice and Jay looking at her as if she'd just announced she'd struck oil in the bottom of her tea glass.

"I thought we were looking for a penny-candy counter," he reminded her.

"We are. Sort of."

"These dolls don't look sort of—or even remotely—like any penny-candy counter I've ever seen."

"That's because you have no imagination."

Their gazes locked across the table, above smiles held in place purely for Lillian's benefit. "Oh, really? You would be surprised to know how very active and colorful my imagination is at this very second."

"How unseemly," Maxi retorted. With a narrowed gaze and a one-shoulder shrug, she managed to pull off a credible rendition of a woman offended. "Need I remind you of your responsibilities?"

He didn't flinch. "Need I remind you of your deadline? You have no time to waste sitting around here—"

"Really, Jay, taking time for a glass of ice tea is hardly going to set me so far behind that I miss my deadline."

"I'm not talking about the damn...darn tea." He shot a quick, uneasy glance at Lillian.

"Oh, don't mind me," she said, laughing as she misread his concern. "My husband was a merchant marine. Believe me, I've heard worse."

"Sorry anyway," he muttered, then turned his attention sharply back to Maxi. "You're supposed to have the concept of these spots all worked out and ready to shoot. Instead, you're sitting here thinking about changing everything, impulsively, on a whim, simply because you happened upon—"

"I'm not thinking about changing everything," she interrupted. "I'm merely trying to enlarge upon the theme."

"With dolls?"

"That's right."

"How?"

Actually she had no idea, but the skepticism expressed by his upthrust chin was so irksome that Maxi refused to own up to even a shred of uncertainty. Matching his smug smile, she said, "Wait and see," before quickly turning to Lillian. "I know you said you haven't had a chance to examine the dolls, but could you possibly quote me a price on these three now?"

Lillian bit her bottom lip lightly as she considered the bride doll and her attendants. "It will be very high, I'm afraid. Each is rare enough individually. To find three in a set is a collector's dream."

Maxi felt her joy at discovering the dolls pierced by frustration. No matter how wonderful a touch they would provide, she couldn't afford to squander a large sum on so minor a detail. She was about to admit defeat when it came to her—impulsively, on a whim—that there might be another way.

Later, sitting beside Jay in the front of the truck, with the three dolls, carefully wrapped in fresh tissue and protective batting, secure beneath a tarpaulin in the back, she tried not to gloat.

She drove—it made her feel more in control—and they rode all the way back to the main road in silence. Maxi didn't need to see his expression to know that falling under his direct gaze would be about as pleasant as going on a forced march with a stone in your shoe. It was just as well he kept his face turned away.

Beyond his open windows was a solid wall of maples and oaks, their leaves still mostly green but looking as if someone had taken a brush dipped in crimson and gold paint and shaken it at them. When Jay finally did speak, he continued to stare out the window, as if she were somewhere out there among the trees.

"Okay. You're right. I acted like a jerk back there."

"I didn't say that."

"You were thinking it."

"No, I—" She suddenly remembered who she was lying to. "All right, so I thought it. Big deal."

"I'm not exactly inspiring confidence in you."

"Is that what you're trying to do?"

He turned at that, shrugging, but the expression in his eyes was anything but careless. "No, I . . ." He shook his head and his tone turned ferocious. "I just want this whole thing over with."

Hearing how eager he was to get rid of her brought Maxi a jolt of disappointment she couldn't have explained. "Me, too," she forced herself to say. "Of course, I know you have a lot more at stake than I do."

"Maybe that's why I'm overreacting to everything that happens." There was a heavy current of self-disgust in his tone.

Maxi tried not to chuckle and failed. "I'm sorry, Jay, but it was funny back there, watching how hard you tried to complicate what was really a very simple matter between Lillian and me."

"I couldn't believe she would just lend you the dolls without getting something out of it."

"You heard her. She will be getting something out of it, the pleasure of seeing her dolls on television."

"I meant something substantial."

"Pleasure *is* substantial, Slick. You meant money."

"It seems reasonable that she would want to be paid for letting you use something belonging to her. I mean business is business."

"Where have I heard that before? Ah, yes, standing in my kitchen this very morning." It pleased her to see Jay shift uneasily on the seat. "Besides, you heard me offer to pay her for the use of them. She wouldn't hear of it."

"Exactly. That's when I really became suspicious. I figured she might be trying to set you up for something."

"Dollnapping?"

"Go ahead, laugh. I'm the one who's responsible for looking out for you."

"And you're doing a wonderful job." The sincerity she was trying to project was ruined by the sudden bubble of laughter that followed the compliment. "I just think that trying to get Lillian to sign a waiver saying I wouldn't be held liable for any 'personal injury' the dolls might suffer while in my possession was going above and beyond the call of duty."

He folded his arms across his chest and stared straight ahead. The set of his jaw was somewhere between angry and granite. "I was trying to sound like I knew what I was talking about."

"I guessed that. Unfortunately mentioning dolls and personal injury in the same breath was a dead giveaway that—oops, there's that *D* word again, sorry."

"Knock it off. There's no reason you can't say the word *dead* around me."

"That's not what you said the last time I said it."

"That was different."

He was looking out the window again, his expression grim. Who could blame him? thought Maxi. Suddenly more than anything, more than finding the penny-candy counter, more than making the commercials a success, more than forcing Dave and the rest of her family to admit she could do it and do it on her own terms, she wanted to make this man smile. She wanted to distract him for a few seconds from a problem bigger than any other she could imagine. She wanted it so badly that she didn't bother censoring the possibilities.

"I think I'm beginning to catch on," she said. "I mean about you and the word *dead*. It's sort of like that old George Carlin joke about what you can and can't say on television. It's all right to say you pricked your finger, but you can't say you fingered your..."

Her voice trailed off as Jay swung his head around, certain he knew where the joke was headed. He stared at her in disbelief. All right, so maybe it wasn't the sort of joke you ought to tell someone in his position; at least it had worked. His laughter started as a quiet rumble and soon surrounded her, a deep, rough, uninhibited, wonderfully masculine sound. It was the first time she'd ever heard him really laugh, Maxi realized—smug chuckles and knowing grins didn't count—and she liked it. She wondered if he'd heard the one about the female robot and the man with the bionic arm.

"You're really something," he said before she had a chance to ask. "I can't remember the last time I laughed that hard."

"Of course you can't, you dummy. You can't remember anything else, either, remember?"

It wasn't an especially clever remark, not worthy of the joint burst of laughter that left them both a little winded and giddy, their defenses down. When Jay reached over and squeezed her shoulder, the touch was spontaneous and affectionate—and enough to make Maxi feel like every nerve ending in her body began and ended at that spot.

"I realize that I don't remember anything," he said, sobering, "but I told you about these feelings I get, and I have a feeling that laughing wasn't a big part of my life before. At least not this silly, good kind of laughter."

"There's a bad kind of laughter?"

"Sure. Laughter that's nothing about fun or joy, but about cynicism or how you're expected to respond to a certain comment."

"Laughter shouldn't be that complicated. Sounds to me like you ran with the wrong crowd."

"Maybe. I keep thinking that maybe if..."

"If what?" Her words were very soft, no more demanding than the flutter of butterfly wings, yet they slammed Jay's shoulders tight against the tan vinyl truck seat.

"Never mind," he said roughly. "It never would have worked anyway."

For just an instant Maxi took her gaze off the winding two-lane road ahead and met his gaze. That instant was enough to remind her how close laughter was to other feelings on the emotional roulette wheel.

"Right," she said. "It never would have worked."

They were at last on the outskirts of the town of Scituate, she noted with relief. It would take all her concentration to locate the shop she was looking for. Suwaski's had been out of business for some time, but, according to the friend who'd told her about it, when she was growing up in Scituate it had been home to the biggest, shiniest penny-candy counter in the world. All gleaming mahogany and sparkling glass, it sounded like exactly what Maxi was looking for.

They drove nearly the whole length of the three-block stretch that was the small town's business district with no glimpse of the shop she was looking for. Maybe her friend's directions were wrong or the shop had been reopened under a new name. Maxi reached for the smooth crystal hanging from a gold chain around her neck and rubbed it, hoping the streak of good luck she'd come to associate with the piece of rose quartz would hold, and suddenly there it was.

The rusted metal sign above the door was slightly crooked, but its red letters were still legible against the chipped black background. Suwaski's. She stepped on the brakes, hard, without thinking and without warning, and grimaced as she saw Jay's head jerk forward, then back. Bracing his hands on the dashboard, he glared reproachfully at her.

"The brakes stick," she said quickly.

He closed his eyes. From the slight movement of his lips Maxi suspected he was counting to ten silently, but all he said was, "Right. Is this the place?"

"Yes."

"I think we're a little late," he said, squinting at the shop's front window, where only a shoe polish display remained. Dusty and empty, it, like the shop itself, looked disturbingly forlorn. "Like maybe half a century."

"That's the point. I'm hardly going to find an authentic penny-candy counter in a 7-Eleven. My friend Marcia warned me that the shop closed a few years ago, but she thinks the owner, Elwin Suwaski, still lives upstairs. I just hope he hasn't gotten rid of the store fixtures," she added as they climbed from the truck.

Peering through the grimy glass told them nothing, so they climbed the narrow stairs to the apartment on the second floor.

"Are you Elwin Suwaski?" she asked the man who opened the door.

He nodded, and Maxi's heart took flight.

One look told her that Elwin Suwaski was a genuine character. Instant camaraderie. His bushy mustache and the crescent of hair he had left were softly turning from gray to white, and he had a cuddly form and a round face complete with the wire-rim spectacles that seemed to be standard issue for dear-old-gramp types. If Norman Rockwell were alive, he'd be running for his brushes.

"What do you want?" he demanded before she could say anything else.

The gruffness in his tone and his icy-eyed glare didn't fool Maxi, who knew such crotchetiness always concealed a heart of gold. That candy counter was as good as hers.

As succinctly as she could, she explained about Robert Chandler and the commercials and her hopes of finding exactly the right penny-candy counter. She sensed more than heard Jay's impatient sighs as he stood close beside her in the stuffy hallway with its faded fox-hunt wallpaper. Even as she spoke, she offhandedly registered that the wallpaper might be a nice touch for the inside jacket of the Wild Horses album. Jay's sighs grew louder, his not so subtle hint that it wasn't necessary to relate how she'd come by the assignment in the first place and how important it was to her.

Maxi knew better. That was just the sort of personal touch needed to melt a lonely old man's heart.

"So you see, it would mean so much to me if you could come to my rescue with your candy counter, Mr. Suwaski," she concluded. "That is, if you still have it."

"No."

Unbelievably the door began to shut. Maxi was so startled it took a few seconds to realize that the only thing that prevented it from slamming in her disappointed face was the rapid motion of Jay's foot.

"You sold it?" she asked.

"No."

"Then you must have given it to someone? Perhaps they..."

"No."

The noes were getting progressively more hostile. In the background she recognized the sounds of *Wheel of Fortune* and decided that must have something to do with his impatience.

"Mr. Suwaski, would you like for us to step inside while we discuss this so you won't miss—"

"No," he interjected. "There's nothing to discuss. I didn't say I don't have the counter, I said you couldn't use it."

"But why not?"

"Why should I?"

She quickly abandoned the notion that he might get a kick out of seeing it on television. "I'll pay you."

"How much?"

"Well, I would only need it for a few days, and it's just sitting there gathering dust anyway. How does one hundred dollars sound?"

"Lousy," he said without hesitation. He turned to Jay, directing a pointed look at his foot. "Move it or lose it, fella."

"How does one thousand dollars sound?" she heard Jay ask, and her first instinct was to laugh. It had to be a joke.

Elwin Suwaski didn't share that realization.

"That sounds more like it," he said instantly. For the first time he smiled. Not like a grandfather. Like a shark. "I'll just go and get you nice folks the key to the shop."

As soon as he moved away from the door, Maxi turned on Jay. "What's wrong with you?"

"Nothing. You wanted the counter, I made sure you got it."

"Right, and nearly bankrupted me in the process. Jay, I thought I pointed out that one of the reasons I was given this project was because I was willing to work—"

"Cheap?"

"On a budget. A very tight budget. One that doesn't allow for grandstand gestures. When you don't have much cash, you have to have a lot of smarts."

"I thought it was pretty smart of me to get him to rent you the counter. He sure wasn't bowled over by your offer."

"Did it occur to you that there's a lot of room for compromise between one hundred and one thousand dollars?"

For a second he appeared perplexed by the question. Then his mouth twisted into a rueful grimace. "No, it didn't. My instinct is to go all out for whatever I want."

"I can't afford your instincts. And as soon as Mr. Su-waski gets back I'll tell him so."

"Then what?"

"I'll make him a reasonable offer."

"You're dreaming, Maxi. Suwaski will never come down on the price now."

This time her instinct was forced to agree with his. "Then I'll just have to go down there, take a quick look at the counter and tell him that I'm sorry, but it's not quite what I was looking for after all."

"So we can waste time running around in circles looking for another one? You could well end up spending nearly that much anyway or, worse, not find another one and have to admit to Duvall that you couldn't pull off your original concept so you had to come up with a different—second-rate—idea."

With an uneasy sigh Maxi stared at the wall, watching countless foxes pursuing countless hounds as she weighed one thousand dollars against having to eat crow à la Du-vall.

"Here you go," Mr. Suwaski said, returning with the key, which he held out to Jay. "As soon as you give me my thousand dollars you can go on down and have a look-see at the goods."

"First, we'll look, then we'll pay," Jay countered without reaching for the key. He glanced at Maxi as if waiting for permission.

"All right," agreed Suwaski, "have a look first. And, of course, it goes without saying that you're responsible for moving it and getting it back here on your own."

"How heavy is it?" Jay inquired with, it seemed to Maxi, infinitely more concern than he had shown over spending her money.

The old man's chuckle was like fingernails on a blackboard. "Plenty heavy. Hope you ate your Wheaties this morning, fella."

"Maybe we oughta—" began Jay.

But Maxi had just made up her mind. She reached for the key. "No problem. He'll manage."

Later, after Maxi had deemed the penny-candy counter perfect and Mr. Suwaski had returned upstairs with his check for one thousand dollars, instructing them about how to lock up on the way out, Jay gave the counter an experimental push. It did not move so much as a fraction of an inch. Turning to her with a disgusted expression, he mimicked her earlier words.

"'No problem. He'll manage.' Would you mind telling me exactly how I'm supposed to manage?"

"It's obvious, isn't it?" Maxi replied, indicating with a casual sweep of her hand how simple the whole matter was.

"Not to me, it's not. I'm looking at a problem that's six feet of solid wood and leaded glass that stands as tall as you—correction, I think it stands a bit taller than you—and I'm looking at hauling it outside, down a step and across a very wide sidewalk so I can hoist it into the back of a pickup truck that I don't know will even withstand the weight, and I would like for you to explain to me your very obvious solution to all that."

"You know." She waved her hand again and rolled her eyes impatiently. "*You* know. Remember last night?"

His irritated, confused expression abruptly gave way to one of disbelief. "You mean..."

"Of course."

"Have you lost your mind?"

She stood as tall as she could. "No."

"Then you must think I've lost mine."

"Why? You're supposed to be helping me, aren't you? It would really help me right now if you could blink or wiggle your nose or do whatever it would take to get this counter into the back of that truck."

"I don't wiggle anything," he told her through gritted teeth. "I just concentrate."

"So concentrate."

"Absolutely not."

"Go ahead, just try. It seems obvious that if you can walk through walls, you—"

"This is my fate we're talking about here, Maxi," he interrupted. "Forever. The whole ball of wax. Even if I knew how to, I'm not about to go flying furniture through the air as if this were some sort of stupid situation comedy."

"You could try it just this once. After all, you don't really know for sure that you're not supposed to do it."

"I know."

"Why would you have been given these powers if you aren't supposed to use them?"

"It's a test. Can't you understand that? It's all a test. And I'm not about to flunk it by taking the easy way out of this."

"Fine." She tossed her handbag on top of the counter and crossed her arms. "So we'll do it the hard way. Any suggestions as to what that might be?"

He frowned, giving that some thought before nodding. "As a matter of fact, I do. We passed a gas station about two blocks back with a gang of young guys hanging out front. I'll bet we could pay them to—"

"Pay them?" she interjected.

"Do you want to get this thing moved or not?" He barely waited for her disgruntled nod. "We can give them a few bucks each for helping us get it onto the truck."

"All right, but this time I'll handle the financial arrangements. If they so much as hesitate, you'd probably throw in a pension plan to sweeten the deal."

It took the five guys and Jay over two hours to get the counter onto the truck. Most of that time Maxi and the others spent playing cards out front while waiting for Jay to disassemble the door jamb in order to widen the doorway, which they discovered was an inch narrower than the counter. Finally it was loaded. She paid the guys for helping out while Jay neatly stacked the pieces of the door jamb inside the shop. He would hammer them back into place when they returned the counter in a few days.

Groaning, he lowered himself to the shop's front step to drink the can of soda Maxi had bought for him. She sat beside him, watching as he tipped his head back and drank half the can in one gulp. His smooth forearms were slick with sweat and there were dark patches under his arms and across the back of the black T-shirt he was wearing. His hands were marked with assorted nicks and cuts that she didn't remember seeing before his stint with the hammer and crowbar.

"Jay, you don't ordinarily do a great deal of physical labor, do you?"

He shrugged and pressed the cold, wet can to his cheek, then his forehead. "I don't remember."

"Let me see your palms," she said.

He glanced sideways at her with a wary expression. "My what?"

"Palms. Let me see one."

"Oh, no, don't tell me you read palms."

"Just give them to me," she ordered, sticking her own hand out.

He placed one of his hands, palm up, on top of hers.

"Just as I thought. The closest you usually come to physical labor is sharpening a pencil. You're definitely an office rat, Slick."

"Really?" He looked intrigued in spite of himself. "What line tells you that . . . not that I believe in any of this."

"It's not so much a line as a circle; an oval, really."

"An oval?" He lowered his head to examine his palm more closely.

"Yup. Specifically, this one right here," Maxi said, pointing to one of the new blisters at the base of his fingers. She laughed as he jerked his hand away.

"Very funny."

"Who jumped to conclusions that time? I never said I read palms."

"I just figured you looked the type."

She matched his irritated frown. "Very funny. Anyway, under the circumstances I don't blame you for hoping I could tell you what your future holds."

He leaned back on his elbows, the soda can balanced on one knee. "Actually I was more interested in what my past holds. It's odd, not knowing who you were or what you did or who the important people in your life were, that sort of thing."

"I guess it must be. Who knows, you might even have a wife somewhere." Maxi made the suggestion offhandedly and was startled by the way the mere possibility unsettled her.

Jay squinted across the street as if he didn't at all like what was on the other side. His sigh was rough yet strangely wistful. "No, I didn't leave a wife behind. Don't ask how I know. It's just one of those things I know. No kids, either. In fact, I have this hunch there wasn't anybody especially important in my life, or anyone to whom I was important. I was sort of hoping you might be able to tell me that hunch is wrong."

He turned his head away, looking off down the street, leaving Maxi grappling for something gracious or comforting to say. Nothing sprang to mind, so they ended up sitting in the sort of silence that makes you suddenly, acutely aware of how many noises there are in any given moment.

Overhead birds noisily chased each other from tree to tree, while somewhere around the corner children played their own version of the same game, their shouts loud and excited. The tires of passing cars made a low-pitched whirring noise on the blacktop, punctuated by the steady scuff of sneaker toes on cement as a little boy made his way along the sidewalk toward them. As he drew closer, Maxi could hear the raspy, tuneless sound of his whistle.

The boy had a yo-yo, and as he walked he repeatedly let it drop, tried unsuccessfully to make it climb the string back to his hand, rolled it up and proceeded to try again. His movements were so rough and jerky he was doomed to fail.

Maxi found herself suppressing the ages-old adult urge to jump up and say, "No, do it this way." So it wasn't a total surprise to her when Jay suddenly shot to his feet and yelled, "No, not like that!"

What was a surprise was the vehemence in his tone. He caught the yo-yo just as the startled little boy finished making another wild toss with it. Holding it captive in his hand, he said, "What are you trying to do? Break a window with this thing?"

"N-no," the boy replied, eyes wide and frightened.

Maxi quickly righted the soda can Jay had sent flying and hurried over to play mediator, but as if he had also heard the harshness in his reprimand and regretted it, he immediately gentled his tone. Crouching so that he was at eye level with the small boy, he held his hand out for the other end of the string.

"Here. Let me see if I can give you a few pointers. I used to be real good at this when I was your age."

Curiosity seemed to take the edge off the boy's fear. "When you were seven like me? No kidding?"

"Well, maybe just a little older than you," Jay replied, his smile working the same magic on the boy that it always did on Maxi. "But I started when I was about seven, and I practiced every chance I got, just like you're doing, and pretty soon I was the best yo-yoer in my whole neighborhood."

"A champion? Did you win any trophies? My friend Ryan's brother won a trophy. A big gold one."

Jay shook his head. His head was bent, his attention focused on the red plastic yo-yo he was carefully rewinding, but Maxi saw the muscles in his cheeks clench. "No, I never won any trophies. After a while I just quit playing with it."

"I'm never going to quit," the little boy announced with his whole seven years' worth of certainty. "Never."

"I hope you never do," Jay said, his smile back in place. "I'll show you what I know, and maybe someday you'll win a trophy for both of us. What do you say?"

"All right," the boy replied with a vengeance.

"But first you have to get what I call the knack."

The boy's shoulders slumped as he went from a picture of elation to dejection. "I won't be able to get any knack. My mom said this is the last yo-yo she's ever buying me, and if I lose this one..."

"No, no, a knack isn't something your mom has to buy," explained Jay, fighting a chuckle just as Maxi was. "A knack can be a lot of different things, but when you're talking about yo-yoing, a knack is like a...a spring. A spring that's hidden right here in my wrist." He touched a spot at the center of his wrist. "It's hidden there in your wrist, too, and I'm going to show you how to use it."

Maxi marveled at Jay's patience and his ingenuity as the boy struggled to duplicate the moves he was demonstrating. She sat nearby, watching as the boy tried in vain again and again. Finally, in a stroke of brilliance, Jay moved him to the curb, providing him a few extra inches of height, and showed him how to use them to his advantage. Once he was able to make the yo-yo climb back, he quickly mastered the trick of moving around and keeping it going at the same time and finally walked off, still whistling tunelessly, but with a new, confident rhythm in the way he moved his wrist.

"You really do have a knack," Maxi told Jay as they stood watching him go. "And not just for yo-yoing."

His smile was relaxed and full of satisfaction. When he looked down at her it turned playful. "You mean you're only now noticing that?"

Laughing, she replied, "Let's just say I'm only now noticing that you have a knack for charming kids, too."

"I figured I owed it to him," Jay admitted, helping her into the passenger side of the truck and climbing behind the wheel before Maxi realized she was being outmaneuvered. She was too tired to protest. "After the way I yelled at him, I mean."

"You did come on a little strong," she agreed. "Even I jumped a few inches when you yelled."

"Yeah, well, I guess that's what happens when you get too tired, too hot and too hungry all at the same time. Why don't we stop on the way home and pick up something for dinner?"

"I can't wait that long. I know just the place for us to have dinner. It's on the way home. Sort of."

"Do you mean this place is sort of on the way home or you sort of know where it is?"

"Relax, I know where it is."

"And we can go there dressed like this?"

"Sure. No one will even see us. Trust me."

"It must be an indication of how hungry I am that I'm willing to even consider trusting your sense of direction."

"Of course you're hungry. Do you realize we forgot to eat lunch?"

"I wouldn't say I forgot, exactly. My stomach kept reminding me. I just didn't expect it to take all afternoon to get this thing loaded on the truck."

"Me, either. And Jay?"

"Yeah?"

"I want to thank you for all your hard work. I also want to apologize for griping about the offer you made Suwaski. The truth is, I'm not sure I would have been able to pull this off without your help, and you know how much it means to me and . . . well, thanks."

"You don't have to thank me. In fact, I'd rather you didn't. I did it for myself." His tone was at once sharp and detached. "Whatever I do, I do for myself."

"What about helping that little boy?" Maxi inquired, puzzled by his abrupt change of mood. It was as if an invisible glacier had passed through the truck. The easy laughter they'd shared only a moment ago was gone. "Did you do that for yourself, too?"

"That was nothing."

"It was a lot more than nothing to him."

''For Gòd's sake, don't go getting all misty eyed over the fact that I talked to some kid.'' He twisted in his seat to meet her gaze directly.

For Maxi, looking into his eyes was like looking through a window on a starless night. She knew there had to be something out there, but all she could see was a shiny black void.

"I thought I made it clear that the reason I'm helping you is because it's what I have to do to help myself. You'd be wise not to forget that."

## Chapter Seven

It was such a blunt, unequivocal warning that there was little Maxi could say in response. Jay almost wished it wasn't so. Her silence unsettled him more than any protest she could have made.

They weaved their way across the northern part of the state, following a maze of narrow winding roads. Several times his stomach growled and hers replied. Afterward they both sat stone faced, pretending not to notice. Jay kept his eyes on the road ahead and after an inane remark or two about the foliage, kept his mouth shut. Maxi spoke only when absolutely necessary to tell him to take a left or a right or slow down for the mammoth bump just around the next bend.

As a navigator she was one of a kind. She didn't know street names or route numbers but had total recall of bumps and bends and forks in the road. Twice he asked, in a carefully pleasant tone of voice, and twice she insisted she knew exactly how to get to the restaurant. This was, she announced as he negotiated a hairpin turn that brought them perilously close to the edge of a pond, a shortcut. Jay resisted the urge to point out that it seemed more like an endurance test. Theirs was definitely not the sort of silence that welcomed witty observations.

Not that it was an angry silence. It wasn't even particularly unfriendly. Instead, it was marked by an unmistakable sadness, and Jay was stunned to realize how much more devastating that could be. Unreasonable as it was, Maxi was hurt by what he had said about being in this for himself alone. He'd caught on to that without her saying a word, and every shred of decency he possessed told him he ought to say something more, offer some explanation, try in some way to make her feel better.

The problem was, he had nothing to say, no soothing explanation to offer, no way to sugarcoat the truth. He *was* in this for himself, first, foremost and right to the bitter end. Oh, he would uphold his end of the bargain by helping her. He was, in his own way, a very honorable man. It was because he was honorable and not a hypocrite that he refused to let her harbor the notion that he was doing any of this for altruistic motives. He was doing it because he had to, because he had no other choice, and he'd been sincere in warning her not to forget that . . . as he almost had. It had taken a gawky kid with a yo-yo to bring him to his senses.

When he'd first noticed the kid, Jay had barely given him a second glance. He'd been too mired in his own thoughts. From the very start of this he'd told himself it would be best not to dwell on the past or the future, and he tried hard not to. It wasn't easy. Being alone with Maxi today had made it impossible.

Trading jokes with her and making plans for the commercials had drawn them closer, and it had started him thinking. He hadn't expected to enjoy any of this, but even working as hard as he had this afternoon was tolerable when she was nearby. More than tolerable, actually. It had been fun. It had felt right, and comfortable. What it hadn't felt was familiar, and that thought stuck with him like an itch in a spot he couldn't reach.

All day he had tried. He'd strained to break through the wall between him and his past, to try to recall if there had ever been someone like Maxi in his life, someone who could inspire him to anger and laughter and sometimes back again within a matter of seconds. Maxi made him feel things deep inside, in a place he had a niggling suspicion had never been touched before. It wasn't a satisfying thought. Rather, it left him feeling frustrated and vaguely pissed off, wondering what the hell could have been so damned important in his life that he'd never had time for feeling this good.

As much as he wondered and struggled to remember, however, the past had remained a tormenting shadow in some distant, darkened corner of his mind—until that kid and his yo-yo turned a spotlight on it.

It had happened quickly, the way even the most long and complicated dreams supposedly do. Over and done with almost before he knew it, leaving him with questions and impressions and a haunting desire to see more, to go back and finish it to his satisfaction. What he had glimpsed so briefly was himself at about age nine or ten. It had been strange, as if he were back there living it again, feeling the same feelings he'd felt as a kid, and yet at the same time looking on, filtering it all through an adult perspective. Strange and confusing.

He saw himself playing with a yo-yo, amazing his friends—and himself—with his ability to control it. He performed trick after trick, even taking requests from the gang of kids watching in awe. Around the World, Baby in the Cradle, nothing was too difficult for him. For once, he was really somebody. Then he had attempted Walk the Dog, a cinch trick, except he hadn't checked to see how close he was standing to the cellar window. He'd let the yo-yo rip and immediately heard the sickening sound of shattering glass.

The next image he'd had was of himself walking down the front steps of that same house with a ratty looking duffel bag clenched in one hand and tears soaking his face. Sitting on Suwaski's shop step beside Maxi, he had felt all over again how hot his face had been that day and he remembered the shame. He had been mortified to be seen crying in public, yet unable to do anything to stop it.

It wasn't his own home he was so upset at leaving, but a foster home. One in a long series. And his leaving was unrelated to the broken window, although he hadn't understood that at the time. Back then all he had known was that once again he had tried as hard as he knew how to fit in, to do the right thing, to be the kind of son people would want to keep around, and that once again he had failed. Only this time when they sent him away, they had kept his little brother, separating them for the first time since his mother had turned them over to the state. Jay wasn't able to recall his brother's name, much less his face, but he knew that after that day he hadn't seen him again for two years, and he knew that he never again picked up another yo-yo. Until today.

He had no idea why that particular memory alone had come back to him, but it left him with a maelstrom of unresolved feelings, feelings he didn't fully understand. He certainly didn't understand any of it enough to share his thoughts with Maxi. All he knew was that he'd left the foster home that day with the beginnings of a philosophy of life he had perfected and clung to through the years. Don't depend on anyone else, and don't let anyone depend on you. So maybe he had missed out on a few things because of it. He'd spared himself a lot of pain in the process, and he saw no reason to change the way he did things at this late date. It was best Maxi understood that, no matter how much telling her so had left him feeling like a heel.

The sight of a green highway sign up ahead interrupted Jay's brooding. At last they were at an intersection with a decent-looking road, Route 44, and he breathed a sigh of relief as Maxi pointed east. He even began to see signs of life other than a farmhouse every five miles or a rustbucket pickup truck abandoned by the side of a field. Jay stopped worrying so much that they were lost and felt hungrier than ever.

He switched on the headlights as they drove. No matter what tricks Mother Nature was playing with the temperature, the sun knew this was September. Although it was barely 6:00 p.m., the sun had already dropped behind the trees, leaving what was left of the day colored a watery gray, which seemed at odds with the lingering summer warmth.

At last, after driving two miles that felt more like twenty to Jay's gnawing stomach, Maxi leaned forward with a triumphant smile. "There."

Jay looked at the flat-topped building she was pointing to and at the orange-and-brown neon sign at the side of the road. "A root-beer stand?"

"You don't like root beer?"

"No, I do. I like it. Love it, in fact." After the long miles of silent treatment, he was willing to sound downright cloying if it would keep her talking.

"Good."

Jay scanned the parking lot, which was about three-quarters full, and pulled into an empty spot along the fence.

"You have to back in," Maxi said.

He looked at her. "Why?"

"So they can see your lights."

"So they can see my lights?"

"Right." Her tone suggested he wasn't very bright.

Obviously not, because he had about a dozen questions running through his head, starting with "Who are *they*?" and "Who cares if they see my lights?" He didn't ask them because, as faulty as his memory was, he still had some social savvy of the man-woman variety. It had to be a natural instinct, like the one for survival. It warned him that in this very tense situation Maxi was the offended and he the offendee. If she were to suggest he park the truck on its hubcaps, it was his responsibility to keep the peace by doing it.

He turned the truck around and backed into the parking place. "Better?"

"Much."

"Good." He reached for the door handle.

"Don't get out."

Jay threw his hands in the air. "I give up. Just tell me what you want me to do, step by step, and I'll do it."

"There's no need to be so touchy. I only told you not to get out because this is a drive-in restaurant, for Pete's sake."

"So? I did drive in. I even backed in. Now it's time to eat."

"The kind of drive-in where they come and take your order and then bring your food to the car."

"Oh." He looked around, noticing for the first time the young women in brown slacks and orange-and-white striped shirts scurrying about the parking lot with trays and order pads in hand. "You'll have to excuse me. I thought carhops were extinct."

She gave a smug smile. "Live and learn."

"Believe me, I'm trying, on both counts."

The smile vanished.

He decided to try being solicitous. "You've obviously been here before. What do you recommend?"

"Root beer."

"A very innovative selection. What else?"

She shrugged, clearly struggling now to remain aloof. "The chili dogs are good. Of course, you should make your own decision. Choose whatever's best for you."

Ouch. "Listen, Maxi, I didn't mean..."

"Hi, I'm Janelle."

Jay turned in response to the lilting greeting to find a young woman with a friendly grin and auburn hair pulled back in a ponytail peering in the window of the truck.

"Are you ready to order?" she asked.

He shook his head. "No."

"Yes," Maxi said.

He smiled. "I meant yes. We'll have two roots beers, large. And some chili dogs, three for me...Maxi?"

"Two."

"That makes—" Janelle tossed her ponytail as she figured it out "—five altogether."

"And a large order of French fries," Maxi added.

"Two large root beers, five chili dogs and a large fry," Janelle repeated in sing-song fashion. "Okey-dokey."

As she walked away, Jay glanced at Maxi, hoping to tempt into bloom the smile he saw her fighting to suppress. "Carhops never change. What do you suppose they become when they grow up?"

"Old car hops," she shot back, still without releasing a smile.

She was made of stronger stuff than he'd thought. He tried again, and again. She responded politely to his attempts to get a conversation going, but there was no humor, no warmth, no Maxi. He missed her, damn it, and he hated feeling this way, so...lonely. It was ludicrous. It wasn't even possible to feel lonely when you weren't alone, was it? It was a relief when he spotted Janelle heading their way carrying a tray.

"Please roll your window up five inches," she instructed, then deftly anchored the tray to it with the attached rubber grips. "We're having a little trouble with the grill, so the chili dogs will take a few minutes longer than usual. I brought your drinks while you're waiting."

"No problem," Jay assured her, groaning inwardly as she bounced away. More excruciating time to fill. He lifted one of the frosted glass mugs from the tray and offered it to Maxi. "Here you go."

"Thank you."

"You're welcome."

He took a drink from his own mug. It was beyond ludicrous; it was absurd. He was sitting here feeling as bad as she obviously did and not knowing how to fix things, wishing he could tell her he was sorry and without any idea of how to begin.

Worst of all, on top of that, at this most inopportune moment, he wanted her. He could no longer push, cajole or will that fact from his mind. Maybe not wanted in the biblical sense, exactly, although he sure wouldn't want to be tested on that score. For now he would settle for being close to her, very close, a holding-her-in-his-arms kind of close. He wanted it in a way he suspected he shouldn't and with a fierceness that was growing stronger all the time and that he wasn't sure he could go on ignoring much longer.

With a sigh he twisted on the seat, permitting his arm to stretch toward her, wetting his lips, getting ready, a hundred different thoughts running through his mind.

Maxi turned to look at him. With her head tilted a little to one side she looked alert, curious, expectant, absolutely beautiful. Jay willed himself to say something about how he was feeling, something portentous.

He cleared his throat. "Great root beer."

Quickly lifting her mug, Maxi muttered something from behind it that could just as easily have been, "Yeah, great root beer" or "Who asked for your opinion?"

Jay chose to assume it was the former; it gave him a theme to expand upon. "Yep. Really great root beer."

It was such an innocuous remark it startled him when, with a stubborn set to her mouth, she suddenly swung her knees onto the seat and thrust her mug toward him. Visions of having the contents poured over his head flashed before him.

He pressed his back against the seat. "What are you doing?"

At his alarmed tone she froze, kneeling with one arm extended in front of him, her body close enough to his to make him sweat. She gave him an odd look. "Putting my glass back on the tray. It's cold, and holding it is making my fingers numb. Do you mind?"

"Of course not," he said, feeling like an idiot. "All you had to do was ask."

"You mean ask you?"

Sheepishly, wondering if he ought to mention the drips of condensation from her mug that were soaking his pants leg, he said, "Yes, I guess that's what I meant."

She opened her eyes wide. "Never. I wouldn't dream of asking you to do something for me, something you wouldn't get anything out of personally, that is."

The set of her lips was defiant as she leaned over him to finish putting her mug on the tray. As she did, her breast brushed lightly against his arm.

Jay pretended not to notice as pleasure rushed up and down his spine.

It was suddenly hard to think.

She shifted, and the top of her thigh pressed against the side of his.

Instant temptation. It pulsed inside him, hot and thick and insistent.

The only coherent thought he could manage was that he shouldn't. Couldn't.

Instead of feeling relieved when she began to pull away, the way he ought to, Jay's senses rebelled. Before he could stop it, his hand was in her hair. The strands sifted through his fingers, feeling just the way he'd imagined, cool and silky against his overheated skin. If he'd ever had a chance to begin with, it was lost. Her skin, when his fingers closed gently around the back of her neck a second later, felt so smooth and soft he would give anything to go on touching her.

*Anything?* taunted an unwanted voice of reason within. His fingertips strayed to the side of her throat and found the pulse point there. It was racing with excitement to match his own. Anything.

"Oh, what the hell," he heard himself mutter as he reached to pull her closer.

It wasn't a difficult task. At his slightest nudge her body yearned toward his, as if she were freezing and he was the sun. Gracefully she twisted and fit her small body into the space between his chest and the steering wheel. What might have been awkward was instead a slow dance of the most excruciating anticipation. It was as if they had been rehearsing for this moment all their lives.

She settled into the crook of his arm, lifting her face to his, waiting. Her lips were slightly parted in invitation. Their eyes clung, as if there were nothing else in the world to look at. The deepening shadows outside added to the spell. They were alone, and whatever lay beyond the confines of the small truck cab ceased to matter.

With a small groan Jay cupped her chin with his free hand. He caressed her face with his eyes and with his fingertips as he slowly lowered his mouth to hers. When their lips met, it was as if someone had put a match to the powder keg of desire that had been growing since the moment they met.

For Maxi it was an explosion of the most exquisite pleasure she had ever felt, and she shook from the power of it. Instinctively she clung to Jay's shoulders, and a thrill shot through her as she realized that he was trembling, as well. All the patience and delicacy with which they'd come together a moment ago was swept away in what quickly became a kiss of hunger and desperation.

Maxi tilted her head to the side to give Jay fuller access to her mouth, and with his tongue he quickly seized the advantage. He pressed home, withdrew and pressed again and again. She thrilled to his impatience. Her own pent-up longing would settle for nothing gentler. She welcomed his roughness, opened to it fully, and finally matched it with her own urgency.

Her hands, which had been gripping his shoulders, slid slowly downward to caress his chest. Once more she heard Jay groan and felt it as a deep rumble, a blend of satisfaction and hunger, beneath her fingertips.

When he lifted his head to look down at her, his eyes were dark and shining with desire. His breath was as ragged as hers, his skin as flushed as she knew hers must be. If Maxi needed further proof that he was excited, ready and able, she was sitting on it.

"Wow," he said when his breathing slowed enough to enable him to speak.

"Mmm. Yes."

He smiled that smile she would walk through fire for and began to trace her tender lips with one fingertip. Before he was half through he abruptly bent his head to her again, murmuring, "More. Now. Open your mouth for me."

"Oh, yes," Maxi whispered as his lips took hers.

This time they both displayed more patience, as if the first kiss had appeased whatever part of them feared that the other might evaporate before they got enough. With Jay's strong arms supporting her, Maxi felt as if she were floating in space. The only part of her with an open sensory line feeding her brain were her lips, and they were transmitting slow, detailed messages meant to be savored and recorded forever.

She memorized the sweet, light taste of root beer that clung to his lips and tongue, thinking it was without doubt the most wildly erotic taste in the world. Why did lovers ever bother with champagne? She ran her tongue across his lips in delight, loving the soft, firm feel of them. She flicked his tongue with hers, fully cognizant of the sort of response it would incite, and a heartbeat later was thrilled by the desire and force in his thrusting retaliation.

As their kiss wound on, Jay's hand slid lower, feather-brushing the tip of her breast before capturing it in his cupped palm. Maxi drew a deep breath of delight, swelling into his hand encouragingly. Peeling her vest aside, he lowered his head to kiss her through the soft cotton of her dress. She wasn't wearing a bra, and when the fabric became wet from his eager tonguing, it left the hard point of her nipple clearly visible.

Jay stared at it in fascination, brushing it with his finger-tips as if awed by his power to excite her. He grabbed for the tiny buttons of her dress, but as soon as the first one fell open he brought his impatience under control. His fingers slowed. He unfastened the remaining buttons leisurely, pausing to kiss her throat and her face in between each small conquest. He smiled and scraped his tongue across the upper swell of her breasts with the lazy self-assurance of a man who had performed this sort of intimate task a time or two before.

Maxi, no stranger to Jay's appeal, had no doubt that he had. It was a very different matter for her. Never before in her life had she felt this insatiable hunger for a man. She didn't understand the sudden burning need any more than she understood a lot of other things where Jay was concerned. And right this minute she didn't care about under-standing. She only wanted to feel.

When the front of her dress was open he parted it enough to slip his hand inside and stroke her bare flesh. Maxi shiv-ered and nestled deeper into his lap in a way that ripped a rough sigh from him as he shifted beneath her. Laughing delightedly, she threaded her fingers through the dark waves of hair at the nape of his neck.

He breathed softly against her neck. "You're torturing me, sweetheart."

"I'm so sorry," Maxi whispered with another strategic squirm. "But just think, relief is at your fingertips."

Chuckling, Jay lifted his head to gaze down at her. In spite of his smile, the desire burning in his eyes was fierce. Maxi quivered the way she might before parachuting out of an airplane. In a way this situation with Jay was just as un-precedented and every bit as dangerous.

"At my fingertips, hmm?" Slowly, but very purpose-fully, he peeled back the front of her dress so her breasts were fully exposed to him. Sitting in the shadows, cradled against his chest, she was safe from any other view. "I think maybe I should check this out more closely." He lowered his head. His warm breath washed over her, a moist, arousing tease. "Much, much more closely."

"Here you go, folks, five chili dogs. Enjoy."

The carhop's approach had been silent, but her cheery announcement that their food was ready had the same effect as a policeman's flashlight or a lightning bolt ricocheting through the truck. They lurched apart like guilty teenagers. Maxi was back in her own seat with her dress nearly rebuttoned before Janelle was out of sight. As Maxi adjusted her vest, she kept her eyes straight ahead. Jay steadied himself with a long gulp of root beer.

The silence was amplified by their heaving breaths.

"I want you to know," Maxi said after hurriedly marshalling her thoughts and defenses into some sort of order, "that I was just about to call a halt."

Jay turned from putting his mug back on the tray and looked at her, nodding solemnly. "Me, too."

"Oh, come on," she blurted in flagrant disbelief.

"It's true." He kneaded his forehead with stiff fingers. "I can't believe we let it go that far. I must be even more tired than I thought."

"So you're saying you only kissed me and—and, you know, because your resistance was down? Thanks."

"No, that's not what I'm saying. Lord knows I was enjoying every second of it, but I knew all along we couldn't finish things. It's too much of a risk. *You're* too much of a risk, Maxi."

"I'm too much of a risk?" She forced a nonchalant laugh. For just a second there she had been moved by his sad eyes and the emotional tremor in his voice. Obviously, however, this was one more instance of Jay looking out for number one. Sure he was sad, sad that he couldn't *finish things.* "At least I'm not so much of a risk you have to worry that you'll turn around and find I've walked through a wall and disappeared."

His chin lifted as if she'd struck him. "Have I ever disappeared on you? Or have I been right there for you every time you needed me? Never mind,'' he continued as she fumbled for a lancing retort. He threw his head back, staring at the ceiling before meeting her gaze once more. "Look, let's not fight, okay? I don't want to spoil the memory of what happened a minute ago with a stupid argument over nothing."

"Me, either," Maxi admitted. Her voice, with its raspy note of misery, was barely audible. She couldn't mistake the finality in his use of the word *memory*.

"Good." He smiled an obviously forced smile. "Let's eat."

They both bit into their chili dogs with less enthusiasm than their earlier hunger had forecast. A car radio nearby was tuned to the oldies station, and Maxi recognized the soft strains of *In the Still of the Night*. The haunting melody suited her mood. The stillness within the truck made it hard to escape from her own thoughts, and she suspected Jay, sitting so quietly at the other end of the bench seat, was suffering his own version of second thoughts.

"Why didn't you come right out and accuse me of lying?" she asked finally.

Jay swallowed quickly, his brow wrinkling as if she'd taken him by surprise. "When?"

"A few minutes ago when I said I was about to call a halt."

"Were you? Lying, I mean?"

"You should know."

He shook his head firmly. "I don't. I told you I can't read your mind, Maxi. It's only once in a while that I get these—"

She nodded impatiently. "I know, I know, impressions."

"Right."

"And you didn't get the impression that I was lying when I said that?"

"No." He spoke quietly. "Maybe I was too busy hoping you were lying to pick up on anything else. I liked thinking that you were enjoying it as much as I was."

"Oh, Jay, you should know that I was enjoying it. Much too much. That's the reason I want to clear this up between us."

She dropped her hands to her lap, fiddling with the edge of the wax paper her chili dog had been wrapped in. "When I said I was going to call a halt, what I meant was that if I had been thinking straight I definitely would have called a halt. I don't usually just let myself go that way with a man, especially not with a man I've known such a short time and, well, somehow I just wanted you to know that."

"I already do know that. No, not through any special power," he quickly added when she gave him a disgruntled look. "I know it because, in spite of what you just said about us hardly knowing each other, I do know you. For instance, I know that underneath that impulsive, live-and-let-live attitude of yours, you're a woman with very strong ideas and values and that you're not easily swayed from them."

"Now you *are* reading my mind," she accused lightly. "That's more or less what I wanted to tell you. I didn't want you to draw the wrong conclusion about me."

He smiled at her. "You mean you didn't want me to think you would melt for just any guy who walked through a wall into your life?"

The corners of her mouth lifted in a brief, reluctant smile. "Something like that. You know, sometimes I'll meet a man, just a nice regular guy, a banker or something, and we'll go out, and about halfway through the evening I know that the reason he asked me out was because he looked at me and at the way I dress—" she plucked at the purple cotton ruffles of her dress "—and maybe at what I do for a living, and he thought, 'Oh, boy, here's an easy target—artsy, wacky, nice and loose.' Don't laugh, it's a common misconception among certain groups of men."

"Yes, and I'll bet you always set those men straight before the night is over."

She returned his grin. "I try. They're not always very gracious about it."

"Is that why you need Godzilla standing guard downstairs?"

"Don't make fun of Rudy. He's a wonderful friend."

"What else is he?"

There was no mistaking the seriousness in Jay's tone. Even if he couldn't read her thoughts about this, Maxi wasn't about to hedge on the truth. She swept her hair back from her face and met his gaze. "Rudy and I were lovers. But that was a long time ago. Now we're just good friends."

Jay reached for his remaining chili dog and shook it loose from the wrapping, as if trying to punish it. "I had to ask."

"Does it bother you?"

Jay sighed, looking first out the window, then down at the hot dog in his hand and finally straight at her. "I know it shouldn't. I have no right to be upset over anything in your life, never mind in your past, but, yes, it bothers the hell out of me."

Maxi said nothing, afraid that if she spoke the absurdly giddy joy she was feeling would come through. Later, when she was alone, would be time enough to ponder and dissect and think over what it might mean that Jay was jealous of Rudy.

"So what happened with you two?" he asked offhandedly between bites, as if he was only making idle conversation and not desperately interested in her answer. Maxi, struggling to maintain the same sort of casual demeanor, knew better.

"Eventually we both realized that no matter how much we wanted it to work, it was never going to," she revealed. "Chalk it up to basic philosophical differences, I guess. For me, sex and love are all tied up with commitment. Appearances aside, I'm very old-fashioned. And Rudy..."

She sighed, considering how best to put it, an affectionate smile curving her lips. "Rudy is a free spirit in every sense of the word. From day to day he never knows how he's going to feel about a particular person or thing until he wakes up in the morning."

"How did you ever get involved with such a zero— Excuse me," Jay apologized as she arrowed an annoyed look his way. "With a guy like Rudy Bannon in the first place?"

She shrugged, her weak laugh more resigned than amused. "I think the reason qualifies as my fatal flaw, my own personal catch-22. Rudy is zany and fun and sensitive. We like the same movies, listen to the same music. I was attracted to everything about him . . . just as I'm always attracted to men who can't commit. The men I meet who value stability and fidelity and all that home-fires-burning stuff never turn me on."

"Yet that's what you want . . . someone to keep your fires burning always." In his silkily abrasive voice the words alone were enough to make Maxi feel warm. "It's important to you that a man be willing to pledge himself to you forever?"

"Very. I didn't always know how important, but I do now. I gave my heart away once with my eyes closed, and it hurt too much when I finally opened them. The next time I give myself to a man, I have to know up-front that we both want the same things from a relationship. It doesn't necessarily have to be white lace and a three-tier cake with cute little plastic dolls perched on top, but I need to know that our love has a future."

"I see. Quite a coincidence, isn't it? A future is one thing I definitely cannot offer you, Maxi, love." His tone was light, his movements oddly taut as he scrunched the wax paper into a tiny ball and hurled it back on the tray. "So I guess that's that."

"Yes," she said softly, having no choice but to agree. "That's that."

## Chapter Eight

It took three days to finalize arrangements for the next shoot. Maxi located a candy-supply company and ordered enough penny candy to fill the display case. She spent hours fine-tuning the script and coordinating schedules. Jay agreed with her that voice-overs would not be as effective in this spot as having the candidate on the scene, interacting with the residents of the Hillside Nursing Home, where she had arranged to do the filming. That meant finding a time that would fit into Robert Chandler's busy schedule and also be convenient for the nursing-home staff.

After much debate it was determined that the only possible time was the following Friday afternoon. For Maxi it would mean going directly from the taping to the first of her status-reporting sessions with Peter Duvall, but it couldn't be helped. Friday offered the added bonus of being bingo day at the nursing home, and she instructed Jay ahead of time to get some footage of the home's residents at play. The mention of bingo started wheels turning in her head, and she phoned Hillside's activities director to see if there was a horseshoes court on the grounds and to ask if she might get some volunteers to play a few rounds for the camera. She wasn't sure how much of what Jay shot would end up in the finished commercial, but didn't want to overlook any opportunity.

Even with all her careful attention to detail, however, Maxi wasn't prepared for the scene that greeted her and Jay when they arrived at the nursing home on Friday afternoon. Ned had agreed to let them borrow Mickey along with his camera equipment, and Mickey had volunteered to drive out to the nursing home early to begin setting up. From the looks of things, he'd been very busy.

Bingo tables were set up at one end of the long room. At the other were two long tables draped in yellow holding a punch bowl and the catered sandwich buffet Maxi had ordered to express her appreciation to the nursing-home staff and residents for their generous hospitality and cooperation.

During one of several scouting visits earlier in the week she and Jay had determined which areas of the room offered the best lighting, and she had mentioned them to Mickey in passing. Now in the exact corner where she had envisioned it stood Suwaski's infamous penny-candy counter. The glass sparkled and the wood gleamed, the result of a full evening's labor on Jay's part. The silver trays inside the case were filled with everything from sour balls and squirrel chews to lollipops. On a small wicker table nearby stood the bride doll and her attendants, as well as an old hand-operated coffee grinder and a wooden canister of coffee beans, an estate-sale find Maxi had known would come in handy one day.

The scene was perfect, like something in an old sepia-toned photograph, and Maxi couldn't help throwing her arms around Mickey, who was hanging around the candy counter, grinning and chewing on a piece of red licorice.

"This place looks fantastic," she told him. "I can't believe you did it all by yourself."

"Actually I didn't," Mickey admitted. "One thing there is no shortage of around here is volunteers." Dropping his voice he added, "Maxi, do you have any idea what a big deal this is to these folks? One of the nurses told me that anything that breaks the monotony around here is tantamount to a holiday, and this—" he indicated the camera lights and props, the platters of tiny sandwiches and fancy pastries "—is the biggest thing since Christmas."

Maxi hadn't considered it before now, but as she followed Mickey's gaze to the elderly men and women already gathered in small clusters at the opposite end of the room, she could see he wasn't exaggerating. They were all wearing their Sunday best in anticipation of what was clearly a very special occasion for them.

The same women who on Maxi's last visit had shuffled along the corridors in housecoats and slippers were wearing dresses with bright stripes or floral prints with dainty collars, tucks and pleats. In general the men were less obvious. Most had settled for pulling on a cardigan sweater over a plaid sport shirt, but here and there she spotted a sport coat and tie.

Excitement was evident in their smiles, as well, and in the sidelong glances they slanted her as they patted their freshly permed silver hair or struck an impressive pose with pipe clenched between teeth. It was as if this were a casting call for a big Hollywood production. And she, Maxi realized suddenly, was the casting director.

She immediately excused herself from Mickey and looked around for Jay, finding him off in a corner sweeping two beaming elderly ladies off their feet. It didn't require much effort on his part. What woman wouldn't be charmed by his undivided attention? Even wearing a ratty black T-shirt, he'd been a seductive force to contend with. Today, dressed in loose-fitting khaki trousers and a forest-green cotton shirt, sleeves rolled to the elbow above his tan forearms, he was irresistible.

These clothes also were courtesy of Rick Grecco, but this time they had been hand-chosen by Maxi. After watching Jay suffer through one day in fashion hell, she had taken pity on him and gone downstairs to personally rummage through her obliging neighbor's closet. The following afternoon she had talked Jay into going shopping for more personal items and a pair of black boots to replace the designer loafers, which she insisted clashed with his new look.

The boots had been a point of contention. Jay had automatically veered toward the dress-shoe display, but in the end, after a quietly fierce power struggle, he had agreed to take a long look in the store mirror. After a lengthy study of his new image he had conceded to her choice with a simple and unprecedented "You're right."

Unfortunately his appreciation for the clothes and her help did nothing to lessen the unspoken tension that had hovered beneath their careful politeness since that day in the truck. Maxi was a big girl. She knew only one thing could put an end to this kind of tension, and that one thing was off limits.

After locating Jay in the crowd, Maxi hurried across the room to his side. Based on staff recommendations, she had earlier in the week made her selection as to which Hillside residents would actually appear in the commercial. Now she gripped Jay's arm to draw him from his conversation so she could announce a last-minute change in plans.

"Tape them all," she told him.

"What are you talking about?"

"These people," she replied, waving her arm to include everyone in the room. "Look at them, all dressed up as if they were going to their high school prom. Have you ever seen anything so sweet?"

Jay glanced around, trying to see what was so sweet and compelling about a few polyester dresses and motheaten sweaters. He shrugged. "No. Never."

"Neither have I," said Maxi, "and I want you to tape them all."

"Sure. So what if it's the longest political commercial in history? Duvall will be thrilled you made the record book."

She shook her head impatiently. "I know they can't all be included in the final cut, but at least I can have copies of the tape made for them to enjoy. I noticed they have a VCR in the TV room. It's obvious how much today means to them."

Jay opened his mouth to warn her that what she ought to be thinking about was how much today meant to her, but he was stopped short by her eager expression. Snap out of it! he wanted to shout. Forget about these old folks playing dress up. Worry instead about whether Chandler will show up on time and whether he'll be a stiff in front of the camera and about what last-minute monkey wrench Duvall might throw our way in an attempt to screw everything up. Look out for yourself, honey, he longed to tell her. Because nobody else is going to. It was honest, hard-earned advice, the best he had to offer, but for some reason, staring into Maxi's bright, unguarded eyes, he couldn't bring himself to say it.

Instead he swung the camera he was holding to his shoulder, smiled at her and said, "I'll take care of it for you."

Maxi gave his arm a grateful squeeze, and as he turned away she quickly switched her attention to the clipboard in her hand, reviewing the list of last-minute things to do. Check with caterer. Done. Check tables. Done, thank heavens for Mickey. Check candy display, done; dolls, done; Bessie.

Bessie.

Maxi quickly scanned the crowd and spotted Bessie Sherlock, her soon-to-be star, sitting on the sofa. She had already reviewed Bessie's few lines with her yesterday and had complete confidence that, barring a severe attack of stage fright, she would be wonderful.

Bessie was a petite woman with white hair, which today was arranged in soft curls and held in place with a beaded hair net. She was wearing the royal-blue dress she and Maxi had selected together. Draped across her shoulders was a lightweight pale pink sweater, anchored in front with a pearl sweater clasp. It lent a simple, old-fashioned touch. Perfect, thought Maxi.

Bessie lifted her head and smiled as Maxi approached.

"Hello, Bessie, are you all set for your big debut?"

"Oh, my, yes. I can't wait to hear you shout 'Lights, camera, action!'"

Maxi chuckled. "I'm afraid we're not quite that formal."

"Oh." A sigh of disappointment lifted the elderly woman's frail shoulders. "Well, never mind."

"Bessie, if it will make you happy I will personally shout 'Lights, camera, action!'"

"Such a nice girl," Bessie murmured, brightening instantly, like a child who has gotten her way. She slanted a coy little smile toward the woman seated beside her. "Didn't I tell you she was a nice girl, Ida?"

Ida smiled and nodded agreeably.

"I was just remarking to Ida," Bessie continued, "what a shame it is that there is no lemon-meringue pie in that nice spread you have over there. Lemon meringue is my favorite, you know."

"I didn't know, Bessie, or I would have asked the caterer to include it especially for you. I simply ordered their standard desserts."

"My goodness, that's no way to do things. You have to speak up in this life, my dear, or else how will you ever get what you want?"

How, indeed? thought Maxi. The few hours she'd spent with Bessie had convinced her that the woman was as sharp as ever. Now she realized she was crafty, as well. She'd wager there were few things Bessie wanted that she didn't get around here, one way or another. Wanting to abandon the subject before she found herself calling the caterer back to make a special pie delivery, Maxi got directly to her reason for seeking out Bessie.

"Bessie, I'd like you to come with me now," she said. "Linda, the makeup artist who will be working with us today, has just arrived, and she might want to touch up your makeup a bit for the camera."

Bessie accepted help getting to her feet and squeezed Maxi's hand before letting go. "Of course, my dear, and don't you worry about that lemon pie. I prefer the home-made variety, anyway. Not that there's much chance I'll be tasting one ever again."

"Oh, now, Bessie," Maxi admonished vaguely, still hoping to gently change the subject. "Come on with me. I know you're going to like Linda."

They'd walked about halfway across the room, making their way to the out-of-the-way spot where Linda had set up shop on a small folding table, when there was a flurry of activity near the door. Robert Chandler had arrived—and on time, Maxi noted happily. He was flanked by a half-dozen aides in dark suits. Her pleasure dimmed a bit when she realized that one of the men accompanying him was Peter Duvall.

She gave a quick hello wave and was signaling that she would be right with them when Bessie came to a sudden halt. Maxi did the same, bracing herself for more lemon-meringue manipulation.

"Is *that* Robert Chandler?" Bessie asked, her brown eyes as sharp as tacks as they fixed on his tall frame. "Is that the man you've been telling me about?"

"Yes, that's Robert Chandler. I'll introduce you to him as soon as Linda finishes with you so you can chat for a few minutes before we begin."

"But he's a Democrat," Bessie countered. "Don't try and deny it, because I saw him on the news the other night."

"Of course I won't deny it, Bessie. Robert is a Democrat. I'm sure I mentioned that to you."

"Oh, no." She shook her head adamantly. "You couldn't have, or I never would have agreed to any of this. My goodness, my poor old father would roll in his grave if I had any hand in putting a Democrat in the state house. The Sherlocks have always been Republicans. Everyone knows that," she concluded, as if stating a fact as basic as the law of gravity.

"All right, perhaps I did neglect to mention it," Maxi allowed, knowing she had not. "I don't see why it should make any difference. Robert has consistently supported issues that benefit senior citizens. I'm sure your dear old father would be in favor of that."

"Oh, now I just don't know what to do." With that, Bessie wrung her hands and peered off into the distance, the flutter of her faded lashes suggesting that she was greatly perplexed. Maxi fought an urge to grab her by the dainty shoulders and shove her in front of the camera.

"Bessie, you gave me your word that you would help," Maxi pointed out. "And it's too late now for someone else to step in and memorize your lines."

"I do want to do the right thing," Bessie assured her. "But I have my heritage to consider. The Sherlocks are proud people."

Yes, thought Maxi, and so are the Loves, not to mention being extremely image conscious. If she blew this project because Bessie pulled a scene in front of Robert Chandler or, worse, insulted him to his face, the Love family would never let Maxi forget it.

She glanced anxiously at Robert, who was now walking briskly toward them, Peter Duvall at his heels. Mickey was nowhere in sight, and Jay was at the far end of the room shooting the extra footage she had requested. She had about sixty seconds to come to her own rescue.

Fate granted a brief reprieve as Robert stopped to shake hands with a group of people along the way. Maxi touched the crystal pendant she was never without at critical times like today and considered the odds of winning Bessie over

on the basic of logic or plain old human decency. It would
be a long shot. She licked her lips nervously and looked up
to see Peter Duvall catch her at it. Smirking, he dropped his
gaze to check his watch, a pointed reminder that they were
already two and a half minutes behind schedule.

No time for long shots. It was definitely a moment for
desperate measures.

She looked at Bessie, who sighed dramatically and looked
away. "Bessie, I know it's asking a lot for you to put aside
your family's political tradition for even a short while, but
do you think I might persuade you to honor our agreement
if I threw in a bonus? Say—" she drew a deep breath "—a
lemon-meringue pie, for instance?"

Bessie's lined satin cheeks crinkled; her dark eyes danced.
"Homemade?"

It seemed to Maxi an inopportune time to mention that
being made in her home was not exactly grounds for the
Good Housekeeping Seal of Approval.

"Of course homemade."

"You've got yourself a deal, my dear."

Quickly, with tremendous relief, Maxi delivered Bessie
into Linda's capable hands. Robert had been sidetracked
once more, so she stood by while her frail extortionist was
rouged and combed, anxious to get started before it occurred to Bessie to up the ante by demanding chocolate
mousse, as well. As soon as Maxi caught Jay's attention, she
beckoned for him to join her.

"Glad to see Chandler got here on time," he said after
making his way to her side. "If everything goes well, we'll
have a few hours after we finish up here to plan how we're
going to approach tonight's meeting."

"That won't be necessary," Maxi told him.

He cocked an eyebrow. "Pretty confident for a lamb
scheduled to appear in the lion's den, aren't you?"

"I meant it won't be necessary because *we* aren't going to
the meeting. I am."

"You're kidding."

"No. I don't have time to kid. Or to argue. I'm the art director on this project, and I'll make the presentation at the meeting. Alone." She turned away from his incredulous frown. "It won't look good if I need to have my cameraman there to help me over the rough-spots."

"It also won't look good if you go belly-up the first time, Duvall throws you a curve."

"I won't go belly-up."

"Sure you won't. And the sun might not rise tomorrow. Honey, you don't know the kind of guy you're dealing with here. Duvall—"

"Is my problem," she interrupted. "And I'll handle him. I have to. I might not wholeheartedly agree with your 'me first' philosophy, Jay, but one thing I do agree with you about—the time comes when you have to look out for yourself, no matter how tough the going might be. I'm always preaching to my family about wanting to do exactly that. Tonight is my chance to prove it. To them, to you . . ." Her smile was vulnerable as she softly added, "Maybe even to myself."

Maxi expected him to argue, to try to change her mind, to insist that he be allowed to come along in case she needed him. All right, part of her even wanted him to insist. He didn't, however, and the look of admiration he gave her instead was worth facing a thousand Peter Duvalls.

"Okay," he said. "Just remember, if you need me—"

He was interrupted as Robert, having shaken about every hand in the room, finally made his way to her side. "Here you are, Maxi. It certainly looks as if you're doing your part to turn out the seniors vote."

She shook his hand, smiling with genuine affection as she reminded herself that, problems and personality conflicts and professional ambitions aside, she was doing this because she truly wanted to see Robert elected governor.

"I'm trying, Robert. I hope this ad does more than turn out elderly voters, though. I've worked hard to see that it appeals to a cross-section of your constituents. The idea is to project the kind of images that can touch the memories everyone has in their hearts. Then, by having you appear, we'll try to trigger an association between you and the values that are most important to all of us."

Robert nodded enthusiastically. "I knew I could count on you to come up with a different approach. I read the outline for this spot that you sent to my office, and I think you're on to something here. Just tell me what you want me to do."

"I think you should begin by—"

"Yoo hoo... Maxi."

She broke off midsentence, turning to discover that the gentle tug on the sleeve of her sweater was made by Bessie. Maxi had hoped to have a moment alone with her, to clarify exactly what she was and was not to say in front of the others, before introducing her to Robert. Pie or no pie, she didn't completely trust Bessie. The determined gleam in the older woman's eye, however, made clear that she was not to be brushed off even temporarily.

"You can begin by meeting the lady who'll be appearing in the commercial with you," she said to Robert. "Bessie, this is Robert Chandler. Mr. Chandler, Miss Bessie Sherlock."

Robert's smile was warm, giving no hint that this was a routine chore for him as he reached out to clasp Bessie's delicate hand in his. "Miss Sherlock, it's a pleasure to meet you. And I'm flattered that a beautiful lady like yourself sees fit to help me in my bid to be elected."

Maxi held her breath.

Bessie let her gaze drift downward as she responded to the compliment with a pretty blush. A nice touch, but still no guarantee of what she would do next. One word about her dear old Republican father rolling in his grave and the pie deal was definitely off.

With great elegance Bessie lifted her chin, squeezed Robert Chandler's hand and smiled so brilliantly Maxi thought she ought to be the one running for office. "Enchanted, I'm sure, Mr. Chandler... or should I call you Governor?"

Robert beamed. Bessie fluttered her lashes. Maxi exhaled, at last, and wondered where she could dig up a simple recipe for lemon-meringue pie.

Cream of tartar?

Maxi leaned down and blew away traces of flour to take a clearer look at the cookbook open on the counter before her. She had been up late last night, recounting for Jay her triumphant meeting with Peter. Maybe her eyes weren't fully awake yet.

The memory of last night's meeting caused her mouth to curve in a very satisfied smile. She had dazzled Peter, there was no other way to describe it. The rough cuts of the commercials she'd brought along spoke for themselves, as well as for Jay's genius with a camera. Even Peter had acknowledged the freshness in his approach.

Maxi suspected he did so partly because it was unavoidable in view of the enthusiastic response of the other campaign workers present and partly because he felt certain he could score his points later, when the time came to discuss the legal and financial aspects of the spots. She'd been ready for him. With Jay's help she had organized the receipts and signed release forms, completed a schedule for the remaining work and written a meticulous and comprehensive progress report that was utterly Duvall-proof. The only tense moment for her had come when she opened her briefcase and couldn't find the folder containing all of it.

Suppressing a natural urge to panic, she had excused herself to check for it in the car, rummaging through the trunk and crawling over the seats, all without luck. She'd returned to the conference room trying to decide if it would be better to try winging it or admit that she was the scatterbrain of the year, when some impulse moved her to check her briefcase again and—miraculously—the folder was there.

*Miraculously* being the operative word. From that moment on she hadn't felt quite so alone in that big room. Of course Jay, all wide blue eyes and innocent shrugs when she questioned him later, had denied having anything to do with the reappearing folder. Unconvinced, Maxi had proceeded to wheedle, implore, tease and ultimately give up. In the week and a half they had been together she'd learned that when Jay didn't want to do, eat, see, hear or reveal something, he didn't. He was a man of steely, impenetrable, utterly maddening control.

If only. . . She immediately crushed the thought. If she'd learned anything lately, it was that thinking about the impossible only caused more frustration. With a small sigh she gave her eyes a cleansing blink and turned back to the cookbook. That's what it said all right, cream of tartar.

She had remembered that the recipe called for cream. The kid stocking shelves at the all-night supermarket had made a halfhearted attempt to stifle a yawn and asked if she wanted heavy cream, light cream or sour cream. Of course, having no idea, she had bought some of each. Now, with three assorted pints of cream waiting in the refrigerator, it turned out it wasn't heavy or light or sour cream she needed, but rather cream of something called tartar. Whatever that was. It sounded gross. Like something you'd pick up at a dental supply shop.

She reached for the hand mixer. Terrific or not, this was one lemon-meringue pie that was going to be made without it. She had been up since six, wrestling with a pie crust that had more holes than imported Swiss cheese and producing a rather lumpy version of lemon filling. All that remained was to whip the topping, which was where the mysterious cream of tartar came in.

Or rather, where it would have come in, if she had any. It hardly seemed worth making another trip to the store for a quarter teaspoon of the stuff. How much difference could such a small amount possibly make? Determinedly she started the mixer. She'd just go ahead and whip without it. With any luck, Bessie wouldn't know the difference.

The unfamiliar whirr of the electric mixer woke Jay. He momentarily burrowed his head in his pillow, refusing to think about what Maxi might be doing in the kitchen, of all places. She had helped him fix dinner the other night, and when he'd finished chipping from the bottom of the pan the last of the blackened remains of what had started out to be linguini, he had vowed to never again set foot in that room with her.

Unfolding himself from the sofa, he stood with his hands braced on the small of his back, doing waist bends to get the kinks out. He folded his sheets and put them away, not because his hostess demanded, or even noticed, that he did so, but because doing so made him feel marginally in control of the chaos surrounding him. Next he dropped for fifty push-ups, having discovered that his body was programmed to do them first thing each morning, then went to brush his teeth. He brushed the way he did everything, methodically, thoroughly, and was surprised when he emerged from the bathroom some time later to hear the alarming sound of Maxi at work with an electrical appliance still flowing from the kitchen.

His desire for a cup of coffee was stronger than his resolution, it seemed, because after only a brief inner debate he joined her. He was wearing only the faded black cotton gym shorts Dave had provided for him to sleep in, and Maxi wasn't wearing a heck of a lot more. She was barefoot, and although her short black robe covered all the essentials— barely—it had a tendency to slip and slide in very distracting ways. Jay knew, because for days now it had been for him a prime source of both frustration and fantasy.

Fortunately Rudy hadn't stopped by for coffee for the past several mornings, or Jay would have been forced to order her not to wear the damn thing in front of him, and there was no question about the sort of defiant response that would have drawn from Maxi. She didn't even like him telling her to put her shoes away so he wouldn't trip over them and break his neck. Rudy, he'd been pleased to learn, was spending his mornings and nights with a woman he'd met at one of the clubs the band played. Jay had studied Maxi's face closely when she told him about it, looking for some trace of sadness or regret. There was none, which pleased him even more.

So as long as they were alone here, he said nothing about the robe. He could handle temptation. He'd been doing it for days now, hadn't he? In fact, he was becoming a master at it. To prove that to himself, he paused in the door of the kitchen and watched as Maxi moved the hand that gripped the mixer in slow circles, causing her hips to move in slow circles of their own. The black silk rustled and shimmered enticingly. It wasn't anything he couldn't handle.

Beneath the silk he detected a faint ridge across her hips that he knew must be made by her panties. Probably that pair he'd seen hanging in the bathroom last night. The lavender ones with the lace panel in front and sides so skimpy he could snap them with his fingers. The ones that had felt as soft as rose petals between his fingertips when he'd sneaked a feel and had smelled fresh and flowery, the way Maxi herself always smelled. He shifted his weight from one foot to the other. This was not a problem. He could handle it. A cup of hot, black coffee would fix everything.

As he made a move toward the coffeepot, Maxi bent slightly to peer into the mixing bowl, and as she did the robe lifted in back to reveal the point where her thighs, firm and slender, rounded into something softer and lavender-covered and infinitely more tempting. Jay came to a dead halt, his breath turning to dust in his throat. All right, so she had a sweet tush; this was not news to him. He was strong enough to handle this situation. Then, before he could manage a swallow, she tossed her hair back in that unbridled way she had, as if utterly exasperated with the concoction before her.

It was her damn hair that did it. He had no idea why, but it had come to symbolize Maxi's unique blend of sexy and vulnerable, and it got him every time. It plucked some erotic chord deep inside, and suddenly all he could picture was that robe coming off her shoulders, being stripped away by him, black silk sliding over soft tawny flesh, her back bare to him, and those delicious, rounded hips . . . He squeezed his eyes shut. No man was strong enough for this.

Cold shower now. Coffee later. That was his only hope. Before he could retreat, however, Maxi switched off the mixer and immediately whirled to face him. Had he been panting so loudly she'd heard?

She smiled. "Good morning. Did I wake you?"

"No, I smelled the coffee," he replied, keeping his hands carefully, strategically clasped down low in front of him.

"Help yourself," she invited in a distracted tone, already turning back to what she was doing.

"Thanks." He quickly made his way to stand against the counter, taking advantage of Maxi's preoccupation to shift position inside the snug shorts. Almost two weeks of this to go yet. How was he going to get through all those days—and nights—resisting what he wanted most in the world? As he lifted the cup of black coffee to his lips, he at long last permitted himself to consider the question he'd been ducking for days. Did he really want to resist?

He knew he probably should. It was the wise, safe, prudent thing to do. But did he *want* to?

For the first time in his life Jay wasn't stone-cold certain of the right moves to make, and he hated it. He hated feeling so unsure of himself. By now he'd recalled enough bits and pieces of his life prior to the accident to know that he had spent most of it figuring out the rules of the game, playing by them and winning. Now suddenly there were no hard-and-fast rules to guide him, only instinct.

He gulped his coffee, observing above the rim of his mug the incongruous sight of Maxi absorbed in a cookbook. The hot liquid scorched its way down to his belly. Let it burn; it was nothing compared to the fire already down there. As his longing gaze slid the length of her bare legs all the way to her bright red toenails, it occurred to him—and not for the first time—that perhaps from the very start he had been making this whole thing too complicated. Perhaps Maxi and Maxi alone was his mission here.

It was a tantalizing possibility. She seemed to be the one thing he had never wasted time looking for...an honest, loyal, loving woman. Without recalling any particulars, Jay knew that for him the war of the sexes was resolved in one tidy equation: women equal pleasure. Period. If he'd been sent to watch over the sort of woman he was accustomed to dealing with, he'd be home free now. He would know exactly what to do—or not to do—and how to keep himself emotionally detached.

But Maxi was something new. She kept him off balance. She kept him wondering if maybe he'd been wrong all these years. Maybe she was for real. Maybe not all women had the same lack of courage and integrity as the mother who had dumped him and his brother in a state orphanage and never, in spite of all her promises, come back for them.

Yeah, he thought, taking another swallow of coffee, and then again maybe he was losing his objectivity in a major-league way. Stay detached, stay loose—wasn't that what he always told himself, and hadn't it always worked to his advantage? He just wished he could get back that old feeling of being in control of his own destiny.

On more than one occasion lately, as he struggled to get to sleep, he had this vision of what was going to happen when this was over. He saw himself getting to wherever he was going only to find a bunch of seedy-looking guys, clearly life's big losers, gathered around a table playing cards and chewing tobacco. In response to his hopeful inquiry one of them would look up, shoot an expert stream of brown tobacco juice from between his teeth and say, "Heaven? Buddy, heaven is where you just came from. You had nearly four solid weeks there. What you did or didn't do with the time is your problem."

Jay ran his fingers through his uncombed hair. Thoughts of heaven and Maxi had become hopelessly tangled up inside him. Was that insight? Or wishful thinking? If only he could be sure. There was so much at stake, and leaps of faith weren't exactly his forte. Some sort of sign would be helpful. It didn't seem like such an outlandish thing to request, considering how outlandish his being here was to begin with.

It didn't have to be a sign of epic proportions, either. He wasn't asking to see anyone turned into a pillar of stone or the words GO FOR IT spelled out in lightning bolts. Just some small sign that Maxi was really all she seemed to be, that he wasn't simply looking at her through lust-colored glasses.

Taking slow, uncertain steps, he erased the distance between them. For minutes he just stood there, close behind her, and let her scent fill his head, diluting his already weak reservations.

"What are you making?" he finally thought to ask, mostly because it gave him an excuse to move closer still as he peered over her shoulder.

"Well`...'" When she lifted the beaters the glossy white mixture flowed back into the bowl. "It's supposed to be a lemon-meringue pie."

"A pie, huh? Maxi, pies are round, solid-looking things, and lemons are yellow—"

"Oh, stop. The pie is over there." She pointed at the counter behind them, where something yellow and tan and vaguely resembling a pie did, indeed, sit. "This is the topping."

"That's more like it. Yes, I can see where that looks a little like—"

"It's a disaster," she interrupted. "I've been whipping forever, and nothing is happening."

"Maxi, love, you're a fantastic art director, a very beautiful woman, a terrific checkers player, but..."

"But?" She spun toward him, armed with a plastic spatula, as he searched for a gentle way to phrase it.

There wasn't one.

"But you're definitely a contender for the Chef from Hell Award. Whatever possessed you to try making a pie?"

She tilted her head to the side in a beguilingly sheepish gesture. "It's sort of a bribe."

Amused and enchanted, he reached for a lock of her hair and wound it around his finger as he spoke. "Maxi, you don't need to go to nearly this much effort to bribe me. In fact, all I want—"

"It's not a bribe for you," she interrupted, her words laden with amusement that quickly squelched him.

"Then who?"

Maxi widened her eyes at the sudden, unexpected harshness in his demand. He was jealous. She filed the knowledge away with an assortment of other conflicting insights she had garnered over the past days. It wasn't an easy process. Since his rare show of emotion in the truck, Jay hadn't directly said or done anything to encourage her to think he wanted her in the intense, unflagging way she was stunned to find herself wanting him. He was friendly and helpful, affectionate in the way one of her brothers would be.

The only thing that kept her from turning into a giant knot of frustration was her firm belief that it was all an act. The dark fire that smoldered in his eyes at moments when he thought he was watching her undetected was proof that his self-control was being severely tested from within. The fact that he was at this moment openly looking at her in that same hot way was proof he was losing the battle.

He gave a little tug on her hair, just enough to regain her attention, and repeated, "Who are you so intent on bribing?"

The temptation to fuel his jealousy was great. Maxi was well into a taunting, elusive smile when she recalled the absurdity of lying to him. With a sigh she said, "Bessie."

His eyes narrowed in confusion. "Bessie?"

"Bessie Sherlock, from the nursing home, remember?" He nodded and eased his grip on her hair a little. "She had a little last-minute conflict of interest yesterday, and somehow I ended up bribing her with the promise of a lemon-meringue pie to get her to go ahead with her part in the commercial as planned.''

"So why not just buy her a pie?"

"Our deal stipulates a homemade lemon-meringue pie."

"No problem. Claim temporary insanity due to stress and overwork, forget the pie entirely and send flowers instead—something gaudy and extravagant always works. You can charge it to the campaign and include a note saying you were too busy to cook."

He delivered the instructions with the clipped-tone ease of someone accustomed to giving orders and having them followed. For just a second Maxi wished she had a weak enough spine to say, "Yes, sir," and gleefully dump the mess in front of her down the garbage disposal.

Instead, with a resolute shake of her head she turned back to the bowl. "No. I can't disappoint her."

"She'd probably be disappointed for about half an hour, tops, then she'd be so busy showing off the flowers you sent that she'd forget all about the pie."

"Not Bessie."

"Maxi, I know you mean well, but this is above and beyond the call of duty. You hardly know the woman."

"What does that have to do with it?" she asked. The gaze she directed at him over her shoulder was straight and serene and utterly artless. "I know me. And I have to live with me. Whatever lapse in judgment may have prompted it, I made a promise to Bessie, and I'm going to keep it. Even," she concluded with a dramatic wave of the spatula she was holding, "if it takes me all day."

The burst of startled laughter that followed her speech barely registered with Jay. He was as awestruck as if those words he longed to see were indeed written in lightning bolts above his head. GO FOR IT. If a woman was willing—no, more than willing, adamant—about taking time she couldn't spare to do something she didn't want to do for an old lady she barely knew, what would she do for the man she loved?

The answer drifted slowly to the surface of Jay's mind, amazing, liberating, filling him with wonder. She would do anything, give anything. A woman like that would always be there for him. And, even more significant to him at the moment, a woman like that was worth any risk, any sacrifice, worth whatever price he would ultimately have to pay for what he was about to do.

He lifted his hand to her face and slowly stroked the backs of his fingers along her cheek, wanting to savor every sweet instant of his surrender.

"I am sorry, Jay," she said, biting back another chuckle. "I guess I got a little carried away at the thought of spending the entire day cooking."

His bewildered gaze followed hers to his chest, which was splattered with dollops of white meringue. He hadn't felt them land but realized now it must have happened when she shook the spatula, which explained both her laughter and her apology.

"The least I can do is clean you up," she said, reaching for the linen dish towel hanging nearby.

She made several passes across his chest with it. In his current mood the contact was as arousing as if she were caressing him with her fingers instead.

"Forget that," he said suddenly, grabbing her wrist and tossing the towel aside. "Let's see just how much of a disaster this topping is." Still holding her wrist, he guided her hand in a circular motion across his chest so that the remaining traces of meringue clung to her fingertips, then he lifted her hand to his mouth. With her fingertips resting lightly on his bottom lip, he stared into her alert, questioning eyes and murmured, "Let me taste."

Maxi watched breathlessly as Jay drew her fingers inside. His mouth was the hottest, wettest thing she had ever felt. But then, she already knew that from the time they had kissed. With the same lazy expertise he had demonstrated on that occasion he now slid his tongue across the pads of her fingertips. He nibbled lightly, playfully, and then with a look that was anything but playful, released all but one finger and sucked the one all the way into his mouth.

Maxi heard a broken, whimpering sound and realized it had come from her. Her knees were suddenly about as substantial as the concoction in the bowl. She leaned back against the counter for support, and Jay immediately responded by moving in closer.

"Not a disaster at all," he whispered, sliding her finger back and forth across his lower lip. "It's sweet and salty and creamy."

She gave an awkward little smile. It was all the sophistication and pizzazz she could manage, and she prayed it didn't give away the fact that he had her senses reeling out of control. Sweet and salty and creamy? Was he talking about the meringue? Or her finger?

"Exactly," he went on, kissing her fingertip, licking it, making her tummy tilt deliciously, the way it did when she drove fast over a dip in the road, "the way I know you're going to taste."

Maxi drew a shuddering breath. He definitely was not talking about the meringue. *The way she was going to taste.* The words lingered like a cloud of steam, heating the air around them. Not the way she might taste or the way he thought she would taste. No, the way she was *going* to taste. He said it with quiet assertion, as if the taste of her on his lips was already a fait accompli. Excitement swirled inside her, along with confusion.

There were so many questions she wanted to ask him. What about his reason for being here? What about the rules and playing it safe and forever and ever, amen, and the big risk he was taking by just kissing her?

She never got a chance.

## Chapter Nine

Maxi felt his lips, hot and hungry, as they took hers in hard, broken kisses. She felt his body crowding hers, first his chest and shoulders, pressing her backward against the counter, and then the inward swing of his hips and the firm muscled length of his thighs opening wide to encase hers. He was touching her all over, bestowing a rush of pleasurable sensations.

Feelings merged and flowed, one into the next, sweeping over her in a thrilling blur, save for one... her piercing awareness of his arousal, hard and strong and flagrant, an excitingly violent demand pushing rhythmically against the soft cradle of her femininity. It burned through his cotton shorts and the silk of her robe. She was on fire, exultant. This is what she had wanted, dreamed of, prayed for. She closed her mind to stop questions and doubts from intruding. Later, later she would think.

With eager, seeking movements of her tongue she kissed him back, matching his wildness, urging him closer still with her arms wrapped tightly around his middle. He bent his head to kiss her neck, teasing her with his tongue and teeth before sucking her skin between his teeth in a sharp bite that made her gasp with pleasure.

Jay laughed at the sound, a deep, satisfied rumbling sort of laugh that tapered into a groan as she slid her hands down his back to the elastic waist of his shorts, then up, and once more down. Up. In spite of the fierce longing inside, she couldn't seem to get her hands to obey her command to explore him more intimately.

Bringing his lips close to her ear Jay blatantly urged her to do precisely that, but all Maxi could do was stand with her fingers curled into his firmly muscled shoulders, trying to distract herself from the concerns niggling at her closed-for-business brain. It was no use; the unwelcome thoughts refused to be banished. They were grating and persistent, like a cat scratching to get inside on a cold night.

When Jay, deciding to take matters into his own hands, stepped back and reached for the sash on her robe, Maxi took advantage of the moment to bolt past him and flee to her bedroom.

She slammed the door behind her.

She had barely made it across the room, collapsing onto the old piano stool in front of the vanity, when the door swung open. Jay stood framed in the doorway, his eyes glittering, black with fury, his breathing ragged. Maxi, watching him in the oval mirror above the white wicker vanity table, tried not to notice the way his bare chest rose and fell. It was hard enough trying to catch her own breath without new provocation.

Seeking something to distract her as she willed her heart to slow down, she reached for the brush lying on the silver filigree tray before her and began pulling it through her hair.

Jay remained where he was, asking in a voice taut with frustration, "What the hell do you think you're doing?"

"Brushing my hair."

"Why? Your hair looked just fine to me the way it was."

She hesitated, her furious strokes slowing as she considered her reply. "It doesn't matter what it looked like. I always brush my hair when I'm upset."

"Did I upset you, Maxi?" he asked, his deep voice changing, hitting a cajoling note.

"No," she answered quickly. Then, unable to help herself she met his gaze in the mirror, her smile fragile and reluctant. "Yes, obviously, or I wouldn't have run."

"Why did you run? I was under the impression you were having as good a time as I was."

"I was. It was…wonderful," she admitted, dropping her gaze and then forcing it back to his. "But it was wrong."

"Wrong? Pleasure?" His dark eyebrows lifted above a sardonic smile. He rested his shoulder on the door jamb. "Isn't that attitude just a bit archaic? Especially for someone who's…how did you describe your look? Artsy-tartsy-easy? Or was it teasy?"

"I said I wasn't easy," she snapped, twisting on the seat to face him. "And don't you dare poke fun at me or condescend to me. You know very well what I meant. I meant that it would be wrong for you…because of everything that's going on. It's you I was thinking of, you ingrate."

She suddenly became aware of the laughter he was holding back, and she hurled the brush at him. He ducked. It hit the door and bounced to a rest by his feet.

With a toss of her head she squared her shoulders and glared at him. "I wish now that I had just gone ahead and let you do it, damn your soul."

Jay stared at her clenched jaw, her cheeks flushed with anger, and at the wide eyes shooting green sparks at him, and thought to himself that it was a hell of a moment to fall in love. "I wish you had, too, Maxi, love."

"Wish I had what?" she asked, thoroughly distracted by the way he was looking at her. If she were to fantasize about a man looking at her in a way that was enough to make her melt with longing, a look that was at once hot and tender, seductive and protective, this was it.

"I wish you had gone ahead and let me do it."

She shook her head. "No. Are you crazy? What about playing it safe and the angel's code of honor and—"

"Forget all that," he broke in. "It doesn't matter."

"You have gone crazy."

"Exactly the opposite," he said, his smile as easy and unconcerned as his tone. "I've finally come to my senses. And not a minute too soon. In fact, I'd say we have a lot of time to make up for and not much time to do it."

His eyes burned as darkly as they had when he first slammed her door open, but with an emotion far from anger.

"Jay, I think you ought to go take a shower, a cold shower. You're letting your hormones do your talking."

"No, it's definitely my brain talking." Without taking his gaze from hers, he bent and retrieved the hairbrush and started toward her. "My hormones are humming." With the back of the hand that held the brush, he stroked the side of her neck. "Can't you hear them?"

She was sure the only sound she heard was the blood rushing to her head, but she nodded anyway.

"I want you," he said simply.

"What about—"

"Forget all that."

"You said you were afraid that—"

"I was wrong."

"How can you—"

"Because I do."

"You can't—"

"I can."

"But—"

"I know I'm right about this."

"Stop it," shouted Maxi. "Stop reading my mind."

"I'm not," he told her, smiling. "At least not the way you think. I've gotten to know you so well that I understand how worried you are for me. That's very sweet, but it's not necessary."

"Since when? If I remember correctly, only a few days ago you were plenty worried about a measly little kiss or two."

He decided to let the "measly" remark go for the moment. "I told you, I was mistaken. It was stupid of me to think that making love to you could ever be considered wrong. Loving you will be the rightest thing I've ever done."

"How can you be so sure?"

"Because I've made up my mind."

"Oh, that's a terrific reason. And here I was worrying." Maxi threw up her hands in raw frustration. "This is insane. Why am I arguing? I feel as if I'm back on the high school debating team, assigned to defend the side I don't believe in."

"Good. You can stop defending—" he rubbed his knuckles across her bottom lip "—and start surrendering."

Catching his hand, she pressed it tightly against her cheek, her gaze locked with his. "Don't joke about this. I'm scared for you, Jay," she whispered.

"Don't be. I know what I'm doing."

"Do you mean this is one of those things you just somehow know is right?"

"No, it's not like that at all," he admitted, watching her hopeful expression dim. "This comes from inside me. I finally realized that it was my decision to make, and I made it. I decided that it's worth . . . that *you're* worth any risk I might be taking. I'm willing to live and die with my decision and to stand before anyone, anywhere, anytime and defend my need to make love to you. This feeling can't be wrong."

He smiled and ran his fingers through her hair, over and over, letting it sift free, only to catch it again. Maxi nibbled her lip as she watched him, her green eyes clouded.

"You're still worried about my salvation," he observed with a wry smile. "Don't you see? Maxi, sweetheart, you are my salvation. I never had time, never *made* time in my life for loving anyone. Please, let me make time now."

"Oh, Jay."

She attempted to rise from the seat, reaching for him, willing to let his words work magic, free her from unwanted doubts and questions. Now it was he who held her in place with a firm hand on her shoulder.

"There's only one thing that could make me turn and walk out of this room," he told her. "And that's you."

Dropping to a crouch at her feet, he locked his hands behind her neck, using his thumbs to stroke her cheeks. His smile faded. "Maxi, one thing hasn't changed. I still can't promise you forever... unless you have a very modest definition of the term. I wish—"

He stopped himself short on the verge of saying that he wished he had met her years ago, while there was still time, that he wished he had a future for no other reason than to spend it with her. It was all true, but it wasn't fair to say it now. If she came to him, he wanted it to be with her eyes open to the reality of their situation.

"The fact is, I can't promise you much of anything," he said quietly.

"Shhh." She pressed her fingertips to his lips. "I don't care. You see, I've made my decision, too. Days ago, actually. I made up my mind that if I ever had the chance to—"

She broke off in sudden embarrassment, the soft skin of her cheeks heating beneath his touch, reminding him of how vulnerable she was. He needed to be sure. He needed for her to be sure.

"You understand that in all likelihood this will only be for two weeks? If that," he forced himself to add.

"I don't care if it's for only two days... or two hours."

"That will be enough?"

"The way I feel right now, two lifetimes wouldn't be long enough. But you're enough. I'll take whatever I can get."

"That's the most totally illogical explanation I've ever heard," he told her with great satisfaction.

"It so happens I don't believe in logic. Instead I firmly believe that there are times when you have to take a chance. When you have to just close your eyes and jump, and hope you get lucky."

"In that case," he whispered, "close your eyes."

Eager and obedient, Maxi closed her eyes. She sensed him getting to his feet, felt him swiveling the stool beneath her. With a gentle touch he tipped her chin up. She waited for his kiss and was startled to feel instead the pull of the brush through her hair. When she opened her eyes she was facing the mirror and Jay was standing behind her, grinning at her disgruntled expression.

"I thought . . ." she began.

"Patience," he chided. "Patience."

"I have been patient."

"And now I'm going to reward you." He lifted her hair and ran the brush underneath. "Slowly. Very, very slowly."

She leaned back, pressing her head and shoulders against his midsection. "This isn't a reward, it's torture."

"Yes, but who's torturing whom?" With a yearning groan he pushed her upright, so that he was touching her only with the brush. His gaze found hers in the mirror. "I've been remembering some things from my past."

The revelation, made in a lazy, inconsequential tone, as if he were commenting on the weather, caught Maxi by surprise. "You mean you've remembered who you are? Where—"

"No," he interrupted. "Nothing that specific. Mostly it's little stuff from long ago, when I was growing up. It's as if my mind is this murky black pool and every once in a while something breaks loose and floats to the surface."

"Tell me about it."

Maxi watched closely his reflection in the mirror, wondering at the way his jaw tightened and his blue eyes grew shadowed for a few seconds. She was famished for information about him. She wanted to know everything, but instead of satisfying her curiosity, he flashed an elusive smile and lifted the hair off her neck. Bending to her with a courtier's grace, he placed a quick kiss on the sensitive spot beneath.

"Sometime I will," he said, his tone light yet final. "Just now I was remembering something I once read. For a while when I was about eight or nine, I was fascinated with Indians. I read about this one tribe in which a warrior's honor was measured by the care he took of his woman. One way he did that was by doing exactly what I'm doing now, so you could tell how much a woman was cherished by looking at her hair."

As he spoke he drew the brush through Maxi's hair in long, soothing strokes. The brush he was using was an antique one she kept around mostly because she fancied it added a touch of elegance to the room. It had a long, engraved silver handle and very soft, very dense bristles. The brush she usually used was much firmer to the touch, so the sensation she felt now was unfamiliarly light and teasing.

"Of course as a kid I found the notion of a warrior brushing a woman's hair pretty funny," he continued.

"And now?"

He gazed at her from beneath the black shadow of his half-lowered lashes and smiled in a way that sent desire shooting through her. "Now I think those warriors were on to something damn clever. That's what I want to do for you, Maxi, what I've never before done for any woman, cherish you. Will you let me?"

"Oh, yes, please."

"Then relax." The command had a silky, hypnotic quality. "Close your eyes."

She did. He brushed slowly, lifting her hair in a way that made her scalp tingle. Gradually the air around her filled with the fragrance of her shampoo; it crackled with static electricity, heightening her awareness of each touch, fueling her anticipation. Maxi hadn't known it was possible to shiver and sweat at the same time.

When he lowered the brush and slid the bristles along the side of her throat, Maxi gave a little start. The caress was unexpected but gentle, both rough and soft, and incredibly arousing. She opened her eyes to find him watching intently for her reaction. When she smiled with pleasure, he repeated the movement, this time bringing the brush around to trace the slant of her collarbone.

Maxi held her breath as the bristles brushed her skin, mesmerized by the sight of his strong dark fingers on the silver handle. He took his time, stroking the brush up and down in the V of her robe, making her skin tingle. A split second before the pleasure became abrasive, he slid the brush inside her robe to caress the upper swell of her breast. Her nipples tightened in response, jutting against the black silk. With his other hand Jay reached around to slide his palm over her breasts, the scant pressure enough to bring Maxi to the edge of her seat with excitement.

While she continued to watch, his hand dropped to the sash at her waist. Deftly he loosened the knot. Watching his unhurried movements, seeing his eyes darken and glitter with desire as strong as her own, was arousing Maxi to a point beyond what she had dreamed possible. Part of her wanted to throw herself into his arms and force the pace to a hasty completion. Another part wanted the slow, sweet yearning unfurling inside to go on forever. She might have yielded to impatience if not for her certainty that Jay would never allow himself to be rushed.

Trembling, she forced herself to sit still as he peeled back the robe and slipped it off her shoulders, letting it slither to the floor between them so she was left sitting there in only the briefest of lavender panties.

His whisper was as roughly caressing as the instrument he wielded. "Lady, you are more than worth all the waiting I've done."

She blushed in spite of herself, so that her face matched the skin of her shoulders and chest, which was already heated and rubbed to a delicate apricot shade.

"You're beautiful." He nearly groaned the words. "So beautiful I can hardly bear to wait."

Maxi reached up and grasped his arms. "Then don't. Don't wait. Don't make me wait."

"I'll make it worth your while." He trailed the brush lower, dancing it beneath her breasts, across her ribs. "I promise."

The soft bristles circled her stomach, causing her to sway on the stool. Jay moved in closer to support her with his thighs. He skated the brush along the top of her panties, teasing, tantalizing, then moved lower.

"Open your legs for me." It was part order, part request, wholly exciting.

Hesitantly, her breath a solid core of heat locked deep inside, Maxi drew her thighs apart.

"Wider," he urged softly, and as she complied he used the brush to drizzle a caress along the inside of one thigh, then the other, sliding up and down on her sensitive skin until she was trembling with need. Finally, when she knew she wouldn't be able to sit still another second, he pressed with a firm, circular motion against the lavender satin covering the damp, swollen petals of flesh that burned for his touch.

Maxi moaned softly, arching her neck in a sinuous, yearning movement, and as she did her gaze lifted and collided with his. The passion in his eyes pushed her over the edge.

"Jay, I—"

"Me, too," he said before she could say more.

He tossed the brush aside and, laughing, pulled her to her feet, holding her with one arm as he struggled out of his shorts and dragged her panties off.

Maxi was laughing with him, which was hard to do when she was already breathless. "Somehow," she said between pants, "somehow I expected that you would finish with as much finesse as you started."

"I would...if I weren't trembling. Seeing you this way...touching you...blows holes in my technique, sweetheart." At last they were both free of their clothes. Maxi stepped back to glance at him, as comfortable looking at his body as she was having him look at hers. He was golden in the morning sunlight, aroused and magnificent. She told him so, lovingly caressing his hair-roughened thighs and in-between, as he had her. With a harsh, impatient sound that revealed how hungry he was for her, Jay grabbed her hand.

"Not so fast," he muttered hoarsely.

"Oh, no," Maxi said, laughing softly. "Turnabout's fair play."

"I'll turn you about later," he shot back with a wicked half smile. "Promise. Now come here."

He hauled her against him for a desperately uncoordinated kiss, at the same time lifting her in his arms. For Maxi it seemed the most natural thing in the world to wrap her legs around his lean waist. He groaned and shifted his hips, and when she settled against him a second time, he drove deep inside her.

Maxi gasped and dropped her head to his shoulder, eyes closed, mouth open to the hot, salty taste of his skin. At his husky command she held on tight as he backed up a few feet and found a piece of wall to lean against. With his back safely braced he began to move with hard, strong thrusts that were like fire inside her, burning higher and hotter.

She clung to his shoulders so she could move, too, wildly, fiercely, desperate for the long overdue explosion now within reach. She was out of breath, climbing, tumbling, following his lead and drawing him on, all at the same time. When she finally climaxed, it was with an unprecedented fury that rocked her entire body. She collapsed against Jay's chest with a muffled cry of satisfaction, followed instantly by his deeper, rougher, exclamation.

She couldn't even lift her head and marveled at his resources of strength and coordination as he walked across the room with her still locked in his arms and gently lowered her onto her brass bed. He lay on his side next to her. Stretching like a well-fed cat in the sunlight that streamed through the window above their heads, drenching the unmade bed with warmth. Maxi slid closer to him, pressing her sweat-slick body to his.

"Mmm," Jay murmured, kissing the top of her head and rubbing her back down low. How did he know she liked that?

Maxi responded to his contented murmur with the only words on her mind. "I love you, Jay."

The rubbing stopped as suddenly as if she'd dropped a ton of bricks on his arm.

She waited.

Jay felt as if he'd just been blindsided by the second in a combination of body blows. The first had been the onslaught of his own explosive, uncontrollable passion. He had intended to make love to Maxi for the first time with slow, meticulous attention to detail. He definitely had not intended to do it standing up, pumping into her as if satisfying his own reckless, insatiable desire were all he could think of. Not that Maxi seemed to mind. She'd been voluptuous in her response, erotic, as unrestrained as a hurricane breaking around him. She was a woman of incredible passion. Hell, she was incredible, period. And now this sweet, totally inappropriate declaration.

After a moment of silence, which Maxi found very revealing and quite endearing, Jay cleared his throat and tipped his head back to peer down at her. "Don't say that."

She met his concerned look with one of straightforward confidence. "Why not? It's true."

"I thought..." He drew a desperate-sounding breath and ran his fingers through his hair. "I thought you understood how things were."

"I do. I understand completely."

"Then you must understand why you can't say..." He paused.

"The *L* word," she supplied, smirking, totally unruffled and not exactly surprised by his reaction. She'd known it was his hormones talking earlier. Too bad the rest of him wasn't as clear-sighted as they were.

"Yes."

"Why not? Not saying it won't make it any less true."

"Maybe not, but it will make things a whole lot less painful in the end. Maxi, I tried to tell you before that there were limits—"

"You also told me there was nothing wrong with how we felt," she interrupted to remind him.

"And there's not."

"Well, that's how I feel. I love you."

"That's not exactly what I was talking about. I meant there isn't anything wrong with our wanting each other, or with giving each other pleasure while we can. But, damn it..."

"Darn it," she corrected with amusement.

"Damn it," he repeated more loudly, "you have to keep what's happening in perspective. Enjoy what we have together, but save the rest for someone who can return it. There is a limit to what I can give you."

"Did you hear me asking for anything?"

A small smile broke through his bleak expression. "Not in so many words."

"Then relax."

"Like hell. I know you, Maxi, and I know that if I encourage you to talk that way, think that way... it's only going to make it harder on you in the end."

For a moment the words "in the end" hung over them like a blanket of ice.

"Nothing's going to make this easy, Jay," she pointed out at last. "So you handle it your way, and let me handle it mine." Lifting her chin, she confronted him with a look he suspected she intended to be defiant. It came across as poignantly naive. "I love you."

I love you, too, his heart screamed.

"Suit yourself," he said.

Maybe he couldn't stop her from saying it, but he could stop himself. And he would. It seemed ridiculous to lie there with her naked in his arms, his body stirring once again in response to the gentle, persistent play of her fingers, and think of ways to keep some distance between them, but that's exactly what he had to do. He knew that each emotional bond he allowed to form between them now would be like a choke chain on Maxi's heart after he was gone.

Regardless of his warnings and her self-assured claims, Maxi was too emotional, too impulsive, too much of a starry-eyed optimist to keep matters in perspective. If anyone was going to keep a rein on this situation it would have to be him. Making love to her had created new complications and challenges in a situation that was already plenty challenging. Yet, as she rolled him onto his back and straddled him with total, utterly welcome impudence and a very purposeful smile, Jay didn't—couldn't—believe that this had been a mistake.

It was late afternoon when they finally made it to the nursing home to deliver the lemon-meringue pie. Maxi's qualms that Bessie might not consider the sickly creation a good-faith attempt to fulfill Maxi's part of their bargain proved needless. Bessie appeared as amazed as Jay had been that Maxi had taken time to honor her promise.

The elderly woman beamed, not uttering a word about how the topping was brown on one side and white on the other, or how it hung like gooey Spanish moss over the crust. Without the cream of tartar it had not stiffened into little peaks the way the recipe said it should.

When at one point Maxi had been driven to hurl the beaters in frustration, Jay wrapped his arms around her and told her not to be so tough on herself.

"You know," he had whispered, nuzzling her throat and letting his raspy drawl caress her ear, "you might not have much luck with pies, but you make me very, very stiff."

Maxi maintained her grip on the mixer. Would Julia Child let herself be so easily distracted? "Thanks for the compliment. Unfortunately I can't arrange you in little peaks on top of Bessie's pie."

"Peaks?" he echoed, trailing his tongue down the back of her neck. "If it's peaks you want, all you have to do is ask. Come here."

His embrace was overpowering, his tongue persistent, utterly irresistible, and she was no Julia Child. Thank goodness. She doubted any world-famous chef had ever embarked on such a stimulating and creative adventure with a bowl of meringue. Of course the pie's completion had been further delayed while they showered afterward and started from scratch on a replacement batch to use on the pie.

Obviously the distractions and delays hadn't mattered, she decided, extracting herself from the steamy warmth of her memory. Judging from Bessie's smile and wetly gleaming eyes as she pressed a dry kiss of appreciation on Maxi's cheek, it might have been the most perfect pie ever baked. Her duty done, Maxi felt buoyant and free, very much in the mood for celebrating.

Jay and Maxi ate dinner at Maxi's favorite Chinese restaurant, a Formica-topped-table, plastic-covered-menu sort of place on Providence's Smith Hill, where the spicy food more than compensated for the rather rough location. Seated in a dimly lit corner booth, they shared several dishes, feeding each other in a way Maxi ordinarily would have found too cute for words. Suddenly she was reveling in all those stereotypical romantic things she never thought she would be caught dead doing.

When they left the restaurant, they walked with their arms laced around each other's waists, their steps rambling and unhurried. They were still a block from where they'd parked her car when, with a small squeeze, Jay removed his arm and bent to grab the handle of a parked car they were passing. Not just any parked car, a shiny, low-slung, black Jaguar.

Instantly the high pitched scream of an alarm emanated from the area of the car's deadly looking hood ornament, quickly followed by a crash as the door of a nearby bar was slammed open, and then a loud shout.

"Yo, sucker."

It was a common form of greeting in many local neighborhoods and could mean any of several things.

"What's your hand doing on my wheels?" demanded the very tall, broad-shouldered man approaching them at a fast clip. Actually it was more like a fast launch. A rowdy crowd of observers gathered in the open door of the bar, beer bottles in hand.

The most striking features of the man doing the asking were his greased back black hair and pointy-toed white cowboy boots. Maxi couldn't be absolutely certain of what such an individual did to be able to afford a seventy-thousand-dollar automobile, but judging from where he hung out, it most likely involved frequent trips south of the border, a very accurate small scale and violence of the messy variety. Goose bumps chased up and down her spine.

"I asked you a question, man."

Unbelievably, as if he didn't see or hear the hulk materializing right before their eyes, Jay turned to her with a look of excitement. "Maxi, this is my car."

"What are you talking about, man?" exclaimed the car's owner, giving Jay a shove that made Maxi's stomach turn.

Jay recovered from the contact with a gracefully athletic spin, ending up facing the other man with nowhere near the apologetic air Maxi thought the situation merited. "Do you have a problem?"

"Yeah, I got a problem," the other man retorted, grinning in what Maxi considered a very menacing way as he eyed Jay up and down. "I got a problem with you touching my machine."

Jay glanced sideways at the car, as if hearing the alarm for the first time. "I'm sorry. I own one just like it, and I didn't stop to think..."

"I guess you didn't." The man put his hands on his hips, intentionally dislodging his jacket enough for them to glimpse the knife pocketed inside. "Maybe I ought to bang some sense into you so's next time you do stop and think."

Not a muscle in Jay's entire body moved or tightened. The threat he radiated came totally from his eyes.

"You're welcome to try," he said quietly, his gaze on his adversary as steady and sharp as a diamond cutter's chisel.

The silence alone made Maxi queasy. At last the other man lifted a shoulder in a disgusted shrug.

"What the hell," he muttered, "you ain't worth getting my shirt messed up." He circled to the driver's side of the car and used his key to silence the alarm, watching Jay the whole time.

"I'm sorry about the inconvenience," Jay told him as Maxi, eager to get away, grabbed Jay's arm and yanked hard.

"Not as sorry as you're gonna be if you ever mess with my machine again," the man warned.

"He won't," Maxi assured him when it became clear that Jay felt compelled to respond with granite-jawed silence. "It was all a mistake."

She heard the man grunt as they moved away. They continued walking, Maxi attempting to jar Jay from his determinedly lazy pace as her heart slowly slipped back into place so she could breathe.

"It wasn't a mistake," Jay said matter-of-factly.

"No?" She shook her head with the sort of fury only panic can brew. "What do you consider a mistake? Touching the car of a man who packs a Magnum instead of a knife?"

"I mean, what I said about the car wasn't a mistake, I owned a car like that. I know I did...do." The excitement quickly crept back in his voice. "Don't you see? It's the first concrete recollection I've had of my life just before the accident, and it bears out what I thought that life was like, what I was like. Somehow knowing about the car makes me feel closer to myself. It's as if I've come up against this wall and I'm over there, waiting just on the other side."

And I'm here on this side, Maxi couldn't help thinking.

Suddenly Jay swung around and looked at her with understanding followed quickly by concern. His smile was tender, warning her not to dwell on things neither of them could change. Pushing thoughts of the future aside, Maxi reminded herself that was precisely what she had resolved to do.

Slinging his arms down low around her hips, Jay pulled her close. "Enough of that. What would you like to do now?" The quick, responsive gleam in her eyes made him chuckle. "Besides that."

"Besides that, hmm?" She pretended to give the question serious consideration. "Besides that, absolutely nothing."

"You have to come up with something, because I have *that* scheduled for later."

Maxi sighed. "You know, Slick, I went along with the appointment book and the financial log and the answering machine, but there is such a thing as having your life too rigidly organized."

"Maybe, but I don't think you need to lose any sleep worrying it will happen to you."

"Are you aware that you're seriously stifling my creativity? Not to mention what you're doing to good old spontaneity."

"You can be as spontaneous and creative as you like...later. You had a busy morning and an exhausting afternoon. I don't want to wear out your—" he hesitated, his gaze warm and indulgent "—smile." He dropped a light kiss on the smile he was so concerned about. "Besides, I said later because I have this intense desire to see you naked in the moonlight."

Maxi glanced at the sky overhead, noting sadly that it was still more blue than gray. "What time do you suppose the moon will come out?"

"I'd say we have plenty of time to drive to Misquamicut and do some scouting around for the shoot on Tuesday."

"Wednesday," she corrected absently. "Madame Bizane called and asked me to change the date because Wednesday will be the third day of the new moon and that's the luckiest day of the month. I cleared it with Robert's staff."

"Wait a minute. You're telling me you changed plans because of something about the moon?"

She regarded his incredulous frown quizzically. "Of course. It makes sense to shoot on the luckiest day of the month, doesn't it?"

His slow nod had something of the air of a man trying to humor a mad dog. "Yes, yes, I suppose that makes some sense. Maxi, are you sure you want to get involved with this Madame Bizane character? I mean, look at the problems Bessie caused, and she isn't nearly as...as quirky as Madame Bizane."

"Of course, I'm sure. Jay, Madame Bizane is an authentic fortune-teller. Her quirks made her what she is, namely, perfect for this spot on looking into the future. Robert Chandler could stand in front of a camera and talk all day about the need for a leader to be able to foresee future needs and problems, but Madame Bizane is an image that will stick in people's minds."

"I won't argue with that," he said with admirable restraint. He was determined not to spoil the evening by arguing with her about anything. Swinging open the car door, he said, "Hop in and we'll go find the perfect spot to tape your perfect fortune-teller."

"Just one question before we go," said Maxi, pausing as she was about to step into the car. "You're not by any chance having conscience pangs, are you? And maybe trying to distract me from my first choice of activity?"

"Never."

"Good," she countered, her smile as direct and unabashed as she was. "Because I think you ought to know there's moonlight on Misquamicut Beach, too."

## Chapter Ten

*H*onky-tonk best described the half-mile stretch of amusements and food stands along Misquamicut Beach, located about an hour's drive from Providence. A few miles east was the seaside resort Watch Hill, noted for its genteel population, the Olympia Tea Room and a famous antique carousel. But here the mood was one of pure, unadulterated fun.

The smell of cotton candy and fried food hung in the air and the sound of waves crashing on the beach was drowned out by the blend of rock music blaring from the roller-skating rink and blues sweeping from a smoke-filled pool room. From the miniature golf course came the sound of laughter and shouts ranging from triumphant to anguished.

Beginning on Labor Day most local concessions reduced the hours they were open to weekends only. Even now the separate town beach and the towering, twisting water slides closed at 5:00 p.m. Soon the nights would turn cool and everything here would grind to a ghost-townlike halt until spring. Tonight, however, like a shooting star that burns brightest just before blinking out, the entire noisy, overlit strip was operating at full throttle.

"Are you any good with a bat, Slick?" Maxi inquired as she and Jay approached the batting cages. Beyond the cages lay a procession of one-story, pastel-painted motels and beach houses built on stilts.

He smiled dryly. "Your guess is as good as mine."

"Dare you to find out."

"You're much too eager," he grimly observed as she handed the attendant the five dollars that bought them each three dozen swings at balls shot from a rapid-fire pitching machine sixty feet away. "Why do I have the feeling you had the highest batting average on your high school softball team?"

"You saw the trophy," she exclaimed with mock dismay. Swinging open the door of the chain-link cage, she motioned him inside. "Be my guest."

"Don't you mean victim?" he muttered, stepping into the cage.

He wasn't bad, Maxi noted, but he wasn't one of the stars of the Improv Softball League sponsored by clubs throughout the city of Providence. Maxi was. She connected with thirty-two of her thirty-six balls, trouncing him soundly. Jay watched with obvious enjoyment, applauding loudly when she finished, seemingly not at all shaken by being bested by a woman.

"Have you always been so unflappably self-assured?" Maxi wondered out loud as they crossed to the ocean side of the wide street and strolled along the boardwalk where there were more cafés and fast-food stands. At his shrug, she grimaced. "Right, another stupid question you aren't able to answer. Sorry."

"Don't be. Your questions are normal, it's my situation that's bizarre. I'm not sure if I've always been self-assured or if I just learned to be real good at pretending I am. But if you're referring to what happened back there at the batting cages, I don't think I ever had that kind of experience with a woman before tonight."

"I see. You usually pick women you can beat hands down, hmm?"

He shook his head. "No, it's just that I never...played with a woman before. I mean," he continued, amused by the disbelief expressed in her quickly arched brows, "I never played a real game with a woman, the way you and I just did. I have a feeling women were assigned a different, much more specific role in my life."

Maxi's teasing mood withered. "Oh," she said, both wanting and not wanting to know what sort of colorful memories led him to that conclusion. It was impossible to tell from his expression how he felt about a woman overstepping that specific role.

Searching for a subject with fewer hidden thorns, she glanced ahead and noticed a flashing neon sign. She tugged on his sleeve. "Look, fried dough...and I can see from here that it's even sprinkled with cinnamon sugar. Do you like it?"

"I don't know," replied Jay. "I never tried it."

"Then we can definitely rule out the possibility of your having grown up in Rhode Island. Fried dough isn't so much a local food as a custom, a tradition, time-honored and all that. If as a kid you'd ever been to an amusement park or circus or even the beach around here, you'd have definitely sampled fried dough."

Maxi had been rattling on, unaware of Jay's reaction to her words. Her first hint that Jay didn't feel like bantering was the cold, detached undercurrent in his voice.

"I don't think I ever did...go to a circus or to an amusement park, that is. Or to the beach."

He was looking straight ahead rather than at her, but Maxi knew his eyes wore that same shuttered expression they had the morning when she asked for details of his childhood. He released her hand to shove both of his into the pockets of his black jeans. Maxi lightly touched the sleeve of his shirt.

"Talk to me," she urged softly, and was startled by the vehemence of his response as he jerked from her touch.

"No."

He turned and walked away from her. Stopping by the low stone wall where the beach began, he stared out over the ocean, an endless, shifting shadow before them. Maxi stood silently beside him, willing to wait, willing to do whatever would help him, and having no idea what that might be.

"Your family might have been overbearing, but at least you had one," he said finally. "I never did."

"Jay, I know—"

"How can you?" he interrupted harshly. "How can you know about what I don't even know myself? My memories are like some sort of giant glass picture that's been shattered, and every once in a while I get lucky and two pieces come together so I can see a little bit of the image. That's it. That and this yearning inside me that feels as if it's been there forever. I don't even know what the hell I'm yearning for."

There was a rough catch in his voice, and Maxi, understanding why he had to pause for a moment, standing with his jaw thrust forward, lips pressed tightly together, said nothing to prod him.

"You want me to talk about what I've been remembering. Well, so far most of what I've come up with aren't the sort of memories that are fun to share."

"All right then," she said with sudden determination, "let's make memories that are fun to share. You said you'd never been to an amusement park or to the beach.... Well, you're here now," she pointed out, taking in the pandemonium around them with a sweep of her arm. "Let's...go on the Dodge'ems." It was an impulsive suggestion, made as she caught sight of the arena of small colliding cars up ahead.

"That was my absolute favorite ride when I was a kid," she revealed. "So let me share my childhood with you and in a way, because this is your first time at all this, it will be a little like having you share yours with me."

In spite of a trembling fear that he would think her ridiculous and again shrug away from her touch, she gave him a nudge with her elbow and flashed her most brilliant smile. "What do you say?"

For a few seconds he said nothing. Maxi watched anxiously as a deep breath lifted his broad shoulders and flexed the muscles in his throat.

Finally he turned, and when he looked at her she felt the tension drain away like sand running through an hourglass. "I say, What the hell kind of girl picks Dodge'ems as her favorite ride?"

Tossing her hair back from her face, Maxi said, "This kind. Any complaints?"

Jay let his gaze slide slowly over her with lazy attention to every curve and hollow. "Do I look like a stupid man?"

She winked.

He smiled.

And a moment of sweetness passed between them that Maxi knew she would carry pressed in her heart forever.

After countless rides on the Dodge'ems, they played miniature golf and roller-skated, briefly and under protest from Jay. They ate cotton candy and tossed rings to win a small, lopsided stuffed penguin, complete with top hat and cane, that Maxi promptly christened Slick the Second. Throughout, she laughed and teased and kept carefully hidden from the man by her side her sorrow over the little boy he had once been. A boy who had grown up without any of this and, she suspected, without a great many other, much more important things.

Maxi was determined to fix that. She couldn't erase the past, but she could fill whatever time they had with all the love and laughter Jay had been denied. She would be everything to him, everything he needed. She would be family, friend, lover. He'd hinted that his experiences with women had been primarily physical. She was going to teach him how all-encompassing the act of love can be.

The blind arrogance of her last thought made Maxi's lips curve in a self-effacing smile. It was, after all, a lesson Jay had taught her only that morning.

"You think my shooting is that funny?" inquired Jay, glancing at her before he resumed squinting through the sight of a mounted water pistol for his last shot at the cardboard duck target. He missed.

"No. Honest. Everyone knows these games are rigged. I think you're a regular Billy the Kid."

"No wonder you look so amused."

"That was not an amused smile," she insisted as they began walking. "It was a smile of...anticipation. I'd like to draw your attention to the moon." She pointed overhead. "And the beach." She indicated that, as well. "Now let's see how perceptive you are. Tell me what's missing from this picture of a moonlit beach. Time's up. The answer is, you and me."

Now Jay was amused. Laughter laced his voice as he asked, "Is that a hint?"

"An invitation. Of course, if you're not disposed to joining me for a walk along the beach...the moonlit beach," she added pointedly, "perhaps I can find some other, willing, virile, young..."

His gaze had followed her drifting one to the group of young men gathered at the steps leading down to the beach. They looked to be in their late teens or early twenties, dressed in uniforms of the ripped jeans and sleeveless denim-vest variety.

"Young being the operative word," he remarked.

"Several of them seem to find me fascinating. It must be the mysterious allure of a mature woman."

Jay's mouth quirked as he took in Maxi's typically exuberant appearance in a loose-fitting mint blazer over a hot-pink jumpsuit. With her peppery grin, tousled dark hair and a stuffed penguin clasped in her arms, she did not fit any known definition of a mature woman.

Desire for her was like a constantly smoldering fuse inside him; sometimes burning quietly, sometimes, like now, demanding his full and immediate attention. He glanced toward the dark beach, not obtuse to the guilty way one of the young guys by the steps shifted his gaze away from Maxi when he saw Jay watching him.

"I see what you mean about your allure," he muttered, feeling an irrational and inappropriate possessiveness. The young men's attention to Maxi unleashed in him a foreboding of the time when he wouldn't be around to watch over her. Taking her arm, he led her toward the wide steps, smiling to conceal the turmoil inside.

"No need to tax yourself looking for a replacement," he assured her. "I'm plenty disposed to the combination of moonlight, soft sand and soft skin."

With a husky laugh of anticipation, Maxi let him lead her past the group of youths to the beach. She slipped off her shoes at the bottom of the steps and curled her toes into the still-warm sand. They had reached the end of the boardwalk, and as they walked they quickly left the glare of lights behind. The beach ahead was a wide, inviting ribbon of silver winding through the dunes.

It was a few moments before a sound from behind alerted Maxi to the fact that someone was following them closely. Jay seemed to sense it at the same instant she did. He started to turn, but before either of them could say or do anything, someone grabbed Maxi from behind. At the same time Jay was shoved away from her with a blow so forceful Maxi could hear it above the sound of her frightened scream.

She felt rough hands on her chest, then a quick, sharp pain at the back of her neck. She was getting ready to scream again when she was dropped facedown in the sand. By the time she lifted her head and struggled to her knees, Jay was crouched beside her. His gaze volleyed between her and the two lanky shadows rapidly disappearing into the darkness.

"Two of your admirers from the boardwalk," he said with tangible contempt. He brushed her hair from her face. "They didn't hurt you, did they?"

"No, not really," she said, her hand trembling as she instinctively reached for the talisman at her neck. Her fingers clutched at the front of her jumpsuit. "My pendant," she cried. "It's gone."

"That must be what they were after. Wait here," Jay called over his shoulder as he took off after them.

It took every ounce of Maxi's willpower to do as he said. She fought the urge to follow him or to run to the phone booth on the boardwalk to call the police. At least she would be able to give them a detailed description of their assailants. So much for her allure. No doubt it was her pendant they'd been eyeing all along. They'd trailed her and Jay down to the beach, intending to grab it. It was a common enough incidence in the city, but somehow Maxi hadn't expected it to happen here.

She got to her feet and wrapped her arms around herself against the night, which seemed to have turned suddenly cold. The dark silence allowed her active imagination full rein. What if the others in the gang came and found her here alone? What if Jay caught up to the two guys who had stolen her pendant and was hurt trying to force them to return it? Was it possible for him to be hurt, she wondered, when he was already—

She broke the thought, feeling panic seeping in from several directions. Maybe she ought to go for help after all. Checking her watch, she decided to give Jay five more minutes. He returned in two.

"I'm sorry," he said, panting heavily from the chase. "They had too much of a head start. I couldn't catch them." Wrapping her tightly in his arms, he pressed her head to his chest. "I'm sorry about your pendant, Maxi."

With Jay safe beside her, the realization of what she had lost began to settle in. "I can't believe it's really gone. Why couldn't they have grabbed my handbag like normal muggers?"

"You're lucky they didn't. You would have lost your keys, all your identification, charge cards and—"

"Yes, but all that can be replaced," she interrupted impatiently.

"So can your pendant," Jay crooned in what he thought was a soothing manner. Maxi startled him by breaking from his embrace.

"No. It cannot be replaced."

"Maxi, it was only a necklace, just some gold and crystals."

"Just some gold and crystals?" she countered, clearly not at all soothed. "For your information, that necklace was made of three, not crystals, but gemstones. And it was a one-of-a-kind design created especially for me by a friend."

"Then your friend can create you another one. A two-of-a-kind design is still pretty special." His attempt at levity was a washout.

Maxi shook her head in disgust. "You don't get it, do you? *That* necklace was special. That specific one. It had incredible positive energy.

"No, sweetheart. You have incredible positive energy. The necklace was simply an inanimate object."

"It brought me peace of mind. And luck."

"You just imagined that it did."

"Did I just imagine the fact that aquamarines impart serenity? And that amethyst connects you to your higher self? That pink quartz . . . oh, why am I even bothering trying to explain? It's gone." She shuddered as she added, "I don't even want to think what's going to happen now."

"Nothing is going to happen. At least nothing that wouldn't happen anyway."

Maxi made a disparaging little huff and gazed out at the black sea as if it made more sense than he did.

Grasping her arms, Jay forcibly turned her to face him, his mood of benevolent understanding unraveling a little around the edges. "Maxi, the necklace was beautiful, and your carrying on about crystals and their power and energy is endearing and cute, but . . ."

"Cute?" Her eyes burned in the darkness.

"Yes. Cute. But deep down you have to know as well as I do that rocks do not have any real power over our lives."

She sucked in her breath and let it out slowly.

"Of course, you're right," she murmured agreeably. Too agreeably. "Deep down in some dark little corner of my soul I know that." Her eyes narrowed and her smile sliced over him like a straight-edge razor as she continued in an impassioned torrent. "But every single fiber of the rest of me is sure that unless I get my pendant back nothing is ever going to be the same again."

## Chapter Eleven

They filed a police report of the theft but weren't offered much hope. Over the next few days Jay steadfastly attempted to convince Maxi that her fears were groundless, that the stolen pendant had not brought her good luck and therefore losing it did not in any way doom her to an endless streak of bad luck. It was a hopeless task. What was worse, by Tuesday he found that he was spending almost as much time trying to convince himself.

*A totally unrelated occurrence,* he insisted when they returned home from the disastrous trip to Misquamicut Beach and Maxi snapped her key in half trying to unlock the apartment door. When the cleaners ruined her favorite silk blouse he called it a *coincidence*. His tripping over her red boots was *inevitable*. The night one of her treasured ceramic houses toppled to the floor and shattered, seemingly without explanation, he had hurriedly invented an explanation involving *seismic tremors and inner earth currents*.

Maxi hadn't bought a word of it. She had simply responded the same way she did every time something else went wrong, directing him a long, silent look of pity. By the time the hotwater heater in the basement conked out, condemning them to forty-eight hours of cold showers, Jay found himself looking at the crystals lying around her apartment with new respect.

He didn't admit that to Maxi, of course. Instead he attempted to distract her by insisting it would be fun to heat water on the stove and share the bathtub. It *was* fun. It just didn't wash away his growing suspicion that he'd been as wrong to discount the importance of her missing pendant as he had been about a lot of other things.

He had arrived in Maxi's life with his memory a virtual clean slate, but gradually bits and pieces of the man he was made themselves known, some trivial, some very strong. More fervent than all the rest turned out to be his conviction that love was a misunderstood, basically nonexistent commodity. For him, staying unattached had been a form of self-defense, and he'd refined it to the level of an art form. He's been convinced that while deep down everyone operated under the same rules of self-preservation, some preferred to hide behind the illusion of love. He'd had it all figured out long ago. And he'd been wrong. Maxi was all the proof he needed that love was very, very real.

The possibility that he was just as wrong about Maxi's crystals haunted him. He still wasn't convinced that the stones themselves had the power to zap water heaters or create catastrophes, but he had an all-new respect for the power of the human spirit. Maybe it was a case of mind over matter, maybe it was something more. He was hardly in a position to expound on the mysteries of the universe. All he knew was that Maxi believed the pendant brought her luck and ensured her peace of mind, and so it had. Her faith provided the stones with a power that was real, and faith that strong was not to be snickered at.

Jay would have told her of his change of heart if he didn't think such an admission would fuel her fear that some major disaster lurked just ahead, poised and waiting to wreak havoc with the taping set for Wednesday. No matter how many petty problems and inconveniences arose, he was determined that Maxi's project was going to be a resounding success. Once that was assured, he would tackle the next step, convincing her to put her faith where it belonged, in herself.

The only area of their lives that remained completely trouble free was their lovemaking. No small matter, since making love to Maxi devoured a great many of his waking hours, as well as a few memorable ones when they both drifted in that languorous, heightened state of sensuality between sleep and wakefulness. He loved floating up through thinning layers of sleep to the sweet, moist invitation of Maxi's lips moving over his chest and stomach.

Ned had offered them the use of his studio facilities for editing their tapes, so they spent long mornings there, mixing and remixing and arguing over almost every frame until the first two spots were polished to their mutual satisfaction. The afternoons and evenings were theirs alone, and they were perfection.

On the way home from Ned's they would shop for groceries, choosing simple things that could be easily prepared on their occasional, brief jaunts from the bedroom. They watched movies and listened to music and played checkers. They made love and made plans for the upcoming shoot and carefully avoided any mention of the future.

On Tuesday night Maxi lay curled against Jay's shoulder. Through the open window above the bed came a steady drift of sweet-scented night air, and between the branches of the old maple tree outside they could see the glitter of stars. Jay pointed out constellations to her without knowing how the names came to him so easily.

At one point he felt the sudden, subtle tensing of her muscles as she lay pressed against him and knew her thoughts had inexplicably jumped ahead to the following day. He stroked her hair and quietly reminded her of each detail they had checked and double-checked, each contingency prepared for, each solution they had carefully planned for any problem that could possibly arise. He spoke to her in the gentlest tone he possessed, holding her until she fell asleep in his arms.

In all his talk of cameras and thunderstorms and uncooperative extras, however, he never said a word about her ancient Volvo. The next day, halfway between Providence and Misquamicut, it overheated. Leaving Maxi behind, cursing and kicking tires, Jay hiked to the nearest phone booth and persuaded the auto club to send a tow truck in record time. As soon as he had the car at the service station, the mechanic diagnosed the problem as a faulty thermostat. It was quickly replaced, rendering the Volvo good as new, so that the only thing remaining at the boiling point was Maxi's temper.

"I knew it. I knew it," she repeated under her breath for most of the remainder of the drive, rolling her eyes at Jay's intermittent pronouncements to the effect that things could only get better.

They arrived at the Misquamicut Beach parking lot, the agreed upon rendezvous point, exactly one hour and twenty-seven minutes late. Mickey's van was already there, parked alongside the black Cadillac she recognized as the one Robert Chandler used, but there was no sign of either Ned or Robert or Madame Bizane.

"Relax," Jay urged as Maxi bolted from the car before it rolled to a full stop. "Mickey probably herded them all up to the boardwalk so we'd be all set to go."

"You're right," Maxi agreed, saying a silent prayer of thanks for Mickey.

They hurried toward the wide concrete ramp that led to the beach pavilion, providing easy access to the portion of the boardwalk where they planned to shoot. Before they reached it, a steel-gray BMW coasted to a halt beside them.

Grinning at them, Peter Duvall reached for the button to lower the power window. Maxi braced herself for the worst.

"I have to hand it to you, Maxi," he said by way of greeting, "you really did it up right this time."

The remark seemed to lack the usual heavy note of sarcasm. However, that didn't convince Maxi it wasn't the lead-in for a jab about her being late. Again. Pride stiffened her back. She opened her mouth to retort, but Jay's firm touch at her elbow counseled her to silence.

"Yes, sir," Peter continued, nodding with admiration that appeared genuine, if begrudging. "I was dead certain that putting you in charge of these spots was a mistake. I had you pegged as strictly small potatoes, but when the chips are down you really know how to call in the big guns. Of course, the proof is still in the pudding. I'm looking forward to seeing those final cuts on Friday."

"Friday?" Maxi countered. "They don't have to be ready until Monday."

"Uh-uh, there was a last-minute schedule change . . . sort of like the one you made in switching this shoot from Monday to today. Robert wants to preview the new spots at the rally on Friday night. Didn't you get my memo?"

"No, I didn't get any memo."

"How about that?" His mouth twisted in mock dismay. "I'll have to have a talk with that secretary of mine. You know what they say about finding good help these days." Reaching for the window button, he flashed them another grin. "Wish I could stick around for the fun, but I have things to do. See you Friday."

"Do you believe that?" Maxi asked, sidestepping the gravel his tires sent flying.

Jay, experiencing a potent, barely controllable loathing for Duvall, for no better reason than that the man took pleasure in harassing Maxi, worked to keep his feelings hidden behind an idle smile. "No, I don't. Seven clichés in less than two minutes. That must be some sort of record."

"I was talking about how he switched the deadline to Friday. That only gives us two days to work on this last spot."

"That's more than enough time."

"It's barely enough time, provided everything goes smoothly. If. . ."

"Everything *is* going to go smoothly," Jay said in the quiet, steady tone that had become a lifeline for Maxi during the past few days. Sometimes when he said it, she even believed it.

As they hurried up the ramp, the exchange with Peter replayed in her head.

"What do you suppose he meant by saying I knew how to call in the big guns?" she asked Jay.

He dismissed the matter with a preoccupied shrug. The answer to her question was apparent, however, as soon as they stepped through the cool, dimly lit pavilion into the sunlight brightly reflected from the silver-white sand of the beach below. Black wires and cables crisscrossed the weathered wooden planks of the boardwalk, lifelines to the big, fancy, powerful camera equipment that had been set up everywhere. Bigger, fancier, more powerful equipment than anything Maxi had arranged for or required or could afford.

Her confused gaze canvassed the area. She recognized several local television-news reporters and a writer from the *Providence Journal* among the large gathering of professionals and spectators. A white van with Newswatch 10 emblazoned on the side had been driven directly onto the boardwalk and parked in the spot where she intended to seat Madame Bizane. Robert was standing beside the van, being interviewed, obviously overjoyed by all the publicity. No wonder Peter had been grinning. He assumed she was responsible for bringing the limelight to shine so brightly on his candidate.

She wasn't. Not only had she been hoping to generate surprise and interest when her spots began to air—surprise and interest that would be significantly reduced if bits and pieces of them were revealed ahead of time on every local newscast—she had Madame Bizane's feelings to consider.

"No side show," had been the fortune teller's only warning to Maxi when she agreed to appear before the camera.

If the presence of hot-dog vendors and a man hawking balloons didn't qualify this as a side show, Maxi didn't know what would.

"This is ridiculous," she said to Jay and Mickey, who had hurried over as soon as he caught sight of them.

"This?" Mickey scoffed, waved his hand in the air. "This is nothing. You missed Channel Seven's traffic copter—you know...'Rhode Island's Eye in the Sky'—doing death-defying dives to get close-ups, and the live broadcast of the *Peaches and Waylon Show*."

"Oh, no."

"Peaches and Waylon?" Jay inquired cautiously.

"It's a local early-morning radio show, geared to the more adventuresome commuter," Maxi explained. "It features lots of insulting bantering, off-color jokes and weird news stories." She groaned at the realization that her work had been consigned to that latter category.

"I can see it now," she said with a mixture of despair and mounting irritation. "They'll blow this whole thing out of proportion. Madame Bizane was supposed to be simply a visual image in the background to reinforce Robert's stand on job-training programs and day-care. Instead it looks like I'm orchestrating a circus. And I'm going to look like an idiot. Which at least explains why Peter was so happy."

"Not at all," Mickey told her. "Duvall was real happy about all the publicity."

"Was he also real happy about Madame Bizane?" she asked with disgust. "And the fact that it's going to come off sounding like a campaign based on black magic and superstition?"

"No," Mickey replied, grinning and shaking his head. "The fact is nobody except me has even seen Madame Bizane. She took off into the ladies' room yelling 'I am not a side-show freak' as soon as she caught on to what was happening. She's been there ever since.''

Maxi frowned. ''Then if no one knows about her, why all the hoopla over taping a run-of-the-mill political spot?''

''The thanks go to your brother Dave,'' Mickey explained.

''Dave!'' she exclaimed in disbelief that lasted no longer than a heartbeat. When was she going to learn that where her family was concerned, you volunteered nothing and told them even less?

''Right, Dave,'' said Mickey. ''At least he said he was your brother. He was already here when I arrived. Said he'd like to hang around and see for himself the surprised look on your face, but since you were late as usu—well, since you were late...''

''Yes, I can imagine what Dave had to say about that.''

Mickey shrugged. ''Anyway, the story is that these guys over here—'' he pointed to several men leaning on the wall beside their impressive-looking cameras ''—are cameramen from someplace in Massachusetts. Your brother hired them to give us a hand. As for the rest, from what I gather he called in a few favors to arrange for news coverage, and from there it sort of snowballed, with one reporter following another's trail to the hot story of the day.''

''Right,'' Maxi muttered, blocking off an imaginary headline in the air. ''Freelance Art Director Ends Own Career and Sabotages Campaign. What am I going to do?''

Jay dropped his arm around her shoulders and hugged her. ''I wouldn't consider opening a bakery if I were you. How about a massage parlor?''

''Stop. This is no time for jokes.''

''It's certainly no time for giving up and whining,'' he shot back. ''This is nothing we can't fix.''

''Really? I know you can make yourself disappear, Slick, but do you have the same power over entire crowds?''

''What?'' interjected a bewildered Mickey.

"Forget it," Jay told him, sending Maxi a warning look. "And, yes, together we can make this crowd disappear. But only after using them to our advantage. Duvall assumes that Maxi is responsible for the avalanche of news coverage, right?"

"At first he assumed it," Mickey explained with a hesitant look her way. "He was so impressed, Maxi, talking as if you were borderline genius for pulling it off, that I sort of…confirmed the fact that you arranged it. I figured you'd taken enough of his aggravation, so you deserved a little credit."

"Credit now, blame later." Maxi sighed and managed a smile for Mickey. "But thanks for trying."

"I think he did exactly the right thing." Jay's declaration surprised both of them. "We owe Dave our thanks, as well."

"For being a pain in the butt?" suggested Maxi.

Jay grinned. "For being himself. He actually did us a favor we never would have thought of doing for ourselves. He got rid of Duvall the watchdog."

"I might thank him," Maxi allowed, "if I could figure out what you're talking about."

"In typical big-brother fashion, Dave assumed you needed high-priced help, so he arranged for it, right?" Jay hitched his head in the direction of the cameraman who seemed content to collect union wages for standing around smoking cigarettes and drinking Diet Coke.

Maxi gave an unconvinced nod. "So?"

"So they served a purpose by impressing Duvall and getting him off our backs for a while. He obviously took off with an easy mind, thinking he had left his boy in good hands. By the time he hears that we sent the big guns packing the minute he left, he'll have missed his chance to stand around looking over our shoulders."

"What about the reporters?" Maxi asked, afraid to believe that what seemed an inevitable disaster could be defused as smoothly and logically as Jay's self-assured tone implied. She stopped herself short in the act of reaching for her missing pendant, a habit she wondered if she would ever break.

"The reporters we handle a little differently. We can't order then to get lost without arousing their suspicion that there really is a story here. So, we do nothing . . . at least nothing too interesting. Once we get rid of this mess," he went on, indicating the cameras and lights surrounding them, "we begin shooting. . . ."

"But I promised Madame Bizane—"

"We begin shooting with Robert," Jay continued, "and work around anything unusual. As soon as they get enough footage for a filler on the six o'clock news, the reporters will move on to other stories. Without them, the crowd of gawkers will thin a little, as well." He saw Maxi begin to smile as the pieces fell into place, and he smiled, too. "Then we go to work."

Mickey released a loud hoot of laughter. "It's perfect."

"Perfect," Maxi concurred.

Jay held her gaze and lightly, briefly, touched the front of her yellow cotton sweater at precisely the spot where her pendant ought to be. "And all without outside assistance."

"Don't be so sure. We haven't pulled it off yet," she reminded him.

His smile held both arrogance and tenderness. "We will," he promised.

They did.

After being cajoled out of her initial bad temper, Madame Bizane agreed that Maxi was not to blame for the situation and even came to regard it as something of an adventure. She was magnificent in her small, background role, properly dark and mysterious. At the last minute she warned Maxi once again that there were to be no cheap shots at her profession.

"I have my clients to consider," she insisted. "I cannot be made to seem a buffoon or they will never again trust Madame Bizane."

Maxi assured her that buffoonery, in any shape or form, was not in either of their best interests. Madame Bizane's aversion to side-show tactics did not, however, prevent her from telling fortunes for twenty dollars a shot after they had finished for the day. According to her crystal ball, Robert would, indeed, become governor; Mickey, the top dog cameraman with an incredibly successful business; and Linda, who had once again been hired to handle hair and makeup, a radiant spring bride. Only Maxi and Jay resisted the urge to find out what the future held for them.

It was after six by the time they packed everything into the van and said goodbye to Mickey. The beach, swept by a brisk wind, was deserted except for a stray dog or two and a couple tossing a Frisbee. Without discussing it, Maxi and Jay wandered to the end of the boardwalk and sat.

"So, that's it," Jay said, his fingers gently kneading the tired muscles at the back of Maxi's neck.

His words brought into sharp focus the private fear Maxi had been avoiding for days. It clutched at her down deep inside. "What's it?"

"The commercials, your project, it's finished."

"How can you say that? We still have to edit this last spot. And we should review the others. I've been thinking maybe we ought to cut part of the shot of the bandstand in the first one. I can think of a million things we still have to do."

"You're right, of course, but that's little stuff. Basically we're finished. You did it, sweetheart."

Maxi heard neither the pride nor the satisfaction in his voice, only the words *we're finished*. Her eyes burned with sudden tears. "Don't say that."

"All right," he agreed, missing the point. "*We* did it."

"Don't say that we're finished," she told him. "I can't bear to hear it. In fact, I've given this some thought. If you're supposed to be here to help me with this project, what would happen if I never finished it? I could drag it out, lose the tape, do something—"

"Come here," he said, gathering her into the warm haven beneath his arm.

Closing her eyes, Maxi savored the sensation. It was the most satisfying pleasure she had ever known, more soothing than coming home after a long day, richer than hot chocolate on a snowy night, more thrilling than the first few unhurried moments on Christmas morning.

Jay kissed the top of her head and laid his cheek there, understanding fully her motives for offering to screw up her own work. Her suggestion was just one of the hundreds of desperate alternatives he had come up with on his own over the past several days. He had dismissed each of them as reluctantly as he now did hers.

"It wouldn't work, sweetheart," he said softly.

"It's worth a try. We can just go on the way we are, never officially quitting or admitting failure, but . . ."

"No."

"Why?" she demanded, her voice quivering with frustration he also understood all too well.

"Because I don't want you to quit or fail, and I don't want you to have to live on a razor's edge, always wondering when your world is going to be turned upside down by . . ." He would have preferred to let the thought remain unsaid but clearly understood by both of them. For Maxi's sake he forced the words. "By my disappearing from your life forever, as suddenly and mysteriously as I appeared."

"If it buys us even one extra day, it's worth it to me."

He heard the suppressed tears in her voice and felt pain. "But it won't. Even if I agreed, too many others know that the spots are completed now. Mickey, Robert Chandler, Peter Duvall. They would never believe you lost all the copies. Your reputation would be suspect, to say the least."

"I don't care."

"But I do. Very much. You've done an incredible job, under difficult conditions and with limited resources. You deserve to have everyone know how talented you are. And they will, as soon as they get a look at the finished product on Friday night. Duvall, your family—and most of all, you."

"I always knew the ideas were right," she said, "and besides, I had a lot of help."

"Help is nice. But you could have done it without either me or Mickey. You would have managed. Just the way you've managed without the pendant. You're what makes it happen, Maxi, love, and you don't need the full moon or a piece of pretty pink quartz any more than you need your brother's help or Duvall's advice."

"Is that why you thought I was so upset about losing the pendant? Because I was afraid that without it the commercials would flop?"

"Isn't it?"

"No. I would trade all of it, the commercials, the business, everything, to change what's happening with you and me."

"And I might just let you. Unfortunately, we don't have that option, or any other, for that matter. Whatever happens is way beyond our control."

"I know. That's why it didn't seem so crazy to tap every possible source for a miracle. I've been praying and hoping as hard as I could, I figured putting a little faith in crystals couldn't hurt."

"And that's the reason you were so upset when the pendant was stolen?"

She nodded. "I've always been a great believer in fate. Losing the pendant that way seemed like a very bad omen. You don't have to try so hard to look like you're taking this seriously, Jay. I'm well aware that you don't believe any of it."

The truth was that he was taking it very seriously. He'd come around to accepting that Maxi's faith in the stones had a positive effect on her life. She believed they brought her luck, so she had good luck. She believed they enabled her to be serene, so she was serene. So if she believed they would bring about a happy ending for the two of them, then . . .

It was an absolutely bizarre idea, but he was a desperate man. Grabbing both of her hands, he hauled her to her feet beside him. "Let's go."

"Where?" she demanded, stumbling a little as he pulled her along at a fast pace. "Jay, what's the matter? What are you doing?"

"The only thing I can do," he said, not stopping, not smiling as he glanced at her over his shoulder. "I'm going to get the damn thing back."

## Chapter Twelve

Inside the Silver Pocket Pool Hall it was hot and dark and smoky. Exactly what Maxi expected. It was her first time inside a pool hall—she figured the pool room in the college student union didn't count—and she blinked to hurry her eyes' adjustment to the dim lighting so she could have a look around.

Besides feeling extremely apprehensive, she was curious about what sort of people spent their evenings hanging around a beach-front pool hall. Mostly the slightly disreputable-looking sort of person they had come here in search of, she concluded at first glance.

She and Jay had returned to the section of the boardwalk where they'd been the night her pendant was stolen, on the other side of the long parking lot from the public beach where they had been taping earlier. They hung around, unobtrusively munching cardboardy slices of pizza, until a couple of the guys who had been hanging around the other night showed up.

As soon as Jay began questioning them, his tone credibly threatening in Maxi's opinion, they had become alarmed, insisting they had nothing to do with taking her pendant. While not revealing who was responsible, they had hinted them in the direction of the Silver Pocket.

Maxi, certain she would be able to recognize the guy who had been staring hardest at her that night if she saw him again, was slowly and methodically checking out the men in the place and ignoring the women, so it was a few minutes before she spotted it—her one-of-a-kind gemstone pendant—hanging around the neck of a woman seated at the bar. Even in the smoky darkness the rich glint of gold and the sparkle of the stones against the woman's tight black tank top were clearly visible.

Maxi grabbed Jay's arm excitedly. "Over there. The woman at the end of the bar. The one with the big hair and too much eye makeup. Not that way." With an impatient tilt of her head she indicated the opposite end of the bar. "See her? Black tank top. Tight . . ."

"I see."

That was all he said. Maxi, expecting some sort of strategy planning session, was shocked when he started moving toward the woman and her companion. The man standing beside her had his back to them, but Maxi's racing heart was certain he was one of the men who had followed them to the beach. Somehow he looked bigger in here, not quite so young, and he had a black rose tattooed on one curving bicep. Serious reservations clamored to life inside her.

"Jay, I—"

Tightening his grip on her hand, he continued to lead her across the room at an unhurried pace. The glance he shot back at her was easy to interpret. It said, "Shut up and let me handle this." Truthfully, Maxi was glad to do exactly that.

He gallantly helped her up onto a tall stool with a ripped black-vinyl covering and stood beside her. That must be the way it was done in places like this. Women got the stools, men got to stand and plant one hip against the bar, Old-West style.

"Two drafts," Jay told the bartender when he deigned to amble their way and thrust his chin out in a silent request for their drink order.

Maxi liked cold beer on hot days. This beer was warm, and although it was stuffy in the room, the chill inside her was enough to make goose bumps prickle her skin. Nevertheless, she downed half the glass in the time it took Jay to take two nonchalant sips. How could he stay so calm?

Just when she thought her heart was going to leap out of her chest from the mounting tension, he turned to the man, who was standing directly to his left and said in a voice so coldly lethal it sounded like a stranger's, "I want the necklace back."

The younger man didn't say "What necklace?" He didn't deny it or pretend not to understand or recognize them. He laughed. Then, spinning around so his back was to the bar, both elbows braced on it, his legs crossed at the ankle, he ran his fingers through his stringy dark blond hair and said, "That's a real shame, because Dora sure does like that new necklace. Right, Dora?"

Dora, the woman in the black tank top, leaned forward to drape herself around him like some sort of dark, furry, spineless creature. "Right, Biff. I mean, it's not like real Italian gold or nothing, but it's like real different. Sort of classy."

Maxi wanted to ask what a person who pronounced Italian, "Eye-talian," knew about class, but refrained.

"My lady is quite fond of it, as well," Jay said. He took another leisurely sip of beer and brought his icy gaze to bear on the man beside him. "It has sentimental value."

Biff's shrug said that Maxi's emotional peculiarities weren't his problem. "I suppose," he suggested finally, "you could make me an offer for it."

"I could also call the police and let them settle this," countered Jay.

Biff appeared nonplussed. "And then again, you and your lady could walk out of here the same way you walked in, empty-handed but healthy."

There it was, the threat Maxi had been holding her breath dreading. Jay gave no sign he had even heard it, but she knew he had, that he was right that moment weighing his odds and chances, figuring her presence into the equation. She would be crazy not to be scared, yet at the same time she had absolute confidence that Jay would be able to protect her.

An office rat, she had called him once. He had all the required professional skills and smooth social style of a man accustomed to boardrooms and power lunches. Yet on several occasions now she had seen another, tougher, more physically dangerous side of him that spoke of a life outside the business world, or before it. His dangerous side was fully evident now.

"Or," he suggested in reply to Biff's thinly veiled threat, "we could play for it."

Biff swung his head around. His mouth curved like a snake curling in the sun. "You mean play pool?"

"It seems the most likely choice," retorted Jay, putting his lips to the bottle in his hand.

"Let me get this straight. If you win, you get the necklace back, right?"

"That's how it works."

"But what if I win? I already got the necklace, man."

Jay considered that, turned to Maxi and flicked back her hair to reveal the large hoop earrings she was wearing. "How about these?"

"Oooh, Biff," crooned Dora. "Now they look like real Italian gold."

Biff grinned. "Mister, you got yourself a game."

Jay had good instincts. He knew when he could handle a situation, and he knew when he was in trouble. The minute Biff straightened from the bar, snapped his fingers and barked, "Dora, my stick," Jay knew he was in trouble.

Maxi trailed along behind them to an available pool table, wondering if she should offer to hold Jay's beer the way Dora was holding Biff's. No, her hands were too sweaty.

She noticed that several men who had been at the bar had also drifted over. They leaned against the wall, their bloodthirsty smiles reminding her of the spectators in *The Hustler*. Come to think of it, in that movie Paul Newman had owned his own cue stick, very similar to the one Biff had pulled from its leather case and was now assembling. Belatedly it dawned on her that Biff was a pool hustler. She wondered, a little uneasily, how good a player Jay was.

Jay chalked the tip of the cue stick he'd selected from the rack on the wall, blew lightly on it and then examined it through one squinted eye, as if a milligram too much or too little friction would have an effect on his game. It was a bit of showmanship that would no doubt be the highlight of his performance.

He stood by and let Biff rack up the balls. He even managed a self-assured smirk as he waved off the coin toss and allowed his opponent to break, delaying the inevitable. It's not that he had never played pool before. He was confident he had. The stick felt comfortable in his hands and he intuitively knew how each shot should be approached. He just lacked any sense that he had ever won.

There was a sharp cracking sound as Biff's stick made contact with the white cue ball, then a string of rapidfire echoes as the balls scattered across the green felt surface, ricocheting off the sides and each other. When they finally all came to a rest, both players studied the table intently. Biff appeared pleased with the arrangement, Maxi noted. She cautiously moved her gaze to Jay in order to gauge his reaction. His eyes were dark and inscrutable, but his mouth was shadowed by a small, cocky smile. Oh, yes, she thought.

Oh, no, thought Jay as Biff snapped, "Seven ball in the side pocket."

It wasn't the easiest shot on the table. That would have been the three ball in the corner pocket, the shot Jay himself would have taken. The fact that Biff had opted for a difficult opening move and aced it with ease, confirmed Jay's worst fears.

"Six ball in the side pocket." This time Biff jazzed up his shot by banking it off the side.

"Nine ball, end pocket."

"Fourteen, side pocket."

"Three ball, corner."

There was a steady, efficient rhythm to his shots, sort of like machine-gun fire. Jay resisted the urge to dry his damp palms by wiping them on his jeans.

Maxi frowned as she watched Biff clearing the table with the speed of a banquet hall waiter. This wasn't the back and forth way she'd expected the game to proceed. If Jay never got a chance to shoot, how on earth was he going to win back her pendant? Nervously running her tongue over her bottom lip, she took her gaze off the action long enough to see if he appeared worried. He didn't. When she looked back at the table, there were only three balls remaining, one white, one black and the third one lavender. Her lucky color.

Biff called his shot and quickly fired his stick at the cue ball, kissing the lavender ball. It slicked into the side pocket as if being pulled by a string. Jay kept his eye on the remaining balls as he felt briefly Biff's gaze on him.

He watched as the cue stick slowly slipped into place between Biff's poised fingers, in a place that seemed to have been carved especially for it. The air in the room hummed with the tension of a drawn bow string. This last shot was one Jay knew he would have been able to sink. So when Biff missed, Jay knew just as surely that it was intentional. A setup.

The pressure was red-hot and it was all on him. The shot that now remained, his shot, proved Biff's skill more effectively than all the balls he'd previously sunk. It had taken excruciatingly precise technique to land the last ball in a dead spot between pockets. Biff's confidence that victory was as good as his was evident in the grin he flashed as he presented Jay with this final, impossible chance to win.

"Eight ball in the corner pocket," said Jay, stepping to the table. He could just have easily have said eight ball on the moon. The odds of his making this shot were about the same.

Leaning forward, he placed his fingers on the felt and slid his cue stick into position. He closed his eyes. There was only one way he had any chance of making this shot. All his indignant warnings to Maxi over the past few weeks came back to haunt him. *This power I've been given is not a parlor game,* he'd insisted. *There's too much at stake. I'm not taking any chances.*

The stakes had been high for Maxi, as well, and she had sure taken a chance on him. A woman like Maxi didn't gamble her heart. She sure didn't put it on the line for a lost cause. Yet that's exactly what Maxi had done, and was doing yet.

No matter how levelheaded and realistic she wanted him to believe she was, he'd known all along that she was a dreamer. Her claims that she understood that the future held nothing for them, that he could offer no commitment, no permanence, were honest but naive. It was obvious to him that she harbored a stubborn, rose-colored-glasses hope that things would work out the way she wanted them to.

Her hopes and dreams were all centered in that pendant hanging around another woman's neck. So what that it was ridiculous? She wanted it back. And at that moment there was nothing in heaven or on earth that mattered more to Jay than giving her what she wanted.

He concentrated, not even bothering to open his eyes as he fired the stick forward. It hit the cue ball head on, sending it streaking across the felt to slam the black eight ball and put it almost, but not quite, in line with the corner pocket. He did look then, and along with everyone else in the room witnessed the impossible, a pool ball adjusting its course midroll, like a heat-seeking missile honing in on its target. With the softest, sweetest thump he'd ever heard it rolled into the corner pocket.

"Yes," he shouted.

"Well, I never," muttered one old-timer looking on.

That seemed to be the general consensus. Only Maxi seemed completely unsurprised by the upset victory. She threw herself into Jay's arms with an exuberant shout of "All right, Slick."

Holding her tightly so she couldn't feel him trembling, Jay held his hand out to Biff.

"I don't suppose you'd be interested in double or nothing?" inquired Biff, as they shook hands. "Nah, I didn't think so. That was a once-in-a-lifetime shot, man."

"Yeah," Jay promised anyone who might be interested, "once in a lifetime."

A sulking Dora handed over the pendant. Lifting her hair off her neck while Jay fastened it on her, Maxi couldn't hide her excitement. It seemed to shine brighter on her, thought Jay, and the sight of it back where it belonged assured him he'd made the right decision.

Gradually the amazed silence in the pool room gave way to a confusing babble as everyone in the place either tried to convince themselves that they hadn't seen what they thought they had or recounted the time they'd seen someone make a shot that was *really* amazing. It didn't matter to Jay. He walked out of the Silver Pocket a truly happy man, maybe for the first time ever.

Laughing like two scam artists on a roll, they ran all the way back to the parking lot. It was the best way Jay knew to burn off the excess energy still pumping inside him. At least, it was the best way possible in public. He was reserving some very special energy for when he got Maxi alone later. They were both panting by the time they reached the car. Maxi rested her head against the seat and let her breath slow to normal before turning to him with a lively look of curiosity.

"Jay, I'm not much of an expert on pool," she began, "but that last shot . . . was it my imagination or was it a little—"

He pressed a finger to her lips before she could say more, then bent to gently replace them with his mouth, whispering, "Don't ask."

There was a breathy note of laughter in his voice that told Maxi more clearly than words could that everything was going to be all right. Closing her eyes, she surrendered without a qualm to the heat and ecstasy of his kiss. When he pulled away, he left her body taut with desire. It was a delicious state to be in, knowing as she did that as soon as they got home, they would make love.

For the entire hour-long drive she felt as if she were racing standing still, like an engine set to idle too fast. Music was her usual release valve. Jay grinned, knowing her well and understanding why she popped a rowdy Rod Stewart tape into the cassette player and cranked it up loud.

He had his window rolled down, and the warm wind lifted his hair from his face, emphasizing its clean, strong lines. Maxi couldn't stop looking at him, couldn't stop smiling. It was as if together they had crossed some invisible but very formidable hurdle. She could feel it inside and sense it in his mood, as well.

He was different, more relaxed. By winning that game, he had somehow slipped free of all that had been weighing him down. She couldn't ask, was in fact almost afraid to let herself think about it, but it was as if Jay had finally found his way into her secret dream of a happy ending. And if they both believed it, and believed hard enough . . . who knew what might happen?

When they arrived home she ejected the tape and carried it with her to finish playing it on the stereo upstairs. The infectious beat of "Twisting the Night Away" filled the living room and spilled out through the open windows. It was only nine-thirty. Confident none of her neighbors would complain, she kicked off her shoes and at last heeded the urge to move.

Although flying would actually suit her mood better, she was willing to settle for dancing. Holding out her hands to Jay, who was standing with his shoulders braced against the closed door, watching, she pulled him to the center of the rug. She'd never thought to ask if he could dance. She had held back asking about so many things, afraid to know. But now there would be time for all that, she was sure of it. And, Lord, he could dance.

With both hands linked, they twisted, moving together and apart, spinning, dipping, gliding, laughing. He bent her backward and then hauled her hard against him. Of course, she was light and he was strong, but Maxi preferred to think it had more to do with natural grace and rhythm. Their dance was reckless, flawless, an omen, she told herself. As the final notes were banged out, Jay lifted her in his arms and swung her around in a way that topped all the merry-go-round rides of her life. It left their hearts pounding, their bodies sweaty and aroused.

The tape clicked off. She was still in his arms and when their gazes collided a second later their laughter ceased just as quickly as the music had. Their smiles softened. Maxi touched his cheek, his firm jaw, both roughened by a dark, evening stubble, and finally his mouth.

"I want you," she said softly.

He kissed her fingertips. One dark eyebrow lifted. "In bed, boss? Or will right here do?"

"In me. I don't care where."

His breath shuddered then. He carried her swiftly to the bedroom and lowered her onto the fresh, summery-smelling sheets.

Rolling to her side, she propped her head on her hand to watch him undress. Jay was not at all discomfited by her riveted attention, nor did he play to it. He moved quickly, efficiently, as if unaware of the special allure his beautiful body held for her.

He kicked off his boots. His gaze remained fastened on her, gleaming, hungry, determined, as he unbuttoned his shirt and shrugged out of it. The shadows in the room played over his chest, emphasizing its intriguing ridges and hollows, all the places she longed to touch. Maxi reached for him, but was brought up short by the sight of his hands dropping purposefully to his belt buckle.

He unfastened it, and then the snap beneath. The zipper on his jeans whispered in the silence. With his thumbs he dragged the jeans down and Maxi drew a sharp breath as he kicked them aside and stood naked before her. His body was smooth in places, like polished copper, only better, because he was supple and alive. In those places where it was hair-roughened, his skin looked warm and inviting. Her gaze grew smoky with desire as it followed a natural path lower to the raging proof of his need for her.

"Well? Are you going to stand there all night?" she demanded, her tone revealingly hoarse.

His smile came quickly, relaxed, teasing. "I was under the impression you liked looking."

"Oh, I do, I do." Her gaze moved over him like flickering torches. "But I'd rather touch."

His weight made the mattress dip as he moved to kneel beside her. Desire roughened his voice just as it had hers. "Touch," he invited. "Please touch me."

Rolling to sit with her legs folded, Maxi raised her arms and pressed her hands against his chest, slowly sliding them lower. His skin was so warm; his belly hard and flat. She kissed him there and felt him quiver beneath her tongue.

Drawing back, she caressed his narrow hips, his thighs and finally let her fingers sift through the silky nest of black hair surrounding his arousal, prolonging as long as she dared the breathless delight of anticipation. When her fingers finally closed around him, they both trembled.

He was smooth and hot, pulsing with life. She stroked lightly, up and down. She cupped his heat in her palm, pressing, circling, kneading, seeing the effect of her gentle friction in the violent clenching of his muscles. He gripped the brass spindle of the headboard, the muscled cords of his arms flexed as tight as steel girders, his breathing a steady, shallow rasp. She cherished him as lovingly as he cherished her, making love to him first with her hands and then her mouth.

Jay groaned and arched his back when her lips touched him for the first time. He held her head, sweeping back the silky curtain of her hair to see her face, whispering of his pleasure, his desire, his need for her. A need that quickly flared beyond control.

Pushing gently at her shoulders he lowered her onto her back and came down on top of her. He pressed his open mouth to hers, using his tongue and lips and teeth to capture her in a deep kiss. Her clothes came off quickly. He left only the pendant, the feel of the gold oddly warm and reassuring against her flesh. When their bodies finally touched, Maxi's was heated to soft putty, molding to the curves and bulges of his.

He kissed her shoulders, licked roughly at her nipples until they beat with desire. His hand stroked up and down her thighs, then slid between, his fingers moving through her dewy heat to the core of her desire.

"I love you here," he told her, his words more vibration than sound. "So soft. So silky." He pressed deeper. "So tight. Are you ready for me, sweetheart?"

"Yes, now. Right now."

She shifted her legs to accommodate him and cried out loud as he sank into her with a fierce, splendid thrust. She purred softly as he started to move, starting her own slow, now-familiar climb to ecstasy. She closed her eyes, tumbling willingly into his darkness and gave herself up to the rhythm of his mouth, his hands, his thighs as he transported them both to a world of pure pleasure.

Later, limp and sated, Jay lay on his back with Maxi sprawled on top of him, his body still part of hers. He'd been with her long enough to know that if they stayed like that, he would get hard again. He ought to get some sleep. He ought to let her sleep. He stayed where he was.

She felt so good, he couldn't bear to let her go. He felt good, too. He always did after making love to her, of course, but this was different, better, fuller. It wasn't just afterglow, either. This had started even before he touched her, way back in the car. Actually, he felt too good.

Suddenly suspicious, he stared at the ceiling and thought back to what had happened at the pool hall, wanting to test the fiber of this newfound peace of mind. That had been some stunt he pulled. He smiled, but that was all. The second thoughts and regrets he'd expected to unleash didn't come. If Maxi's happiness was on the line, he would do it all over again.

Could it really be this simple, he wondered. For so long he'd lived with the yearning, with the emptiness, consigning it to a place deep inside that no one could ever see, much less hope to touch. Could it have been this simple all along?

He tipped his head on the pillow so that he could look at Maxi. She was beautiful, everything about her, down to the smallest detail: her silky, expressive eyebrows; her eyes, which could laugh and scold and smolder in a way that made him weak; her mouth, vulnerable, red and swollen from his kisses, curving slowly into an invitation as she became aware of him watching her.

She stirred and lifted her head. He felt the imprint of her body all along his, and deeper, inside him. Was that possible? He didn't know, but he didn't want it to stop. He couldn't help moving against her.

Maxi laughed, a delicate, husky sound that rippled across his chest, and flexed her muscles, inside, down low. Jay felt the contractions as a massage of the most sensitive part of himself. He wanted her again, desperately, everything, all of her. But first . . .

He rolled so that she lay beneath him. Supporting his weight on his elbows he framed her face in his hands and kissed her carefully.

"I love you," he said.

The import of his quiet words was not lost on Maxi. Happiness exploded inside her, flooding her eyes with tears of joy. She gently combed her fingers through his hair. "I know."

"You know?" Very briefly he looked surprised. Then he nodded, as if knowing was proper and inevitable. "I didn't want to love you." He smiled. "You probably knew that, too."

Maxi nodded.

"And then even after I knew that I did, I was afraid to let you know."

Again Maxi nodded, understanding.

"But now...tonight..." He paused, but the words he had avoided saying for so long now seemed to be the only ones at his command. "I love you. I love you," he said again, like a child tasting a sound for the first time. "I love you, Maxi."

With him stuck on semantics, a small prod seemed in order. Wrapping her arms around his neck, Maxi smiled and said, "How much?"

His expression flickered: elation, wonder, adoration. He grinned, took her slowly in his arms and showed her how much, again and again throughout the long night.

When she woke in the morning, he was gone.

## Chapter Thirteen

It was a beautiful morning, very unlike the cool, gloomy days associated with March in New England, and for Rita Ferri it was starting in typically hectic fashion.

"Good morning, Artful Purpose Production Services, please hold," she said into the telephone receiver sandwiched between her cheek and shoulder. She needed her hands to open the mail.

She quickly punched the hold button, then the one blinking for her attention, and repeated the words she now mumbled even in her sleep. "Good morning, Artful Purpose Production Services, please hold."

Back to the first call.

"Sorry to keep you waiting. May I help you?" She pursed her lips in concentration as she listened to the high-pitched voice at the other end of the line ranting about the inappropriateness of Chippendale tables in a pharaoh's tomb.

Three weeks ago, before taking this secretarial job, the conversation would have thrown Rita, but no longer. Now she grabbed her notepad and made every effort to follow what the woman was saying, having discovered how easy it is to scramble messages when they seemingly make no sense to begin with, which was the sort of message received most often around here.

The atmosphere of the Artful Purpose workplace—she couldn't in good conscience call it an office—didn't help. It was busy and often noisy, always set to the beat of music. People, some of them very strange looking, came and went, and the telephone rang constantly. Rita wasn't sure how anything got done on time before she arrived, but she was slowly creating as much order as the situation allowed.

Visually, as well, the big drafty loft in the city's reawakening warehouse district was a kaleidoscope of distractions. Racks of costumes lined the wall, props were piled on shelves and everywhere else. Today Rita had arrived to find her desk flanked on one side by a Christmas tree in the process of being decorated with strings of real cranberries and on the other by a pirate's treasure chest full of toys; tomorrow it could be anything. This colorful chaos was presided over by a stuffed, top-hat-and-tails-clad penguin that her boss had a tendency to talk to as if it were a trusted adviser.

Actually that was just one of the unusual things about Maxi Love, but none of it stopped Rita from being crazy about her new boss. She was funny and easygoing and, unlike the man Rita used to work for, never sighed and pressed her lips together disapprovingly when Rita had to pass along to her a problem she wasn't able to handle on her own. Like this one involving the pharaoh's taste in furniture.

Maxi chuckled when Rita explained the dilemma and picked up the phone to speak with Ms. Sylvie Phipps about one of her biggest current projects. Ms. Phipps was the chairperson for the committee sponsoring a landmark exhibition of Egyptian art at the Rhode Island School of Design Museum. Maxi was the lunatic who had agreed to turn an east-side mansion into an Egyptian palace—complete with costumes and makeup for partygoers—for an opening-night gala. And she was loving every minute of it.

It took her no time at all to ease Ms. Phipps's mind concerning the offending tables. At the same time Maxi got the woman's enthusiastic go-ahead for an idea she had come up with only last night, having special hieroglyphic wallpaper printed to hang on the panels in the foyer. It would be costly, but this was Maxi's favorite type of project . . . one in which money was no object.

She'd landed a lot of that kind of work lately. Robert Chandler's election five months ago had ensured a healthy future for Artful Purpose. In spite of Peter Duvall's last-minute grandstanding, Robert had seen to it that Maxi received full credit for the innovative television spots. They had brought her a great deal of notoriety, highlighted by a feature story in a national magazine in which her work was described as "bold and adventuresome." The phone had been ringing ever since.

Maxi was at last a success, in just about every way the sweet-smelling stuff could be measured. Her family was proud and impressed. Mickey was thrilled to be her full-time cameraman. With him on board, and her jack-of-all-trades experience producing the campaign commercials, she was now a full-service operation, able to provide whatever was needed from props to camera equipment. Hence the addition of the words "production services" to her letterhead.

Everything she did lately turned to gold. Rudy and the band were convinced her Midas touch was partially responsible for their album's unexpected appearance on the national music charts. Even Rita, the secretary she had finally gotten around to hiring, wore a perpetual grin, insisting she had never before had so much fun at work. Everybody was happy. Everybody but Maxi.

She stopped herself short in the act of reaching for the pendant she was wearing. She refused to start that again. Today was the first time since that night in the pool hall she had even worn it. She'd slipped it over her head on impulse, telling herself the aquamarines matched her dress and that it was silly to let such a beautiful piece of jewelry sit on her vanity gathering dust.

She wondered, though, if wearing it wasn't subconsciously a symbolic act, similar to a widow who finally gathers the courage to throw away her husband's favorite chair, a proclamation that she was finally ready to let go. Maxi didn't feel ready.

With a sigh she gazed at Slick the Second, perched atop a nearby filing cabinet. More likely she still harbored some deeply imbedded faith in the pendant and figured it would come in handy at this afternoon's meeting, bringing her... not luck—she had confidence in her work these days and was certain if she really wanted a job she would get it—but rather insight. Did she really want to become mixed up in this particular job?

She'd had misgivings from the start, had in fact laughed when the request to meet with her had first been made, and had every intention of sending her very flattered but final regrets. Then she had made the mistake of mentioning the matter to Mickey.

"Allaire, Cross and Griffin!" he had exclaimed, looking as impressed as if she had announced that the head of MGM had phoned and begged her to help with the sequel to *Gone With the Wind*. "Maxi, they're a big-time advertising firm. I mean, *big-time*," he repeated, dragging the words out.

"Where have you been lately?" she countered. "We're big-time, too."

"Not like them. Those guys are Madison Avenue big."

She patted her chest in a dramatic fashion. "Be still, my heart."

"Maxi, just being associated with them on one job would open up new doors for us."

"Need I remind you that we're having trouble keeping up with the doors already open?"

"I can't believe they called you."

"Thanks a lot."

"I mean, just out of the blue and all."

"It wasn't exactly out of the blue. Evidently one of the partners saw an ad for the Wild Horses album in the *Phoenix*," she explained, naming an underground Boston newspaper. "He persuaded the others that I would . . . how was it worded? Oh, yes, I would 'add a fresh dimension' to their bid for some new account." She rolled her eyes. "Can you imagine them wanting to jump on my little bandwagon?"

"Hey, when you're hot, you're hot. Why fight it?"

"For obvious reasons. They want to use me, Mickey, co-opt a few of my ideas to spiff up their prepackaged, rubber-stamp approach. And I'm supposed to feel flattered. It's condescending."

"What have you seen of their work lately?" Mickey inquired lightly. "Of the rubber-stamp variety, that is?"

"Nothing that I can think of offhand," she admitted. "But I know the type. Big time, big business. Give me the old-fashioned, personal approach any day."

"Now who's being condescending?" he came back softly. "Not to mention smug and narrow-minded. Why is it that big is necessarily bad and you have to be the struggling underdog to have any artistic validity?"

"I didn't say that."

"No, I suppose you didn't."

He had gone back to studying a tray of negatives at that point, and Maxi had pretended to work on the storyboard in front of her.

"So you think I should at least go and hear what they have to say?" she demanded finally.

"I didn't say that."

"But that is what you think, so you might as well come right out and say so."

"All right. I think you should go and listen to what they have to say. You just might find yourself interested." He cracked a smile and cleared the air. "And if you're not, I'll be able to go around telling everyone that my bigshot boss turned down the illustrious Allaire, Cross and Griffin."

"Why didn't you say so in the first place? In that case, I guess I'll go."

And so she had said yes to the meeting and now had to steal time from the pharaohs and her search for the perfect location to shoot Christmas in March for a cranberry advertisement and her work on a six-part PBS series on Edgar Allan Poe, to drive all the way to Boston to meet with three guys she already knew she had as much in common with as Lawrence Welk had with Ozzy Ozborne. At least she'd begged off lunch.

After agreeing to meet with them, she had put the matter out of her mind—until this morning when she was getting dressed. Aside from a second's hesitation over the pendant, choosing what to wear had been a snap. Maxi instinctively knew how to dress to impress the Messrs. Allaire, Cross and Griffin—in a black linen-weave suit with a smartly cropped jacket and a skirt that was straight, interestingly snug and slit in back to enable her to walk in her snappy little Emma Hope pumps. Her blouse had to be silk, plum-toned, naturally, next season's most important color. And over her shoulder, a carelessly draped challis shawl with enough fringe to provide the requisite touch of bold individuality.

Fortunately she didn't own anything remotely like that, so she'd opted for a great blue-green silk dress from the forties that she'd happened upon while shopping for antique lace. Over it she wore a lightweight bomber-style jacket of ultra soft tan leather. Glancing in the corner mirror on her way out, however, she paused, frowning.

Something about the mix of leather and silk, casual and sophisticated wasn't quite right. She looked around, snatched a tan fedora with a wide black band off the hat shelf and dropped it on her head. Perfect, and definitely her. She was a great believer in truth in packaging.

The offices of Allaire, Griffin and Cross were located in Boston's World Trade Center. A wide promenade lined with an international array of flags led to the converted army facility overlooking the harbor. Inside, plush muted carpeting, an abundance of both glass and greenery and open-air balconies bordered by brass rails had replaced all traces of the building's former life.

Hurrying past what seemed an endless string of cafés and shops, Maxi thought it would be nice if they had thought to provide golf carts to get from the parking garage to the waterview offices at the very back of the sprawling complex. She was puffing when she finally arrived and was immediately referred by the receptionist to the office of Mr. Allaire's secretary. A tall, efficient-looking woman in her mid-forties, the secretary straightened her designer-eyeglass frames as she gazed at Maxi, as if that might improve the quality of what she saw. Brushing an invisible speck of lint from her black suit jacket, she invited Maxi to have a seat in the waiting area.

"I should warn you that it may be a while," she said as Maxi sat in one of a pair of surprisingly comfortable petit-point-covered Queen Anne chairs and rested her portfolio on the intricate Chinese carpet. Classy, very classy. "Can I get you a cup of coffee while you wait, Ms. Love?"

"No, thank you," replied Maxi. "But if Mr. Allaire is busy, perhaps Mr. Cross or Mr. Griffin would be able to fill me in on their proposal."

"I'm afraid both Mr. Cross and Mr. Griffin were called away from the office unexpectedly. I'm sure they regret not being able to meet with you personally."

"I'm sure," agreed Maxi, both relieved that she wouldn't be subjected to three-on-one pressure and irked that they had not considered her as important as whatever had called them away. "So I'll be meeting only with Mr. Allaire?" she inquired.

"Yes."

"And he's busy?"

"I believe so," his secretary replied with only the slightest ruffle in her crisp composure. "When I left his office a moment ago, he was . . . ah, involved in a long-distance strategy session."

"I see." Two gone and one busy. Obviously they weren't as desperate for her to work with them as she had assumed. Not that she cared. She reached for the handle of her portfolio. "Actually, my own schedule is a bit tight today, so perhaps—"

The woman cut her off with a professional smile. "Why don't I check and see exactly how long Mr. Allaire will be tied up? I'll only be a moment."

"Thank you."

Grace Belvedere's footsteps were silent as she walked down a carpeted hallway and around a corner. She came to a halt outside the solid paneled door of her boss's office.

All the wood in the offices of Allaire, Griffin and Cross was solid and all the doors were paneled. That's the sort of firm it was. For the same reason, all the furnishings were tasteful and authentically old Boston, and all the secretaries were attractive, well-paid and discreet.

It's because she was so discreet that Grace hadn't mentioned to anyone the reason she never breezed into Mr. Allaire's office with only a perfunctory knock as she had in the old days. The old days being the time before his accident, before his weeks in the hospital when no one had been sure he was going to survive his coma, before the long months of recuperation and physical therapy that followed. Once, shortly after his return to the office, Grace had knocked and entered and almost lost an ear to the dart that came whizzing from behind his desk toward the dart board on the opposite wall.

The dart board was new. Just one of the countless small and not-so-small ways in which her once focused, dynamic, hard-working boss was now different. Of course, even though she never said anything, Grace knew that others noticed it, as well. She had seen Mr. Cross and Mr. Griffin exchange looks on occasion, like the time Mr. Allaire had suggested replacing the chairs in the waiting room with wicker swings suspended from the ceiling. That idea, like most of those he'd proposed since his return, had been received with silence, followed by a polite promise to take it under consideration, and then never mentioned again.

Grace knew that the others hoped, as she did, that his odd mood was simply a temporary aftereffect of the accident, but as the days went by, she suspected they were also beginning to wonder if it wasn't something more. She couldn't see things going on as they were indefinitely, with Mr. Allaire sitting at the weekly partner's meetings thumbing through a copy of the *Phoenix* and offending the in-house talent by insisting on calling in outsiders. Outsiders like Ms. Love. Grace worried about the eventual outcome in respect to her position here, but in the meantime, she adapted.

Drawing a deep breath, she knocked and waited for a clear invitation to enter.

At the sound of the knock on the door Jason hurriedly fired the dart he was holding and then called out, "Come in, Grace."

She opened the door, but remained standing with her hand on the knob. "Mr. Allaire, Ms. Love is here. She's the free-lance art director who—"

Grace had anticipated an annoyed sigh. Instead he came out of his seat so fast he knocked over his pencil stand. "Right, I know who she is," he said, cutting her off. "Why didn't you show her in?"

"Because yesterday when I brought your one o'clock appointment in at one o'clock you said that just because you made an appointment to see someone at one didn't necessarily mean you wanted to see them at that time. I think you called it 'creative scheduling.'"

Jason noticed that Grace managed to relate that without once curling her lip in distaste, the way she did whenever he said or did something she considered particularly outrageous. It was a sad commentary on his life that Grace's curling lip had become a bright spot in his work day.

"You're sure I said that, hmm?"

She nodded. "Yes."

"Well. Can't you take a joke?"

Her lip quivered. Almost, thought Jason, almost.

"I'll send in Ms. Love," she told him.

He smiled. "Thank you, Grace."

When Maxi stepped into Jason Allaire's office several moments later, the door snapped shut behind her, almost, she thought, as if his secretary, having announced her, couldn't wait to get out of there. It increased Maxi's curiosity about the man she was about to meet.

Jason Allaire was standing by the window when she entered, silhouetted by the midday sun slanting off the water. Maxi glanced across the room at him and was filled, body and soul, with a single thought.

Jay.

It had happened to her before, hundreds of times, maybe thousands. She would be going along, getting through life a day at a time, waiting for the loneliness to finally recede, and without warning her attention would be caught by the slant of the shoulders of the man walking in front of her, or the back of the neck of a stranger across the room, or the deep laugh of a man sitting nearby, and time would stop. Like now, she would be overwhelmed by Jay's presence. Not mere memories, but the scent and feel and taste of him.

It was just a mind trick, of course. But this time, the sensation was stronger than ever, so real she had to fight to keep from calling his name out loud.

He turned then, and all the air left her body in a rush.

"Maxi?" he said, his voice soft, achingly familiar. Almost immediately it changed, becoming formal. As if correcting himself, he added, "That is, Ms. Love. Won't you please sit down?"

"Yes."

Somehow she made it the short distance to the chair in front of his desk and perched on the very edge of the seat.

He remained by the window, watching her with an odd expression. It was no wonder, considering the way she was staring at him. Maxi deemed it a minor miracle that she had so far managed to resist the urge to touch him, to see if he was real or if she had at last slipped over the edge, into a permanent fantasy.

"I'm Jason Allaire," he said finally.

Maxi nodded, her mind spinning. "Yes." Jason. Jay. It wasn't possible, and yet . . . "How do you do?"

He made no move to shake her hand. She wished he would. Just once, just one touch and she would know.

"Fine, thank you," he said, stepping closer.

For the first time Maxi noticed the cane in his right hand. Her shock must have been obvious, because he grimaced, a look that was partly sheepish, partly one of self-condemnation. It melted into a smile that Maxi felt like an explosion inside her.

His smile, his face, the way he held his head, it was all exactly as she remembered. She was not imagining this. She couldn't be. But what if she was and she said something? The man would have her committed.

"Well, as you can see, I'm not so fine really," he said. He lifted the cane. "I'd hoped to be rid of this damn thing by now, but . . ."

"Darn," she said under her breath and without meaning to.

He looked at her strangely, his voice cracking as he asked, "What did you say?"

"Nothing. It was nothing."

"I'm sorry if my language offended you."

"No. It didn't really. It's me who should be sorry. That was rude."

"Not at all."

Maxi squirmed on the seat. She had to pull herself to-gether. "So how did it happen? The cane, that is. I mean, your needing a cane."

"I was in an accident."

"An accident?"

"Yes. Last year."

Now her voice grew raspy. "When?"

"September."

"Of course. I mean, of course it must have been quite serious?"

He shrugged. "So I was told. I don't remember very much about that time. I was in a coma for several weeks."

Maxi could hardly hold her thoughts together. My God, it was him. She was sure of it and had already started from her seat when the very obvious truth hit her. The odds were very good that even if she was right, Jason Allaire had no recollection of her or the time they had spent together.

She settled herself again with a jolt she was sure he noticed. She pressed her lips tightly together. Oh, Jay. She wasn't sure which was worse, believing he was gone forever, or knowing he was here, alive and well and as off-limits to her as the Hope Diamond. She looked at his gray, double-breasted linen sport jacket, the properly bold silk tie and coordinating, not matching, handkerchief in his pocket, his perfectly creased trousers, and she slunk a little deeper into her leather jacket.

At the same time she became aware that there was something decidedly odd about the long, gaping silences punctuating this meeting. She knew very well why she was silent and gaping, but what was going on behind Jason Allaire's intensely thoughtful blue eyes?

As if also noticing the awkward mood, he gave a faint shrug and hitched one long leg over the corner of his desk. That was when Maxi saw his boots, black, like the ones still sitting in a corner of her bedroom, and very much at odds with everything else about Mr. Jason Allaire.

"Shall we get down to business?" he suggested. "I'm afraid that my time away from the office—recuperating and all—has left my business manners a little rusty...among other things."

The sight of the boots gave her courage. "What other things?"

He looked briefly disconcerted by the blunt question. At first Maxi thought he wasn't going to reply. Then she realized he was considering his answer carefully, as if it mattered greatly what he said to her. A ribbon of hope, about as substantial as smoke, but hope nonetheless, curled inside her.

"I seem to be rusty at work in general," he told her. "I can't get back into the swing of things here. At first I thought it was natural, that the feeling would pass. Then I thought maybe it wasn't just a feeling, that in the months I was away things around here had changed in some subtle way that I couldn't put my finger on. But in the last week or so I've realized that it's me. I'm what's changed."

"In what way?"

This time he seemed as comfortable with Maxi's question as she was with asking.

"I hate what I'm doing. I don't know how else to say it. It's absurd, I know. I have money, power, freedom. I'm a partner here. It's not just a job, it's my life. At least it used to be. Lately I spend a lot of time sitting here, trying to remember why I got involved in all this to begin with." He gave a small smile. "I started out as a photographer, you know."

"I know." There was an excited lilt in her voice.

His eyes narrowed. "You know?"

"No. I didn't mean that I know. I meant . . . it makes sense."

He nodded, his expression circumspect. "I suppose so. Anyway, I was a photographer, Ben a salesman, and Ted a graphic artist . . . they're my partners."

Maxi nodded.

"Between us we had all the bases covered. We were young, hungry, ballsy." He snapped his fingers. "Instant ad agency, instant success."

"Sounds wonderful."

If he heard the waver in her voice he didn't comment. "I always thought so. At parties I'd hear people discussing the meaning of success, going on about how hollow it can be, and I'd think, 'What bullshit.' Now I'm the one wondering why it is that cinching a million-dollar deal doesn't make me feel as good as getting one perfect shot used to." He stared hard at her. "I also think maybe I ought to go back and find out."

"Go back?" Maxi echoed, her eyes wide, her heart thumping wildly.

"Back to shooting pictures." He must have read her disappointment as disapproval for there was a harsh, almost combative edge to his voice as he added, "Crazy, huh?"

"No. No, it's not at all crazy."

"My partners think I'm crazy. My secretary thinks I'm crazy. My own brother thinks I'm crazy." His chin came up in that way that was both belligerent and boyish, and suddenly the memories Maxi had suppressed for so long came flooding back to her. "There are days," he continued with quiet defiance, "when I'm sure they're right."

"They're not right." Maxi met his gaze steadily. "No one else can tell you what will make you happy."

"But will I be happy?" he shot back. "If I chuck all this, what will I have?"

Such a loaded question. Maxi swallowed, not trusting her suddenly dry mouth to produce words.

"Sometimes," she said finally, "sometimes you just have to take a chance. You have to close your eyes and jump."

There was a silence during which Maxi saw the muscles in his throat clench and loosen several times. Finally, very quietly, he said, "And hope you get lucky?"

"Exactly."

Their eyes met. Held. His features were stark. There was no longer any doubt in Maxi's mind that seeing her had prompted some sort of turmoil inside Jason Allaire. She wanted to grab him and shake him and say, *It's me. Remember? Maxi. I love you. And you love me.*

The reason she didn't was because she was afraid. And she was afraid because somehow she understood that he was, too. If she pushed, he might back away forever. She'd had months to come to grips with what had happened between them and she was still as confused as ever. Heaven alone knew what thoughts were spinning in Jay's head at that moment.

Maybe she could just mention that he looked very familiar and see where that led. No, she cautioned herself nervously, don't push. Pushing would be all wrong. The problem was she didn't know what would be the right thing to do. Who the hell would? This wasn't exactly a situation you read about in your average advice-to-the-lovelorn column.

Letting her memories of their time together flow freely, she concentrated all her energy on them, willing him to take the next step backward, back to her.

A deep, shuddering breath lifted his chest. Maxi's heart seemed to freeze midbeat, waiting, but without saying a word he looked away, absently reaching behind him as if he needed something to do with his hands.

"I'm not sure I'm very good at taking chances," he said without looking at her.

"Oh, but you are," she exclaimed, leaping to her feet and nearly planting herself in his lap in the process. Feeling exceedingly foolish, she clasped her hands together and added in as calm a tone as she could manage. "I'm sure you are."

Again he stared at her. Maxi stared back, struck as she had been at first sight by how handsome he was. Instead of blinding her as it had at first, the sun streaming through the window now illuminated each small, familiar detail of his face.

Love for him was like a tidal wave building deep inside her. She couldn't play this game much longer. It was torture to stand this close, after so long without any hope at all, and not be able to touch him. Fearing she would any second weaken and reach out, she lowered her gaze from the dark intensity of his and saw what it was he had reached to pick up off the desk.

"What is that?" she asked on a harshly exhaled breath.

He glanced down as if unaware of what he was holding in his hands and turning over and over.

"This?" He looked at her a little sheepishly. "It's a crystal. My doctor said to get exercise, so when it was too cold outside I'd walk around Faneuil Hall. There's this shop there... it's called Euphoria," he revealed with a sardonic smile. "Anyway, one day I just sort of wandered in... another crazy impulse. I was there so long I felt stupid walking out without buying something, and the woman there said just buy what feels right. As if a hunk of stone is going to feel right or wrong. Go ahead, laugh."

Maxi wasn't laughing, but she was finding it hard not to grin broadly.

"So I chose this," he went on, holding up the stone in his hands. "It's amethyst, supposed to connect me to the higher self that I'm not convinced I have. I ended up buying these, too."

He scooped up more stones from a tray on the desk. "Aquamarines for serenity. I figured I could definitely use some of that. And this is rose quartz." Maxi nodded as he held out the largest of the stones. With each passing second she felt more giddy with anticipation. "The saleslady said it's supposed to open you up to love and help you to let go of things in the past."

"I know." Maxi reached for her pendant, made up of smaller, cut-and-polished versions of the identical stones, and lifted it for him to see. "But didn't she tell you, Jay, that you should only let go of the bad things in the past?"

He stared at the pendant and Maxi saw a flicker of awareness in his eyes before he closed them tightly. It seemed several lifetimes until he opened them again, and yet it wasn't nearly enough time for Maxi to formulate a coherent thought. Only a wish that seemed to well up from deep in her soul. It was as much longing as wish, actually, one that had always been a part of her and always would be, reality be damned. If it didn't come true, if seeing the pendant that so clearly linked them together and to the past, wasn't enough to jar Jay into remembering her, she had no idea what would.

She wished so hard she couldn't seem to help leaning closer to him so that when he finally did open his eyes, she was standing there, hunched forward, swinging her necklace in the face of a man who was suddenly all stranger. She felt all idiot.

"Actually," Jason Allaire said, his deep voice as remote as his expression had become, "we didn't go into the philosophy of the stones that deeply. Buying them was an impulse, Ms. Love. Most of the time I don't even remember they're here. I certainly don't put any stock in their supposed powers."

His words were like an ax slashing away at her fragile hopes. And they were a lie. Maxi knew that as well as she knew her own name . . . and his. She just didn't know how to tell him so without exploding the illusion that they were merely two professionals meeting to explore the possibility of working together.

She had been so certain he was about to remember everything. Now disappointment flooded her, more bitter and heartwrenching than the pain she'd suffered in the days right after he disappeared, and she'd thought nothing could ever be worse than that.

Whatever innate chemistry had been at work a few minutes ago was gone. She had a feeling that Jay wanted it that way. For right now, for reasons even he probably couldn't fathom, he *needed* to keep some distance between them.

"Maybe we should talk about the reason I asked you to come here this afternoon," he said finally.

Maxi took some solace from the awkwardness in his manner. The fact that she so thoroughly unsettled him wasn't much, but it was a place to start.

"Yes," she replied, "let's do that. Why did you ask me here?"

"Won't you sit?" He gestured toward the chair she'd vacated in such an excited hurry.

"No. Thank you. I think better on my feet."

He responded with a casual nod, but his eyes gleamed, revealing to Maxi that he understood there was something happening below the surface here, even if he refused to acknowledge it.

"I saw the work you did for the Wild Horses' album cover," he told her. "I thought it was a very interesting concept."

"Really? What about it interested you?"

Perhaps the ducks dressed like jockeys, she thought, recalling how they had giggled for hours the night she had come up with the idea in bed. Or maybe he'd been struck by the wallpaper that had been inspired by their visit to Elwin Suwaski's ramshackle apartment.

"The general format, I suppose," he said, sending her hopes tumbling back to the cellar. "There was just a feeling I got from it."

"Déjà vu?"

"No, not that," he replied quickly. Too quickly. "This was different."

Maxi nodded. "I know the feeling exactly. It's like a tingle all over, right?"

He shrugged and attempted to chuckle. "I hadn't really tried to pin it down."

"Try now."

"All right, I suppose it could be called a tingle."

"Sort of like being hot and cold at once?"

"A little maybe."

"And not able to catch your breath?"

"I'm not sure—"

She interrupted. "There's a name for that feeling, you know."

"Really?"

"Yes. It's . . ." *You're pushing,* warned something inside. *Take it slow.* "It's slipped my mind." Maxi wasn't sure if it was relief or disappointment that made him shrug. Damn, maybe she should have pushed. "So did you want to talk with me about working on something like the cover of HorseFeathers?" she asked him.

"Not exactly like it. We just signed a new account, an amusement park, and I thought your offbeat approach might be just what we need."

"An amusement park, hmm? That presents some interesting possibilities." The truth is, she would be interested in working up a promotion for a sewage-treatment plant if it meant working with him.

"My partners aren't convinced you're right for the job, however. Of course, before I asked you to submit even a rough proposal, I'd want more of a commitment from them."

"And I'd demand it."

Jay's chin lifted at her self-assured tone. This time the heartbreaking familiarity of the gesture brought her close to tears. "Is business that good that you can afford to play hard-to-get with a firm this size?"

She forced a smile and nodded. "It's that good."

His smile came from out of nowhere. "Great. That's really great." For just an instant there was real pleasure shining in his eyes, and pride. He shook it off as he slid from the corner of the desk, moving to stand between her and the door in a manner that was clearly dismissive. "So if you'd like to leave your portfolio with us for a while, I can go over it with my partners and try to convince them you can do the job for us."

The last thing she wanted to do was leave with nothing resolved. She wanted him back, damn it. Need for him was a crushing ache in her chest.

But at that moment the stubborn professional inside her who had struggled so hard to establish credibility in this business rose up in response to the casual superiority in his dismissal.

She lifted the leather portfolio from the floor. "That's why you asked me to take time from my work and drive all the way up here? So I could hand-deliver my portfolio for you and your partners to look over?"

"That's it."

She swung the case so that it landed against his chest, forcing him to drop his cane to catch it with both hands. "You got it, Slick."

## Chapter Fourteen

*You got it, Slick.*

The words reverberated in Maxi's head all the way back to Providence. As she drove along, bemoaning Boston's rush-hour traffic and her own impetuousness, and Jay's not remembering her—as well as whatever mysterious power had so thoroughly botched up her life—she came up with a hundred better parting shots.

Now, alone in her car, leaving the man she loved farther behind with each mile, she was able to be cool, witty, thought-provoking, honest and unafraid...all the things she hadn't been when she'd had the chance. Now it was too late.

Refusing to even think about the piles of work waiting for her at the office, she drove straight home and continued to torture herself by replaying the scene in his office over and over again, mentally battering herself with all the things she should have said and done and asked.

A thousand times she reached for the telephone to call him and a thousand times she chickened out. Her second thoughts sprouted second thoughts, and third, and on and on. Most of the night she lay awake feeling as if she were personally testing the infinity theory of whole numbers.

At work the next day her eyes burned from sleeplessness and her brain ached from being twisted around so many different scenarios. She was still at a loss as to what she ought to do next . . . if anything. Her options were limitless and confusing.

She would call and nonchalantly inquire whether he and his partners had reached an agreement concerning her work. Right, in the less than twenty-four hours that had passed since she'd stalked out of his office.

She would have Rita call instead.

She would develop some patience. And go stark raving mad in the process.

She would pull herself together and get on with her life. What life? Since Jay had left, her entire existence revolved around the business, around working days so long and exhausting she was able to fall asleep at night.

She would pull herself together and confront him with the truth.

She would play it cool and let him come to terms with it in his own good time.

She would call and ask what he thought of her portfolio. It would be worth appearing an idiot to hear the sound of his voice.

With a sigh Maxi tossed down her pencil and stared at the worthless sketch on the board in front of her. She'd been working for hours with only this embarrassing mess to show for it. Why bother making plans? Obviously what was going to happen was she would be so preoccupied and miserable she would miss all her deadlines, lose jobs and go bankrupt. And that would be that. Jay Angel might have taken a chance on a failure, but Jason Allaire never would.

"Maxi."

At the hiss of her name Maxi swiveled away from her drawing board to see Rita standing behind her. She had closed the door between the two oversize workrooms that made up the office, and from her expression she'd been trying to get Maxi's attention for a while.

Maxi smiled at her. "Sorry, Rita. I guess I was far away for a minute there."

"I'll say." Her secretary's manicured black eyebrows puckered. "You sure you're okay, Maxi? You're not yourself today."

"I'm fine. Just a little tired. What's up?"

Rita's concerned expression turned businesslike. "He's here."

Instinctively Maxi's pulse quickened. "Who?"

"The big shot you went off to see yesterday. Mr. Allaire. Mickey says he's—"

"He's here?" Maxi interrupted, sliding to her feet, smoothing her hair, wringing her hands.

Rita nodded. "Waiting right outside. I said I'd see if you could squeeze him in. I pegged his type right off—fancy face, expensive suit. Won't hurt to let him know you're a pretty important person, too. You want I should let him cool his heels awhile?"

"No. God, no. I want to see him right away."

"All right," Rita said, clearly disapproving. "But, Maxi, take some advice and don't look so eager. You're as good as he is any day." She got as far as the door and paused before sliding it open. Her dark eyes twinkled as she added, "But he ain't bad. Not bad at all."

A heartbeat later Jay stepped into the room. Without asking permission—and to Rita's disappointment, Maxi was sure—he slid the door tightly closed.

Rita was right about the expensive suit. Armor, Maxi thought, and wished he didn't feel he needed protection from her. Looking at him gave her tunnel vision. The rest of the room, the rest of the world, faded to black. There was only him and her, separated by a few feet and by something neither of them understood.

He lifted his hand and Maxi saw he was holding her leather portfolio. "I'm returning this."

"So I see. Should I duck?"

His mouth twisted. "No. The urge to throw it back at you burned off sometime around midnight."

A thrill shot through her as she watched him place it on her desk. She hadn't been the only one doing some thinking last night. "I'm sorry I hit you with it. Not that you didn't deserve it for dragging me all the way up there for nothing."

"Nothing?"

She had to wet her lips to speak. "Nothing much."

He eyed her thoughtfully. "If I deserved it, why are you sorry?"

"I suppose because you were at a disadvantage... having to use a cane and all," Maxi offered, shrugging. "I'm just relieved you didn't walk in here in a full-body cast."

"You don't hit that hard. Of course it did hurt like hell when they taped my ribs, but..." He trailed off, grinning at her. "You deserved that. I'll have you know I'm pretty agile for a man with a cane."

"I never doubted that for a second."

Silence. Then slowly the air between them began to sizzle.

He knew. The realization was like an explosion inside her head, clearing away all the doubts and second thoughts. The glint in his eye, the tilt of his head, something about him, *everything* about him, told Maxi he hadn't come here simply to return her portfolio.

Miraculously the urge to push and shake him disappeared. She had the sense that everything she ever wanted was going to unfold before her and she wanted to savor every delicious moment of it.

"So what did your partners think of my work?" she asked.

"They didn't like it."

That brought the delicious unfolding to a sudden halt.

"Didn't like it?"

He shook his head. "Not at all."

"So I'm not going to be working with you?" Her voice wavered with disappointment.

"No. You aren't going to be working with me." He let her wallow in confusion for a few seconds before adding, "I quit."

"You can't quit. You're a partner."

"That's what they said. Regardless, I'm not interested in forcing them to buy me out, and they insist they'll keep my name on the letterhead for when I'm ready to go back. But I'm never going back."

She watched as he began to move around the room, examining everything in his path the same way he had that first night in her apartment.

"What are you going to do?" she asked.

"I'm not exactly sure yet." He ran his hand across the wood of the penny-candy counter that now resided here. There was no way his touch could be described as anything but a caress, and his mouth curved with remembered pleasure. When his attention was caught by the penguin perched above his head, the faint smile erupted into a grin. "But I'm open to suggestion."

Maxi couldn't say a word. It felt like a hundred wild horses were galloping inside her chest.

He turned, and when he looked at her all the sharp edges were gone from his expression; all traces of the guarded, carefully speculative look he'd worn yesterday had disappeared. It was as if the past six months had never happened.

He smiled at her. "This is really happening, isn't it?"

Maxi knew exactly what he meant and didn't pretend otherwise. Too much time had already been lost. "It's real," she said softly.

"Not a dream."

She shook her head.

He sighed, a sound blending satisfaction and relief. "And not my imagination, which is what I've been telling myself ever since you walked into my office yesterday."

"At first I tried telling myself the same thing," whispered Maxi. "Thank God neither of us is a very good listener."

"All that time I was in the hospital . . ."

"You were really with me," she supplied when he floundered.

"Then it's true. I figured that had to be it, but I couldn't believe it. I've been getting bits and pieces ever since I woke up in the hospital, and I wondered if it was only some sort of weird, wonderful dream. But it was so real. I'd see some woman in a crowd who had hair like yours, and I'd think I knew her. I'd have to stop myself from—"

He touched her hair briefly, looking as if it took a tremendous effort to stop even now. Don't stop, Maxi wanted to plead. Her fingers throbbed from the force of her longing to touch him, but she also wanted to hear what he was saying, and she sensed he needed to say it.

"Lately the flashes of memory have been getting stronger. Most of the time I tried not to think about what it all might mean." He hesitated, then gave a dry laugh. "Because if it turned out to be just my imagination, then I was really in trouble, and if it wasn't, it meant there was a whole chunk of my life I knew nothing about."

"It's easy to understand why you felt that way."

He reached out to touch her again, and this time his hand lingered on her shoulder, as if needing to feel her. "When I saw you yesterday, part of me wanted to come right out and ask you. But I was afraid, afraid of finding out I really was crazy, afraid you weren't the woman in my head after all. And I wanted so badly for you to be real."

She pressed her cheek to the back of his hand, rubbing against it. "I am very, very real."

"That's what I came here to find out. I sat up all night arguing with myself about what to do about you. I hoped that Ben and Ted would buy me some time by signing you for the new project. Then I could be around you, watch you, get to know you. When they stood firm on using in-house talent, I just walked out, got in my car and headed for Providence." Grinning, he at last pulled her into his arms. "I figured that if I couldn't get at the truth about this in a city named Providence, I'd have to give up."

"Thank heavens for your philosophical streak."

His grin widened. "Exactly. Oh, Maxi," he groaned, pulling her closer. "I'd walk around feeling lonely all the time, and I couldn't tell anyone what was wrong because how do you explain missing someone you're afraid doesn't even exist?"

"I beg your pardon," Maxi interjected, conjuring up an icy glare of indignation. "You have some nerve saying I don't exist when I'm standing right here in front of you, in the flesh, as it were."

His initial surprise gave way to a look of amusement and then sudden heat. "Rest assured, Ms. Love, that your flesh has not escaped my notice."

She tossed her head, her green eyes sparkling. "That's more like it."

"The record album was my first real clue. When I saw that ad for it I finally had something solid to grab on to. It was so familiar to me."

"That's not surprising. I bounced ideas for it off you until you began referring to it as—"

" 'That stupid album,' " he finished for her, flashing an irrepressible grin. "Tell me about it. I want to hear about the album cover and about the rest of the campaign . . . about how you made out with Duvall. I want to know everything I missed. . . ." He reached for her hand, brushing his lips across the back of it. "I want to know about any men in your life now."

"That part is easy," Maxi told him. "There are none."

"Good. That means there's no one I'll have to move out of the way. There's been no one for me, either," he said before she had to ask. He kissed her hand again. "Now tell me the rest."

Maxi filled him in as completely as she could while covering six months in rambling, scattershot fashion. She didn't seem able to concentrate and sometimes broke off midthought to touch his face or sweep her fingers through his dark hair. She finished by telling him how Mickey had coerced her into agreeing to meet with Jay and his partners.

"You do remember Mickey?" she asked when Jay looked doubtful.

"Yes, of course. I was just thinking about what might have happened if Mickey hadn't persuaded you to meet with me." He shook his head. "Good old Mickey. I remember that first day at the park, when he picked right up on what we were doing and helped us put it over on Duvall. God, Maxi, I feel like Rip Van Winkle just waking up. I can remember." It was a declaration, at once arrogant and amazed, boastful and vulnerable, like the man himself. "I can remember everything."

Pulling away to see his expression, she asked, "Everything?" Her voice was tremulous.

"Everything," Jay confirmed. As if that had not been clear enough to bring heat to her face, he went on. "For instance, I remember everything about that last night, Maxi. I can close my eyes and bring it all back. I remember the soft sounds you made, the sweet way you smelled when I kissed your throat, and your—" His eyes flared with passion Maxi remembered well.

"I remember the way you felt," he told her, "so hot and silky. And I remember the mark my mouth left on you . . . right about here," he concluded, settling his finger on her breast, beneath her jacket and dangerously close to her suddenly hard nipple.

Maxi swayed on her feet as he reached for her and once again drew her firmly into his arms. He rubbed his cheek against the top of her head, releasing a rough groan of pleasure before turning her face up for his kiss. It had been a very long time. His touch shattered her tenuous control, and evidently his own, as well. His mouth twisted over hers, hard and insistent, as if six months of hunger could be appeased all at once. Maxi was willing to try.

There was a thrilling edge of desperation to his kiss and to the way his hands thrust beneath her jacket to caress her shoulders, lowering to explore her hips, the backs of her thighs. He dropped the jacket to the floor and kissed her neck, her face, her mouth, again and again.

Lifting her off her feet, he swung around so that her back was against her desk. Without releasing her or taking his lips from hers, he cleared the top of it with a sweep of one arm and pressed her down onto her back. Maxi chuckled at the symphony of sound as paper, pens and telephone hit the carpet.

Jay reared back to look at the rapid rise and fall of her breasts. Her dress had no buttons in front and as his fingers curled inside the bodice it was obvious what he intended. Maxi licked her lips and said not a word about the zipper in back. Life presented a woman with too few opportunities for unconditional surrender to let a few torn seams get in the way.

The sound of ripping fabric was fiercely arousing.

Jay dragged in a deep breath as he gazed down at her, and slowly, tenderly stroked his fingers over the transparent lace cups of her bra. Maxi was racing. She grasped his jacket and had worked it off one shoulder when an insistent buzzing from somewhere near his feet brought them both to a sudden halt.

"What the…" Jay lifted his head, shaking it as if to clear his thoughts. A second later Maxi felt and heard him kick the offending telephone console. It continued to buzz. "Damn."

There seemed little else for Maxi to do but sit up. Laughing she held her hand out expectantly and Jay obliged by picking up the phone and slamming it down on the desk beside her. She pulled the edges of her jacket together as she punched buttons until the buzzing stopped.

Immediately it started again.

This time she lifted the receiver and buzzed for Rita. "What is it, Rita?" she asked.

There was a short silence and then Rita's curious voice. "That's what I wanted to know. You buzzed first."

"No. I didn't..." Maxi stopped, remembering how the console had been lying upside down on the floor. "Sorry, Rita. It was an accident."

"Fine. But as long as I have you on the line, you might be interested to know that your two o'clock appointment is here. Ms. Phipps. Remember?

Damn. Of course she hadn't remembered. Maxi glanced at her watch, not nearly ready to let Jay go.

"My two o'clock appointment is here," she told him regretfully.

"Tell Rita to stall," he said.

"I shouldn't... We can't...." She looked into his eyes and sighed. "Stall," she said to Rita.

"Better yet, tell her to reschedule," Jay advised. "Tell her you're not through with your one o'clock appointment yet."

"Rita, I'm not through with my one o'clock appointment yet," Maxi repeated, her smile starting up again.

"I see." There was no missing the suppressed laughter in Rita's voice. "Do you have any idea when you will be through?"

"She wants to know when I will be through with you."

Jay leaned closer, took the receiver from Maxi's hand and spoke into it. "Never."

Winding the telephone cord around his hand several times, he yanked it from the wall.

Maxi shook her head. "Really, Jay. I don't think your partners would let you do that in their offices."

"That's why I plan to have a new partner very soon."

"Oh? Anyone I know?"

"As a matter of fact, yes. Your business is booming, so I thought maybe you could use—" Abruptly, midsentence, he lost his taste for teasing. He had gone too long not knowing what he wanted to fool around now that he knew exactly. He took her by the shoulders. "Marry me, Maxi."

The demand—it couldn't be called anything as mild as a proposal—caught Maxi by surprise. "I don't know what to say," she confessed. "I think I probably should say that we need time to get to know each other again."

"That's crap," he countered coolly. "Maxi, if anyone ought to know that time together is too precious to be wasted, it's us."

"You're right. Of course, you're right."

"Besides, we already know all the important things, and we have the rest of our lives to catch up on the rest."

She wound her arms around his neck. "How did you ever manage to come up with such an illogical, absolutely brilliant analysis all on your own?"

"I had a great teacher. Somewhere along the line it sunk in that you can't apply logic to a totally illogical situation. And ours isn't only illogical and unprecedented...it's downright impossible."

"Hold on, you don't know that for sure. Do you plan to tell anyone the truth about how we first met?"

He grinned. "Not on your life."

"Neither do I. So for all we know there are hundreds, maybe thousands of couples walking around out here with the very same secret. Think about it. Are either of your partners married?"

"Both."

"Your brother?"

"Him, too."

"See? The possibilities boggle the mind, don't you think?"

"Maxi, love, you boggle my mind," he said, laughing. "God, I've missed you."

She let him kiss her for a long time before gently pushing him away. "Say it," she ordered.

"I just did. I missed you." He nibbled her ear. "Like hell."

"I don't mean that. I want to hear it, Jay."

"I love the way you say that," he murmured. "No one else has ever called me Jay. Say it again."

"You say what I want to hear first," she countered, no longer merely suspecting that he was teasing.

His hands slid along her sides to the hem of her dress, lifting it. "What would you like me to say?"

"What you said to me that last night." She shivered as he ran his finger lightly up and down one stocking-clad leg. "I want to be sure I heard you right."

"You *were* sort of out of it that night." His eyes glinted as his fingers beneath her skirt began the slow climb back up her body. His eyebrows lifted in surprise. "Garters?"

Maxi smiled. "They seemed to go with this dress. It was an impulse."

"An inspired one. You wouldn't believe the fantasies I've been having about a woman with shiny dark hair, beautiful green eyes and garters."

"Don't try to distract me. Say it."

"I love you, Maxi, love, with a capital *and* a small *L*."

"See how easy that was?" she asked, slightly breathless from having first rewarded him with a kiss. "Now for the hard part. Show me."

"You want me to show you the hard part?" he asked with a transparent grin.

He should have known better than to try to shock her, thought Maxi. Nodding eagerly she slid closer to the edge of the desk. "Mmm-hmm."

"Now?"

"Now."

"Here?"

She eyed the desk. "Right here."

"And just how do you propose that we do that in the middle of a work day without being interrupted?" he asked, at the same time removing the phone and brushing away a few remaining papers.

"The phone certainly won't be a problem any longer," she said. "Maybe you should start by locking the door."

He did.

On the way back he lifted the hat she'd worn the day before from the shelf where she had hurled it.

"Now—" began Maxi.

"I'll improvise from here," he interrupted. He held out the hat. "Put this on. Last night I had fantasies about this hat, too."

Maxi placed the hat on her head.

A sexy smile of approval curved his mouth as he looked at her. His hands lifted, lazily coasting over the front of her dress, teasing her breasts. "Now take this off."

With Jay's help she shimmied out of her dress and slip, and sat on the corner of the desk clad only in a white lace bra and garter belt. The pendant glittered in the shadow between her breasts. Beneath his turbulent gaze she turned rosy all over.

She reached for his tie, loosened it and dropped it to the floor on top of her dress. "You don't think we will be interrupted, do you?" she asked idly, freezing when he replied with an equally nonchalant, "You can never tell."

He laughed when she twisted to the side to double check the securely locked door. "Don't you dare pull away. Aren't you the woman who once told me that sometimes, when something is really important to you, you have to take a chance? I'm feeling very lucky today," he added, lowering his voice to a husky caress and opening his arms to her. "C'mon, Maxi, close your eyes and jump."

With a soft laugh of anticipation, Maxi slid forward. Only at the last second did she hesitate, looking deeply, questioningly, into his eyes.

"You'll catch me?" she asked.

Jay's nod was sure, his smile adoring, the arms he held out to her strong and inviting. "Always."

\* \* \* \* \*

# COMING NEXT MONTH

### #607 BEST MAN—Jo Ann Algermissen
Sylas Kincaid detected the pain masked by Alana Benton's brittle poise, and he sensed that masculine cruelty had put it there. But surely the love of a better man would bring her heart out of hiding...

### #608 A WOMAN'S WORK—Laura Leone
Hardworking Marla Foster stunned her firm by capturing Brent Ventura's account. But Brent's dangerously unprofessional mix of irreverence and relentless sex appeal soon proved Marla's job had only just begun!

### #609 THE OTHER MOTHER—Pamela Jerrold
Her suddenly widowed sister left pregnant surrogate mother Caitlin O'Shea high and dry. But prodigal brother-in-law Sam Ellison seemed oddly eager to keep Caitlin's bundle of joy all in the family.

### #610 MY FIRST LOVE, MY LAST—Pat Warren
Rafe Sloan's motives for helping Nora Maddox find her missing son weren't entirely altruistic. The abrupt ending to their old affair had left burning questions, and Rafe was prepared to probe deeply for the answers....

### #611 WITH NO REGRETS—Lisa Jackson
Jaded attorney Jake McGowan rationalized that he was helping beautiful, desperate Kimberly Bennett with her child-custody suit merely to win *him* sweet revenge on Kimberly's shady ex-husband. So why was his trademark cynicism beginning to feel like caring?

### #612 WALK UPON THE WIND—Christine Flynn
A hurricane blew sheltered Nicole Stewart into Aaron Wilde's untamed world. Their island idyll couldn't last, but could she return to privileged society once she'd tasted primitive passion, once she'd walked upon the wind?

## AVAILABLE THIS MONTH:

# A BIG SISTER
## can take her places

### She likes that. Her Mom does too.

## BIG BROTHERS/BIG SISTERS AND HARLEQUIN

Harlequin is proud to announce its official sponsorship of Big Brothers/Big Sisters of America. Look for this poster in your local Big Brothers/Big Sisters agency or call them to get one in your favorite bookstore. Love is all about sharing.

BB/BS 1A